LUCIENNE BOYCE is an a⌐
women's suffrage historia⌐
gained an MA in English Lit
specialising in eighteenth-ce⌐
Mystery, *Bloodie Bones*, was joi   ⌐ ,ʊvel
Society Indie Award 2016, a   ⌐ɩɩɩ-finalist for the
M M Bennetts Award for Historical Fiction 2016. The second
Dan Foster Mystery, *The Butcher's Block*, was published in
2017 and was awarded an IndieBrag Medallion in 2018.

Lucienne has been a member of the Historical Novel
Society since shortly after its foundation. She is also a member
of the steering committee of the West of England and South
Wales Women's History Network. She has been a course
tutor and radio presenter, and regularly gives talks and leads
workshops about her fiction and non-fiction work.

Want to know more?
Find Lucienne Boyce on Twitter: @LucienneWrite
You can stay up-to-date by visiting her website, where you can
sign up to her mailing list for updates: lucienneboyce.com.

DEATH MAKES NO DISTINCTION

LUCIENNE BOYCE

Lucienne Boyce (signature)

SilverWood

Published in 2019 by SilverWood Books

SilverWood Books Ltd
14 Small Street, Bristol, BS1 1DE, United Kingdom
www.silverwoodbooks.co.uk

ISBN 978-1-78132-883-5 (paperback)
ISBN 978-1-78132-884-2 (ebook)

British Library Cataloguing in Publication Data
A CIP catalogue record for this book is available from
the British Library

Page design and typesetting by SilverWood Books
Printed on responsibly sourced paper

DEATH MAKES NO DISTINCTION

Chapter One

If Dan Foster, Principal Officer of Bow Street, had not gone into the office early to escape the chaos of the wedding preparations at home, he would not have taken the case. As it was, he had been the only officer present when the message came. A beggar woman had been found dead in the outhouse of a public house at Holborn. Such deaths were not uncommon on a cold, damp night, especially if the deceased was very young or very old.

"If it's just a matter of disposing of the body," said the night gaoler, peering down at the snot-nosed boy who stood breathless and dripping rain on to the floor of the deserted police office, "you can fetch the parish overseer."

"'T'ain't though," the boy answered. "Missus says she must have a Runner. 'Tis murder."

The gaoler rubbed his stubbled chin with thick, warty fingers. "And who says so?"

"Anyone can see 'tis. Her head's stove in."

"It's all right," Dan said, abandoning his paperwork without a pang of regret. "I'll go with him."

Which was how he came to be standing in a shed at the rear of the Feathers at the top of Hand Court on the north side of Holborn. The dead woman lay on a heap of sacks in the middle of the stone floor, surrounded by empty barrels and bottles in crates. She was huddled on her side with her knees drawn up. Dan crouched down and turned her over. As the boy had said, she had died of head wounds, several of them inflicted by booted feet.

Dan pushed her matted hair aside to get a view of her face. One of the boots had left a mark on her forehead. The pattern of the sole was distinctive: there was a triangular notch near the toe cap as if the owner had trodden on something sharp enough to leave an indentation. A tool carelessly left lying, perhaps, or a shard of metal or glass. Dan took out his notebook and made a sketch of the mark.

While he was at it, he jotted down a description. A young woman, at a guess just turned twenty, hair brown beneath the blood, a face that had been pretty. She was thin; had not eaten for some days. She had not been a beggar all her life: her coarse petticoat and blue cotton dress were ragged at the hems and filthy, but were still recognisably garments, not a patchwork of rags such as the wholly destitute wore. There were holes in her shoes and she had no stockings, apron, cloak or shawl, yet she had tried to keep up a decent appearance. A cheap straw hat lay nearby and her bodice was modestly cut, though she had not worn stays. Probably she had pawned them along with the other missing clothes, but she had kept a white muslin neckerchief to wear across her bosom. It lay in a grimy heap on the floor. Her pockets were empty.

Dan lifted up her hand, examined the dirty skin. Working hands, red and chapped. A servant perhaps. Her nails were ragged and there was skin and blood under them. She had put up a fight.

A fight she had lost long before she died. Her bodice was torn, her breasts bruised and scratched. When her killer had done raping her, she had pulled down her skirt and rolled over on to her side. Too injured to move, she had lain there until she'd died of her head wounds. There was no way of telling if it had taken minutes or hours, but her body was cold.

Dan sat back on his heels, looked at the floor. It bore a mass of confused scuff marks, but as far as he could tell there was only one set of footprints. He ran his fingers over the uneven flagstones, groping for buttons, pins, coins, any small clue that might have been dropped. There was nothing.

He pocketed his notebook, stood up and looked around and behind the barrels. Another fruitless search. He stepped out into the yard, shut the door behind him and inspected the lock. A padlock was attached to the hook, but it was too rusted to work.

He turned his head to the left, looked across the straw-strewn yard and through the archway on to the main road. The morning traffic, passing by on hoof or foot, was steadily increasing in volume. The rain had stopped, but heavy grey clouds still hung in the sky. He walked back and forth across the puddled cobblestones, his head bent, his gaze sweeping from side to side. The rain had done him no favours. It was impossible to tell if she had been dragged into the shed or, which seemed more likely from the way she had arranged the sacks around herself, had crept in looking for somewhere dry to sleep.

The boy watched him from the open stable door, a pitchfork in his hand.

"Were there horses in there last night?" Dan asked him.

"Yes, sir. Mr Jones the wagoner was here."

"Where is he now?"

"Left for Tewkesbury this morning."

"And you found her after he had gone?"

"Yes, sir. When I brought out the empties."

"Does he always leave at the same time?"

"Yes."

"Did he have any passengers?"

"Not today, only some barrels of oysters and butter and a carpet and a parcel he said was a skellington for one of the doctors there."

"When's Jones due back?"

"He sets off on Monday, gets here on Thursday, goes back Friday. You don't think it was Mr Jones, do you?"

Dan ignored the question. He looked around the yard. "You don't have much coaching business?"

"No. Just the Tewkesbury man mostly. The coaches go to the big inns."

A door in the main building opened and footsteps tapped across the yard. A short, brisk woman bore down on Dan in an angry rustle of skirts. Her avaricious little eyes flashed. The thin line of her lips parted to release a shrill voice.

"Haven't you moved it yet? This is a respectable house, this is. And we'll have the breakfasts in soon. And you, Thomas, get on with the mucking out and don't stand there gaping."

The boy ducked back inside the stable.

"Mrs Clarke, is it?" Dan said. "The body will have to stay where it is for now. Until I can arrange for the coroner."

"Coroner? I don't want no coroner here. We've never had an inquest at the Feathers and don't want one. Can't you move it to the church?"

"No, I can't. The woman has been murdered."

"I know that right enough, and it's as plain as day why. Had the effrontery to bring a man on to my premises, tried to cheat him, got what's only to be expected."

"Even if you are right, the law doesn't allow a man to murder a woman because she's bilked him."

"That's rich, that is, when a decent householder can't find a constable for love or money when he's being robbed or burgled. I know my rights, and I won't have the thing on my premises. This is a respectable house, this is. You can take her and your inquest elsewhere."

"The body is staying here. If you're so keen on having a constable about the place, I can arrange for one to come and stand guard until the coroner arrives."

"What, with my customers due in? I'll have something to say about it to your blessed coroner if you do."

"That's up to you. But if there's no need for a constable…"

She opened her mouth, snapped it shut, tossed her head and finally muttered, "No."

"In the meantime, the quicker I can get on, the sooner you

can be free of the body. Did you know the woman?"

"Of course I didn't know her. She came in for two penn'orth of beer last night. I was in two minds whether to serve her, but she was well mannered enough. Not so obvious as they usually are. Turned out she only had a penny so I told her to take herself off."

"Who do you mean by 'they'?"

"You don't look as if you were born yesterday. The Dyot Street whores, of course. That's where all the trouble round here comes from."

"What time did she come in?"

"Late. Gone ten."

"Did you see her talking to anyone?"

"No."

"Did anyone leave at the same time she did?"

"No. I saw her off the premises myself. After we closed, I sent Thomas out here to see to the horses and make sure all was shut up, and the shed was empty then. I've been meaning to get a new padlock, but what with one thing and another it was driven out of my head. To think that the baggage crept back and made free of my property."

"And you didn't hear anything during the night?"

"I was asleep, as any respectable person should be."

"I'll need the names of whoever was drinking here last night."

"I haven't got time to be making lists! Besides, we were busy."

"As many as you can remember, then. I can come back with a warrant if you prefer." He doubted the chief magistrate would sign off on that, but she was not to know.

"It will have to wait until this afternoon. And now if you don't mind, I must go and see to my breakfasts." She spun round on her heel and flounced off.

"Did you give her a pennyworth of beer?" Dan called after her.

Mrs Clarke turned back. "What?"

"She had a penny. Did you give her a pennyworth of beer?"

"No. I told her to take her custom elsewhere."

When she had gone, Thomas bobbed into the stable doorway.

"Is that right?" Dan said. "The shed was empty when you came out last night?"

"Yes, sir."

Dan eyed him sternly. The boy blinked at him, innocent or stupid, or both. Dan judged he was telling the truth. Dan went back into the shed and came out with one of the crates, wedging it against the closed door.

"No one is to go in there. I will know if this is moved, and it will go hard on anyone who interferes with police evidence."

"Yes, sir."

Dan left the boy gazing in awe at the crate.

Chapter Two

Dan walked through the archway and on to Holborn. He glanced back into Hand Court. There was another public house called the Wheatsheaf at the end of the court, and a couple of smart-looking oyster shops. He stopped to decide on his next move. Mrs Clarke could be right about the dead woman coming from Dyot Street. St Giles was where vagrants generally ended up.

Caroline had warned him to be back in good time to change before going to church. He pulled his watch from his waistcoat pocket. He calculated that he could easily get to Dyot Street and still be home for lunch.

There were two kinds of people who passed along St Giles High Street. There were those about legitimate business, be it idling or working, who, as they went by, shrank from the network of stinking alleys, filthy lanes and decrepit buildings that opened out from the thoroughfare. Then there were those who turned aside to creep, shuffle or swagger into the maze, where they were at home. Dan knew there were many amongst them who had little choice in the matter, who could afford nothing better than the crowded, rotten tenements. They included men and women who had failed at their trade; foreign seamen abandoned by their employers once they had sailed their ships into port; Irish families who had come to London looking for work; betrayed women; ruined men; discarded children. Once in, they were soon drawn to all the Rookery had to offer in the way of drink and filth and sin.

Three kinds of people, Dan mused, if you counted the

police, but they did not often venture in. He was something of an exception to the rule. He could not say it held no terrors for him, but it was familiar. He knew such places from his childhood, knew their language, knew the way they worked. Knew that you never left your back unguarded and you never went in unarmed.

He left the High Street and strode past lodging houses where you could have a bed for two pence a night, if you were willing to share with half a dozen strangers. He drove off dogs and pigs, stepped over heaps of muck, swerved around sleeping drunks, avoided half-clad, haggard women reeking of gin and sweat, and ragged children with wicked, despairing eyes.

A few twists and turns brought him to Dyot Street and the Old Blind Beak's Head. The house had been known by that name ever since he could remember, though the faded sign over the door said 'Welsh's Head'. It was one of the drinking dens where beggars gathered to do business with one another early in the mornings before they set off on their rounds. There was a daily market in the hiring out of babies and young children. Some of the children were deformed; Dan knew that many had been maimed deliberately to increase their value.

Others came to prepare for the day's labour by rubbing sores, scratches and ulcers into their own and each other's flesh, or wrapping blood-soaked bandages around sound limbs. Not all the broken bodies were fake. There were sailors injured in battle, ruptured workmen, men and women born crippled or made that way by their labours.

Here too they passed stolen goods from hand to hand and plotted new robberies and murders. And it was to the Old Blind Beak's Head they returned in the evening. Then they laid aside their crutches, eye patches and soiled dressings, and spent the evening dancing, drinking, quarrelling and coupling.

One or two looked up from their drams when Dan entered, recognised him with a spit or a scowl, and resumed their activities. Some looked towards a table in the corner of the room, guessing that it was to its occupant that Dan was heading. This was Peg Long, also known as Dark Peg, perhaps because of the rumours about past foul deeds, perhaps because of a complexion inherited from one of her parents. Peg was a madam, a receiver of stolen goods, and landlady of the nastiest tenements in the Rookery. Her fat body was bundled in an assortment of petticoats, skirts and shawls. She was reputed to have packets of money sewn into the many layers. She had a glass of gin in front of her and a copy of *The Lady's Magazine*.

She looked up as Dan's shadow fell across the page. "If it isn't Officer Foster." She had a deep, gruff voice; angered, it could strike terror into her minions.

Dan pulled out a chair, sat down, stretched his legs in front of him.

She snapped her fingers at one of the slatternly girls by the counter. "Coffee."

The coffee served in the Old Blind Beak's Head, at least that served to Dark Peg, was surprisingly good and Dan did not refuse the offer.

She turned over a page of her magazine. "What can I do for you today, Mr Foster?"

Dan thanked the girl who brought him his cup. She leered at him in surprise, and shuffled away. "I'm looking for information about a woman who may have been seen around here in the last couple of days. In her twenties, brown hair, blue dress, down on her luck."

Peg tore out a picture of a woman modelling a concoction of silks and lace, folded it up and put it in a leather case that hung from the belt around her waist. "As who isn't?"

"I think she was begging, but not working. Had not long been on the streets."

Without looking up from her magazine, Peg called, "Betsy!"

A woman at a nearby table threw down a handful of cards, rose and sauntered over, picking her teeth with a filthy finger-nail. One of Peg's higher-class girls, her dress was tawdry but not tattered, her face splotched with rouge, her lips reddened, her lice-riddled hair curled about her shoulders.

"Yes?"

"Tell Mr Foster about that woman you spoke to yesterday."

"Happy to oblige Mr Foster any time. She came in looking for work, said she'd do anything – scrub pots, empty slops, pick oakum. I told her there was only one kind of work for a woman around here. So then she started wringing her hands and wailing, 'Oh dear, what shall I do?' In the end I says you'll have to sell something if you want money and she says but I've nothing to sell and I says what about that cloak of yourn? And after a bit of face pulling, she sold it me and I took it into Simes's pawnshop this morning and got twice what I gave her for it."

"What colour was the cloak?" Dan asked.

"Dark blue."

"Did she tell you her name? Say where she was from?"

"I didn't ask for her life story, if that's what you mean."

"Just fleeced her."

"A lamb waiting to be shorn, that one. But what's your interest, Mr Foster? She hasn't had a go at lifting some gent's wiper, has she?"

"Not as far as I know. She was found murdered in the yard of the Feathers this morning."

Betsy screwed up her mouth and spat philosophically on to the floor. "Like I said, a lamb."

Dan took out his drawing. "The man who killed her raped her first. His boots left this mark on her."

Peg took the sketch, examined it, then passed it to Betsy. Neither woman could shed any light on the wearer. Betsy shivered, handed it back to Dan.

Peg jerked her head. Betsy winked at Dan and went back to her card game and gin.

Dan pocketed the drawing. "There are beggars, women and thieves on the streets round Holborn at all hours, and most of them come from St Giles. I need to know if anyone saw anything last night. There'll be no questions asked about who they are or what they were doing. If you hear anything, will you let me know?"

Dark Peg shrugged. "We've had men like that on the streets before. We'll have them again."

"But I want this one."

She picked up her glass. "If I hear anything, I'll let you know."

Chapter Three

The service was over when Dan arrived at St Paul's in Covent Garden after he had rushed back to his house in Russell Street to change. The wedding party stood amongst the columns in front of the church door. Eleanor and Sam Ellis made a handsome couple and many passers-by stopped to cheer and wish them well. There were a few whining beggar women offering wilted flowers, and one or two keen-eyed boys who drifted away when they saw Dan.

It was the first time for several days that Dan had seen Eleanor, his wife's younger sister. For the last few weeks she had been living with her in-laws. Mrs Ellis had injured her wrist in a fall and Eleanor had gone to help her look after Mr Ellis, Sam, and his younger brother, Frank. She had been glad to go, and Dan had found things easier without her constant presence. Their paths had crossed once or twice when he got home from work, but his arrival usually brought her visit to a close.

The two sisters looked very much alike, especially today when Eleanor's dress was less plain than usual. The difference in their characters was apparent, though. Caroline's clothes were more flamboyant and worn with more flair; she laughed more, talked more, flirted more. Yet Eleanor was not grave. It was only that her smiles and quieter manner were overshadowed by her elder sister's liveliness. Caroline's gaiety had captivated Dan when they first met, as it captivated most of the men who saw her. Like them, he had failed to appreciate Eleanor. Until it was too late.

Dan had agreed many times since the marriage was announced that he was glad to have brought about the couple's first meeting. Had tried to believe it too. Captain Sam Ellis worked days in his family's carpentry business, nights in the Bow Street patrol. A couple of years ago he had called on Dan about a case they were working on and set eyes on Eleanor for the first time. Not that she had noticed him then. It was Dan who possessed her heart.

He was a good officer, Sam. A good man. Eleanor deserved her happiness: a home of her own, children, a loving husband. Things Dan could never give her. Things she wouldn't take off him now if he could, not since his son Alex's birth. He and Caroline had made a peace of sorts over it, but Eleanor had felt his betrayal of her love for him too keenly. For Caroline's sake they had resisted taking an illicit pleasure, had agreed to live with the pain of their unrequited love. Then he had gone and slept with another woman, who had died in childbed.

He moved to his wife's side. Caroline greeted him with, "You hold your son," and dumped Alex into his arms. And that was all she said to him for the next two hours.

At least Alex was happy to see him. The infant laughed and gurgled at him as he bounced him up and down. He caught sight of Nick on the edge of the group, tugging at his collar, his gaze fixed on them. The jacket was an oppressively new one; Mrs Harper had scrubbed his neck and ears and bustled him into it when he had finished his chores. Dan jerked his head. The boy's face split into a smile and he scampered to Dan's side.

Noah Foster looked every inch the sporting gentleman in polished boots, best linen, expertly knotted scarf, and well-fitting jacket. He was still basking in the proud glow of standing in for Dan to walk the bride down the aisle. Paul, his old friend and assistant at the Cecil Street gym, looked equally as proud, but not so dignified. He was as well turned out as any soldier on parade, but the effect was spoiled by his hideous smile. His teeth and jaw had been broken during the siege of Quebec, a wound which in those rough and ready days had received scant medical attention on the field.

Sam's father and brother stood grinning awkwardly in stiff Sunday best. The mothers, Mrs Ellis and Mrs Harper, nodded their rival hats at one another, each exhibiting a forest of flowers and feathers. Before the wedding, they had entered into competition over who could produce the most food for the feast. Back at the house, the party gathered around the table to tackle the mountain of viands they had prepared. There was also wine and ale from the Red Lion along the street. Caroline's temper improved and she forgot to be angry with Dan.

Sam and Eleanor sat side by side. They seemed at ease with one another, Dan thought. He wondered if, living under the same roof, they had found an opportunity to pre-empt the wedding night, then pushed the thought away from him as unworthy. Eleanor caught his eye, quickly looked away again. She jumped up, smiled at Sam.

"Can I get you some more beer, Mr Ellis?"

Sam laughed. "You can, Mrs Ellis."

Paul chatted with Sam's father and brother. Mrs Harper and Mrs Ellis threw challenges at one another in the guise of old family recipes. Nick sat next to Noah, listening to his tales of the ring and the Fancy.

"Tell it me again, Mr Foster," he pleaded.

"You must have heard it a dozen times, lad."

"Go on. I mean, please."

"Very well, if you must... I first saw Dan at Blackheath when I went to see Tom Johnson against Steevy Oliver. That was long before you were born. Steevy was past his prime, but still a game 'un, and it was no shame to him to lose to the younger man. Not long after, a fight broke out between a couple of divers, by no means evenly matched, but the young one went at it like a game cock. Took a real beating from the bigger lad, but wouldn't throw in the towel. Didn't have a towel to throw in, mind you. Didn't have much of anything but a foul mouth and the moves of a born athlete."

"He had bottom, didn't he, Mr Foster?" Nick said. "And you took him off the streets. Like he has me. Tell me about when he fought Hen Pearce."

Laughingly, Noah rolled his eyes, but did not disappoint. He repeated the story of Dan's fight with the Bristol boxer known as the Game Chicken. The Chicken, he said, was one to look out for; it would surprise no one who'd seen him if he was champion of England one day.

"And he beat him, didn't he?"

Dan stopped listening, thought instead about the day when Alex would sit where Nick sat now, lapping up the same stories. He and his son would go to the gym together, watch fights together, discuss the contents of the sporting papers…

Alex fell asleep. Dan carried him upstairs and put him in his bed, taking his time over it. In the end, though, he had to return to the party. In his absence, they had lit the candles and the men had moved the furniture to the side of the room. Mr Ellis senior had produced a violin, and Frank Ellis a flute. Dan joined in the dancing in spite of himself. Or perhaps because of himself. It was a welcome distraction to whirl first his mother-in-law and then his wife around the hot and crowded room.

The day drew to a close at last. The flautist dried his instrument and packed it into its case. Mr Ellis wiped his violin with a soft cloth and packed cloth and instrument away. Then the family crowded into the hall to wave goodbye to the Ellises.

Dan held out his hand. "I wish you and Eleanor every happiness, Sam."

The sisters embraced. "You know what to expect if you marry a police officer, Nell!" Caroline cried.

Eleanor, her arm through Sam's, blushed. He grinned and pulled her closer. "Your sister knows to expect the best I can give her."

Caroline laughed, a fragile, glassy sound. She glanced at her husband. "Oh, we all expect that. But they can't even be in time for a wedding."

She had passed through the merry stage. A good thing their guests were leaving, Dan thought. At last the Ellis family were out the door, skipping and laughing along Russell Street on the short walk to their home on Long Acre.

Dan gave his final handshakes, closed the door and turned back into the kitchen. Caroline sat by the fire, sipping wine from a brimming glass. Mrs Harper was busy conveying dishes to the sink, food to the larder, empty bottles to the hall ready to take back to the Red Lion.

"Don't you think you've had enough?" Dan said, crossing the room to stand by the hearth.

"Lord! It's my sister's wedding."

"And it's over now. You should give your mother a hand."

"Where's that useless boy? Let him do something to earn his keep. Nick!"

The door opened and Nick hurried in carrying a pair of Dan's boots. "I done your boots, Mr Foster."

"Did," Caroline said, and muttered, "Savage."

Dan smiled down at the lad, took the gleaming boots from him. "You didn't need to do that, Nick."

"It would have been more useful if you'd been helping Mrs Harper," Caroline said.

Nick's face fell. Slump-shouldered, he moved towards the table.

"Go to bed, Nick," Dan said. "And thanks for the boots. They look grand."

Nick slept on a pallet bed in the small parlour next door. It was safe, dry and warm: things he was only just becoming accustomed to. The wild street boy had almost gone. Almost. There was something feral in the glance he gave Caroline as he left the room.

She had already forgotten about him, her attention caught by the sound that came from upstairs.

"What now? Mother, go and see to Alex, will you?" She waved at the table. "Leave all that till the morning."

Mrs Harper bustled in from the larder. "Oh, is he crying? Probably all the noise woke him up, the poor love." She hurried upstairs.

Dan watched Caroline drink. She caught his eye, angrily lowered the empty glass. "For Christ's sake, don't be such a fucking Puritan."

"Don't call me that," he said mechanically. Not that it ever did any good.

"I wouldn't have thought you'd begrudge me a drink at my sister's wedding. It's not something that happens every day, is it? A person can have a good time every once in a way, can't they?"

"I don't begrudge you anything, but I think you're—" He amended 'drunk' to 'tired'. She was right after all. It was only once in a way. "It's been a long day."

She sighed, her temper changing on a sudden in response to the conciliatory note in his voice. "Yes, I think I'll go to bed." She stood up, glanced at the ceiling, listening. "Alex has settled. I think we should put him in Eleanor's bedroom now. It will be nice for him to have his own room. Are you coming up?"

"In a moment."

She nodded and walked, none too steadily, out of the room. Dan sat down in the chair opposite hers, stared into the dying fire. So it was done. Sam and Eleanor were married. And so were he and Caroline, and they'd both been working hard to make a fresh start since she had agreed to bring up Alex as her own. And to give Caroline her due, that's what she'd done. The baby had changed her life. She was happier now than he remembered seeing her in a long time. He shouldn't blame her if occasionally she slipped back into her old habits. As she said, a wedding wasn't something that happened every day.

Chapter Four

On Monday afternoon, Dan was about to leave the Bow Street office when the door opened and the chief clerk, Mr Lavender, came into the room, his arms full of papers. Tom Clifford, the young clerk known to the men as Inky Tom, jumped to his feet and went to help him.

"Sir William wants to see you, Mr Foster," said Lavender, handing his burden to Tom to carry into the cubbyhole that served as his office.

Dan refrained from asking why the chief magistrate wanted him. If Lavender knew, he would not say. The chances were he did not know, for he was wearing his 'no one tells me anything' face. Dan straightened his scarf and jacket and went upstairs.

He heard Sir William Addington's voice while he was still outside the room. Whoever was in there with Sir William had set off the old man's temper. Dan cast back in his mind over the last few days, could not remember anything he had done that might have got him into trouble. He knocked on the door. Sir William fell silent. A drawer opened and slammed shut.

"Come in!"

Sir William sat behind his desk. Dan flicked a glance around the chamber, which was littered with legal documents and files. There was no one else there. He kept the surprise from his face as he obeyed Sir William's invitation to sit down. The magistrate eyed him with a baffled air, as if he had done something unexpected and prodigious. Dan, unable to account for his strange demeanour, said nothing, and wondered.

"Well, Foster," Sir William said at last, "I've got a commission for you."

"Sir?" Dan prompted.

"I have received a request for a principal officer from one of the highest in the land." Sir William folded his hands one on top of the other on the desk and leaned towards Dan. "But not just any principal officer. A particular principal officer." Sir William's jowls shook with emotion. "The request comes from the Prince of Wales, and the officer His Royal Highness asks for by name is you, Foster."

"Me, sir?" Dan gazed back at the chief magistrate in astonishment. "Why would the Prince of Wales ask for me?"

Sir William nodded, as if to say, *my thoughts exactly*. "You have been recommended to him by Mr Townsend."

"John Townsend?"

This was beyond astonishing. Principal Officer John Townsend was on permanent assignment as bodyguard to the royal family. He was especially close to Prince George, whom he accompanied to horse races, theatres, suppers, balls and assemblies.

Townsend and Dan did not have much to do with one another as a rule. Recently, though, they had both been involved in the arrest of a radical anti-monarchist group calling themselves the United Patriots. Dan had infiltrated the organisation and exposed their plot to overthrow the government with the aid of the French, who were itching to invade England. While in no doubt that the United Patriots' actions were criminal, Dan had realised that they were nothing more than a bunch of deluded men whose gimcrack revolution could never have succeeded. What was more, he also had a sneaking sympathy for some of their views, for he was not blind to the corruption and injustice that had goaded them into unwise courses. Which was why Townsend had openly accused Dan of 'having caught the levelling contagion'. Since then he had regarded Dan as only one step removed from the detested radicals himself. Yet now he was asking for him to work for a member of the royal family.

"Mr Townsend wants you with him on a case of personal interest to the Prince. You've heard of Louise Parmeter?"

"No, sir."

"She was a celebrity in her day. The most beautiful woman in the land. She caught that ass Sheridan's eye when she was a girl and was all set for a promising career at Drury Lane Theatre, but she gave it up to be the Prince's lover. That was before George came of age. He was a flighty young man and soon moved on to someone new. They parted amicably and he gave her a generous settlement which meant that she did not have to tread the boards again. A pity, as she was glorious. Especially in breeches parts." Sir William's thoughts drifted off for a moment, came back with a jolt. "And now she's been murdered and His Highness wants the killer brought to justice. You will assist Townsend in his investigation of her death."

Things were getting worse by the minute. Assist John Townsend!

"But I am already working on a case. A woman found murdered at Holborn."

"Yes, yes, I know all about that. You haven't time to go grubbing about in the murder of an unknown whore in the backyard of a tavern. I want your every working hour spent on this."

"I don't think she was a whore, sir. Even if she was, someone killed her and that someone should be brought to justice."

"Pull yourself together, Foster. You are off that case with immediate effect. The Home Secretary has his eye on the Parmeter affair and no effort is to be spared. The Duke of Portland's relationship with the Prince is a delicate one. They were friends once, before His Grace defected from the opposition party and accepted Pitt's offer to head the Home Department. Politicians come and go, but George will be king one day and the Duke is anxious to avoid causing further offence. So, since it's you His Highness has asked for, it's you His Highness gets."

"But, sir, I need to speak to the Tewkesbury carrier. He's due back on Thursday. In the meantime, I've got the names of some of the men who were drinking in the Feathers on the night of the murder."

"With immediate effect, Foster. Believe me, you are not the man I would have picked for this job. You're a good enough investigator, but at times you have a cavalier manner and I advise you to rein it in. I'm warning you that if you are in any way a discredit to me, you'll be back in the foot patrol before you can say Jack Robinson. Do I make myself clear?"

"You do, sir."

Chapter Five

Odd, thought Dan, how dressing up murder in silks and satins instead of cheap cotton prints made it less acceptable. As he strode away from Bow Street, he vowed that he would not drop his case. He would find out who murdered the nameless woman at the Feathers. And if she had been a whore, well there was not much to choose between her and a demirep dead in a mansion in Mayfair.

Behind all that lay the nagging question: why had John Townsend asked for him, when he could have picked any one of the principal officers?

Less than half an hour later, he passed Devonshire House, turned into Berkeley Street and entered Berkeley Square. Louise Parmeter's house was on the west side overlooking the gardens where the young plane trees were beginning to show signs of regrowth after the winter. A couple of constables from the Great Marlborough Street police office stood outside the front door, warily eyeing the crowd on the pavement below. These cheerful idlers kept up the strength for their vigil by frequent forays to the Three Chairmen, a public house on the corner of Hay Hill.

Dan's arrival caused a buzz of excited speculation, with some of those within earshot declaring he was a Runner, and others suggesting he had come to take measurements for the coffin. He pushed his way through the gossips and ran up the stone steps between the spiked railings. One of the men knocked on the door, which was opened after much turning of locks and drawing back of bolts by a constable in the hall.

Dan slipped through while the gawpers craned forward for a glimpse inside.

"Mr Townsend is in the study, sir." The officer pointed to a half-open door.

Dan crossed a hallway as big as his parlour and filled with a bewildering array of flowers, vases and mirrors. He saw Townsend moving about inside the room, stopping to fiddle with an ornament here, peer at a clock there, prod a cushion or curtain with his cane. Every now and again he nodded in the direction of an unseen witness.

"Mmm, mmm."

After each slight encouragement, a woman's tearful voice continued its disjointed murmur.

Dan stepped into the room. There were two occupants, Townsend and a woman in a chair by the marble fireplace. His first thought, though, was for Louise Parmeter, formerly mistress to the Prince of Wales. She sat behind a daintily fashioned mahogany desk, the upper half of her body sprawled across the inlaid surface.

His resentment against the victim evaporated as soon as he saw her. Even in death she was one of the most beautiful women he had ever seen. Long eyelashes swept her delicate cheeks; shapely eyebrows framed large lidded eyes; and her hair was a glory of gold. Her lips were slightly parted, as if on the verge of a smile that must have been dazzling when life animated it.

Her hands and arms were stretched out in front of her, the left palm uppermost, a pen lying by her right fingertips. Her head was turned to the side and her left cheek rested on a sheet of paper half-covered in writing that ended in a jagged, blotted line. Her hair was matted with blood from a glistening wound at the back of her skull. A heavy silver candlestick had been thrown on to the desk, gouging its brilliant surface, the end sticky with gore in which were embedded several hairs. The inkstand had been overturned, its contents obliterating the pattern of the opulent rug beneath.

Townsend thrust one hand into the pocket of the yellow waistcoat straining over his round belly and swished his cane like a school beadle controlling an unruly class.

"There you are at last, Foster."

"Mr Townsend."

Dan met the witness's red-eyed gaze. Her nose was rubbed raw from crying. She wore an unostentatious though well-made dress with a checked apron, a simple muslin neckerchief, and a plain cap. She was younger than Louise Parmeter by some ten years: Dan guessed her to be about twenty-five. She did not have the attitude of a servant, would not have been sitting in her mistress's armchair if she was, yet she had clearly not been Louise Parmeter's equal. A companion perhaps.

"This is Miss Agnes Taylor, Miss Parmeter's protégée," Townsend said.

"Her protégée in what, Miss Taylor?" Dan asked.

"Miss Parmeter and I are both votaries to the poetic muse," Agnes answered. She choked back a sob. "That is, she was."

"Miss Taylor found the body," Townsend said.

"When?"

"I came looking for her when she did not come in for luncheon," Agnes said. "Found her – like that."

"I'm asking the questions, Foster," Townsend said. "You just whip out your notebook and mark down the main points." He tapped his cane on the floor as he counted them off. "Miss Louise Parmeter, a literary lady, works in her study from nine o'clock every morning. At midday she takes a light luncheon. Today she did not go to the dining room. Miss Taylor came to fetch her. Knocked. No reply. Entered. Found the lady brutally slain. Murder weapon: the candlestick on her desk. Have you got that? Obvious how the killer got in and out."

The desk stood in front of a glass door that gave on to the garden, a formal affair of urns, fountains and statues, looking grey and drab on an overcast April day. The long curtains were looped back and the door was ajar.

"How did he get into the garden?" Dan asked. "It's a high wall. He couldn't have climbed it in broad daylight without drawing attention to himself."

Townsend tut-tutted. "I have already established the facts. There is a gate at the end of the garden which leads into a lane at the rear running between Mount Street and Hill Street, where the stables are located. The gate was closed but unlocked when I checked it. It is usually kept locked."

"Have you looked for footprints?"

"Thank heavens you are here to think of it. Of course I have. There are none."

"You must have been on the scene very quickly to have discovered so much."

"Owing to my royal duties, I was as good as on the spot. The Prince was paying a visit to Lady Jersey at her daughter's home, number thirty-eight, when I heard a commotion in the square. Naturally a disturbance in such close proximity to His Highness requires my attention and I came to investigate. When His Highness learned that not only had a brutal murder taken place a few doors away, but the victim was known to him, he was deeply affected. He has asked me to bring the killer to justice with all due despatch – which we will not achieve if you are going to waste time going over ground I have already covered."

Dan, ignoring this harangue, moved towards the desk to take a closer look. He stooped over Louise Parmeter's body. One of her earlobes was torn and bloodied.

"Her jewellery has been taken?" he asked Agnes.

"Yes," she answered. "Diamond earrings and a matching necklace. They were a gift from the Prince of Wales." She dabbed at her eyes.

"She wore diamonds to work at her desk?"

"She often wears – wore – them. She didn't believe in hoarding."

"The question is," Townsend said, "who did the thief have on the inside? The servants are gathered in the hall downstairs under the guard of two constables, and all are accounted for. So whoever let him in is still on the premises. Go down and start taking their statements, Foster. Find out where they say they were this morning, and make a note of anyone who doesn't have an alibi. And send a couple of constables down the lane to find out if anyone saw anything."

Dan thought of telling Townsend what to do with his orders, then remembered Sir William Addington's threat to demote him. There was no point giving Townsend cause to make a bad report of him within an hour of starting the case. Besides, there were several things puzzling him.

"That clock on the mantelpiece is worth a bit," he said. "Not to mention the silver snuffbox on that table over there. The candle snuffers. The decanter and glasses. Any one of the ornaments."

"Obviously he came expressly for the diamonds," Townsend said. "They alone are enough to make his fortune – his and his accomplice's."

"But why come for them while she's wearing them? And why in the daytime?"

"They were kept overnight in a Bramah safe in the butler's pantry. The lock is impossible to pick. It's apparent, Foster, that you are not used to high-class crimes of this nature. There's a bit more going on here than the pilfering of a few bits of lace from a haberdasher's, or the lifting of a purse. It takes a bit of nerve to pull off something like this, and it wants someone with connections to sell the gems. They'll need taking out of their settings, possibly getting over to Amsterdam. This is a professional job."

"Then why did he miss one?" Dan used his pencil to push a lock of the dead woman's hair aside, revealing the glittering diamonds on the drop still hanging from her left ear.

"Because he was interrupted before he got everything he wanted," Townsend said. "Probably when Miss Taylor knocked on the door."

Agnes's hands flew up to her throat. "Oh! Do you mean he was still in the room when I was standing in the hall?"

"Very likely," Townsend answered.

Dan scratched his head with the pencil. "But even with someone knocking on the door, it would have been the work of seconds to snatch the earring. He'd made no ceremony of taking the first. And it's strange, isn't it, that she sat calmly at her desk while someone let themselves in at the door just behind her. She must have known he was there. If she didn't hear his footsteps, he would have blocked out the light."

Townsend rolled his eyes. "Do you have a point, Foster?"

"I think the killer must have been someone she knew."

Agnes let out a scream and collapsed back in the chair in a dead faint.

Chapter Six

Dan revived Agnes with a glass of Madeira from one of the bottles on the sideboard.

"Really, Foster, if you had gone and done what I asked you instead of blundering around upsetting people, we wouldn't have a fainting female on our hands," Townsend grumbled.

"No, no!" Agnes protested, holding out her glass for a refill. "Blame rather my delicate sensibility – my soul is aquiver – my heart overburdened – forgive me – it has all been such a shock."

Dan did not think it needed much delicate sensibility to be upset by finding a bloodied corpse, but only said, "Take your time, Miss Taylor."

He put the decanter away and went back to the desk. One of the drawers was slightly open and the key was in the lock, but there was nothing in it. "Miss Taylor, do you know what Miss Parmeter kept in here? Second drawer down on the left?"

She put aside her glass, hurried to the desk and stared into the empty drawer in dismay.

"Her book."

"What book is that?"

"The one she was writing. Her memoirs."

Townsend went over, put his hand inside, groped around and confirmed that it was indeed empty. "There must have been something valuable in there. Money? A watch? Jewellery?"

"Only the book so far as I know," Agnes said. "She kept it locked away when she wasn't working on it."

Her glance fell upon the body and with a horrified squeak she retreated to her seat and the Madeira.

"Why would someone take her book?" Dan asked.

"I don't know," she answered, "but she often said that there were many people who would prefer *Memoirs of Herself and Others* not to be published. She used to laugh and say she was going to dedicate it to 'the Lords, Generals and Politicians of Great Britain'. Many of them were the others, you see."

"She was writing about her affairs with them?"

"Yes."

"Who knew about the memoirs?"

"Everybody, I should think. She used to amuse her company with some of the stories she had to tell. She never mentioned any names, and there was always a great deal of laughter and raillery as they tried to guess who she meant."

"What sort of stories?"

"A young heir who swore to his family that he had ended their affair long before he had done so; if it came out, he would lose his inheritance. A merchant who promised her a generous settlement, then refused to keep his side of the agreement; she knew a great deal about his tax evasions. One who boasted to his friends of his prowess as a lover when he was more of a Lysander to her Cloris."

"A what to her what?" said Townsend.

"A would-be amorous lover in a poem by Aphra Behn," Agnes replied. "It's called *The Disappointment*. But no one took her remarks seriously, nor, I am sure, were they meant seriously. I don't think anybody really believed the memoirs would ever be finished, let alone published, not even Miss Parmeter herself. It was mere drollery."

"Someone must have taken it seriously," Dan said.

"Now, Foster, don't jump ahead of yourself," Townsend said. "I don't think we need concern ourselves with a few pages from a lady's diary. It's the valuables I'm interested in."

"If someone took the book, it was valuable to them. So did they kill her for the book, or for the diamonds?"

Townsend snorted. "Oh yes, that makes sense. The killer

stood here and thought, let me see, what shall I take, a book or some priceless diamonds?"

"But he took both."

"Of course he did. He used the book to wrap the jewels in."

"If he needed something to wrap them in, why not take one of these loose sheets scattered on the desk? If it came to it, why not use a handkerchief or scarf, which could be used to tie them much more securely?"

"How do I know what was in his mind? He panicked and grabbed the first thing to hand."

"But the manuscript wasn't the first thing to hand. He had to go to the trouble of unlocking a drawer to get to it. And, since he was interrupted before he had a chance to take all of the jewellery, it was the book he went for first."

"Let's stop wasting time with groundless speculations. I want you—" Townsend was distracted by the sound of the front door opening and closing. "What the hell is that noise? I told them no one was to be admitted."

It was too late. Rapid footsteps crossed the hall. A domineering voice announced, "I'll show myself in."

The study door opened to admit a vision stuffed into tight breeches and gleaming boots, an exquisitely cut blue jacket, a yellow striped satin waistcoat, snowy white shirt and stock. A corpulent vision with a peevish turn to the mouth, true, but a royal one: once seen, the Prince of Wales was impossible to mistake. Dan had often spotted him when he was on duty at Drury Lane Theatre with other Bow Street officers whose job was to protect the theatre-going crowds from pickpockets, drunkards and beggars.

Agnes produced a high-pitched cry from her repertoire of screeches, started to her feet and gave a clumsy curtsey, while Townsend jumped to attention and made a smart bow. Dan recovered his surprise in time to present his own bow. It was as awkward as Agnes's curtsey, neither of them having much experience of playing the courtier.

"Your Royal Highness!" Townsend cried, hurrying forward. "Let me escort you from this awful scene."

The Prince shook his head, almost dislodging his artfully tousled curls. "It's this awful scene I've come to see, Towney."

Townsend followed him to the desk and shooed Dan out of the way. George glanced enquiringly at Dan.

"My assistant, Officer Foster," Townsend said.

George nodded. "Towney's told me a lot about you, Foster. I never attend public fights now, you know. I once saw a man killed in a bout of fisticuffs. Though I gather that such things are very unlikely nowadays, the rules being much stricter than they were."

The remark puzzled Dan for a few seconds, until he guessed that Townsend must have mentioned his interest in pugilism. Why he should have done so, Dan could not fathom. It could have no bearing on his abilities as an investigator.

Having no idea of the etiquette when addressed by royalty, Dan thought a straightforward response best. He bowed again and, following Townsend's example, said, "Thank you, Your Royal Highness, but I do not fight in public competitions."

"Well, I'll leave all that to you," George said vaguely.

Already distracted from the subject, he gazed down at the body. Some of the natural colour left his cheeks, throwing spots of artificial pink into relief. He stroked the pale forehead with the back of his fingers.

"Poor Louise," he murmured. He caught sight of the ragged ear. "What's this? Her jewels snatched from her?"

"The villain did indeed so violate the lady's remains when he had done for – slain her," Townsend said. "He came for her diamonds."

"Not the ones I gave her?"

"Yes. With your leave, I will ask your jeweller for a detailed description."

George waved his hand. "Of course, of course, whatever you need."

Townsend pointed at the half-open garden door with his cane. "This is how he got in and out. It's what we call an inside job, Your Royal Highness. Someone let the thief in. We are about to start questioning the servants."

"Good God! You don't think it was one of them?"

"Sadly, sir, greed is a besetting sin of the lower orders. Surrounded by all this wealth, is it to be wondered at that many succumb? I see it all too often in my line of work."

The Prince shivered, possibly because the room was growing cold as the neglected fire sank low. With a sigh, he moved away, noticed the open drawer and halted abruptly.

"Her book is missing."

"Yes, Miss Taylor has drawn my attention to the fact," Townsend said.

"If that book gets out, Towney, it'll provide the greatest entertainment we've seen for many an age. There will hardly be a noble house left unblushing."

"I understand that the book is likely to cause a great deal of embarrassment."

"Of the most delicious kind. I am almost tempted to offer a reward for its publication."

Either, Dan thought, this is the coolest performance I ever saw, or the Prince really has nothing to fear from Louise Parmeter's book. But how can that be, if it's about her affairs with the great and the good? Unless he already knows that the book has been safely disposed of.

Dan realised that he was staring at the Prince. Too late. George had already read the suspicion in his eye.

"You think that would be unwise of me, Officer?" the Prince asked. "But I am not in the book."

Dan could bluster a denial that he'd thought anything of the kind, but what would be the point? The whoring, hard-drinking, buffooning royal disappointment of the newspaper gossip columns was altogether sharper than he was given credit for.

"Can you be certain of that, Your Royal Highness?" he asked.

"I must apologise, sir, Foster is not accustomed—" Townsend began, but George held up a silencing hand.

"Damn it, Towney, I like a man who can look me in the eye. Let me set his mind at rest. I can say with absolute certainty that I am not in the book. There are, you see, the diamonds."

Townsend sucked in his lower lip and stared up at the ceiling.

"Oh, come, Towney, let us not be coy," George said irritably. "We're all men of the world."

Dan was not a man of the Prince's world, but he grasped his meaning. It was how women like Louise Parmeter obtained security for the loss of youth and beauty. Jewels, annuities, houses, carriages, paintings: such things were given in exchange for keeping letters private, or memoirs unpublished. Blackmail, dress it up how you will. Had other men also been paying a price for her silence? And had one of those men grown tired of the arrangement and decided to take steps to ensure his story was never told?

George was already ahead of him there too. "I say, Towney, do you think they'll realise what they've got when they look at the memoirs? Do you think it's even possible that they already know? That they took the book because they're in it? Now that would shake some ancient foundations!"

"Why – I – I – yes, I was asking that very question before you arrived."

Dan swung round and looked at Townsend, who ignored him and continued, "Yes, it's what you might call a quandary. Howsomever, that's a question we can settle when the villain is in custody. To my mind, following the diamonds is the best way to go."

"Well, you know best," George said. "And now, I had better get back to Lady Jersey. She will be growing impatient, and you know what a termagant she is when that happens. Be sure to keep me informed of progress."

"Your Royal Highness," Townsend said, bounding forward to open the door for the Prince.

Chapter Seven

"Can I be of further assistance, Mr Townsend?" Agnes Taylor asked when he came stomping back a few moments later. "There are the – the arrangements to consider."

"Of course, ma'am," Townsend muttered, hardly noticing her going.

"We should ask her if she knows who's mentioned in the memoirs and who might have a reason to stop their publication," Dan said when they were alone.

"We are not going to waste time on the damned book."

"But the Prince seems to think it's important."

"Never you mind what the Prince thinks. In any case, find the diamonds and we'll find the book. If it hasn't ended up down somebody's privy as bum fodder by then, and I don't see how I can prevent that, though God knows I'll do my best for him."

"The Prince wants us to find it?"

"It's nothing to do with you what the Prince wants. Like I said, I want you to question the servants."

"Why does he want the book, if he's sure he's not in it?"

"Because he does." Townsend glowered at Dan, then relented. "He thinks it might contain information that could be useful to him. He wants us to find it and give it to him. Discreetly. You understand, Foster?"

"He hopes Miss Parmeter's revelations might give him something to use against political enemies."

"What he hopes is none of your business. I'm going to Jermyn Street to speak to the jeweller. I'll join you back here later and you can make your report." Townsend stalked out of the room.

"Fool," Dan muttered.

Townsend was right about one thing. Find the diamonds and the book would not be far away. The question remained, though: which had the killer come for?

Dan looked at the huddled body. Louise Parmeter couldn't answer his questions for him. Starting with the servants wasn't such a bad idea.

He went down to the basement where he found two constables standing at the open door of the servants' dining room. Inside, the servants were gathered around the table, drinking coffee and talking in subdued voices. In answer to Dan's query, the younger of the two officers suggested that the butler's pantry would be a suitable place to hold the interviews. As Townsend had directed before the Prince arrived, Dan sent the other man to pair up with his colleague in the hall and go and make enquiries along the lane at the back of the house.

The butler's pantry was a combination of storage, work and office space. There was a deep sink with a wooden draining board on which stood a tray of decanters and wine glasses waiting to be cleaned. Above it a barred window looked out on to the area railings. The walls were lined with shelves of cleaning materials. A brown apron hung inside the door. At the side of the room, a heavy iron door fitted with one of Bramah's unpickable locks led to the strongroom where the jewellery, household plate and cash were stored.

Dan piled the account books and receipts on the desk to one side to make space for his notes and sat down. Two sets of footsteps sounded on the flagged passageway. The young constable knocked and brought in Dan's first witness, and what was even more welcome: a cup of coffee. Here was a man with a bright future in the police service, Dan thought, sending the constable back to the servants in the dining room.

The newcomer frowned at the disarranged desk. "I am Mr Parkes, the butler."

Admittedly, Dan did not have much experience of butlers, but he had thought they were chosen to look impressive at their employers' glittering tables. There was no faulting Parkes in the matter of dress, but he was narrow-chested and spindly-legged and had a sallow, bony face that must look like a death's head at the feast.

Dan motioned him to a chair. "Who has the key to the safe?"

"I keep the only one. It is on my person at all times."

"And the house keys?"

"The housekeeper has the indoor keys. I have all the outer ones."

"Including the key to the gate?"

"Yes."

"Does anyone else have one?"

Parkes hesitated.

"If anyone else has a key, you need to tell me. Otherwise I might have to think that it was you who opened the gate."

The butler sucked his lower lip, finally brought himself to answer, "Miss Parmeter had a key."

"I didn't find one in her study. Where did she keep it?"

"You will have to ask Miss Dean, her lady's maid."

Dan made a note. "So Miss Parmeter could have opened the gate herself and admitted a visitor without anyone else knowing about it."

"My mistress is – was – entitled to her privacy. For years she was the subject of scurrilous and malicious gossip."

Hardly surprising given her history, Dan thought.

"Was she expecting someone this morning?"

"That I do not know."

"But if she was, would you have any idea who?"

"No. Again, that is a question for Miss Dean."

"Where were you this morning?"

Dan noted down a lengthy account of consultations with the cook about the evening's dinner arrangements; trips to the cellars; correspondence with the vintner; work at the accounts here in his room; the issue of instructions to the footmen; and a host of other mundane duties.

"What will you do now? Seek another position?"

"I shall not remain in service. After working for Miss Parmeter, I could not work for anyone else. I have always had the ambition to set up as a grocer, selling to the quality, you understand. We shall bring our plans forward."

"We?"

"Miss Evans, the first housemaid, and I plan to marry."

"Expensive, starting out in business. Not to mention getting married."

"She's a capable woman, will be an asset to the business. And I have some money put by. And if I had not, I would not line my pocket by killing the best mistress a man ever had." He paused, then said in a rush, "I knew her when she was a girl, working with her mother as a dresser in the theatre at Bristol. You'd never think she was going to turn into a beauty if you'd seen her then, so gawky as she was. No one was more surprised than I when I heard she'd become a fashionable figure in society. I was in desperate straits myself, had lost money on an investment in a Newfoundland fishery. I applied to her when all other sources of help had failed me. She remembered me and offered me work. I have been with her ever since."

"She didn't mind that you knew about her humble background?"

"She never denied it. So, no, she didn't mind."

The housekeeper came in next. She was a quick, busy woman in her late thirties, with a manner as rigid as her whalebone casing. She confirmed what Parkes had said about the keys. Her morning had also been a productive one: sorting the linen cupboard with one of the housemaids; preparing the tradesmen's weekly orders; checking that the housemaids had dusted furniture and polished grates to the required standard.

"Will you look for similar work?" Dan asked.

She smiled coyly. "I think not. I am expecting to go into the grocery business."

Dan glanced back through his notes. He had definitely written that Parkes intended to marry Miss Evans, the first housemaid. Hastily, he brought the conversation to a close.

The housekeeper was followed by Sarah Dean, the lady's maid. She was an attractive, fashionable young woman, who would have spent more time with Louise Parmeter than any of the others. It had not lowered her opinion of her mistress and her grief seemed genuine. She told Dan she had spent the morning tidying Louise Parmeter's wardrobe, added that her mistress was generous in the matter of cast-off petticoats and gowns.

"You'd know a great deal about Miss Parmeter's private affairs?"

"If you mean affairs of the heart, of course."

"Was there one? An affair of the heart, one that she wanted kept secret?"

Sarah regarded Dan for a moment before answering, "You think a lover killed her?"

"I don't think anything yet."

"Come now, Mr Foster, you think like a law officer. A lover murdered her and so she brought it on herself."

"I've never known a murder victim yet who was to blame for their own murder."

She arched her eyebrows. "Then perhaps you are in the wrong job."

"It will help me to find Miss Parmeter's killer if you answer the question."

She considered this for a moment, then said, "She had recently been close to Mr Cruft of the banking family. Young Mr Cruft. But she had begun to find him tedious, since he asked her to marry him."

"He's a rich man. It would have been a good marriage."

"It would have been, like all marriages, a prison. And why

would Miss Parmeter shackle herself to a husband? She had money of her own, and independence."

"How did Cruft take his dismissal?"

She smiled. "He tried to stab himself."

"You find that funny?"

"So it was. He burst in on one of Miss Parmeter's literary gatherings, produced a small knife, flung himself around the room declaring his love for her, then pinked himself in the arm. If he thought she was the sort to swoon over a drop of blood, he soon realised his mistake. When she had finished laughing, she told him he had a promising career in comedy and said she would recommend him to Mr Sheridan. The man's a fool."

"Even fools have their pride."

"Considering how he howled over a tiny scratch, I doubt he has the courage to commit a murder. I've never seen such a nerveless creature."

The weak, Dan thought, could sometimes be surprisingly ferocious, if goaded sufficiently. If Cruft went to Berkeley Square to confront Louise and the conversation grew heated, rage got the better of him, the candlestick as murder weapon came easily to hand, the diamonds hastily snatched to make it look like an ordinary robbery, the memoirs removed for fear of embarrassing revelations…

"Was it Mr Cruft she was expecting to pay a secret call this morning?"

Sarah looked surprised. "She wasn't expecting anyone."

"But she did secretly receive visitors in the mornings?"

"In the past, when circumstances demanded. But there has been no one for some time now. And there was nothing secret about the affair with Mr Cruft. Not all her lovers were so feeble, though. Lord Hawkhurst was very put out when she ended their affair. The man is a philanderer, has used and abandoned a score of women, but like all such creatures he cannot abide to be the one who is abandoned. He took to sending Miss Parmeter gifts: a pair of black mourning gloves; a black hatband; black ostrich feathers; a silver coffin plate engraved 'Here Lies a Whore'. But it all stopped months ago."

"Did Miss Parmeter keep any of the gifts?"

"Of course not. She threw them in the rubbish where they belonged."

"Where did she keep her key to the garden gate?"

"In a jewellery box in her bedroom."

"Can you show me?"

"Now?"

Dan shut his notebook. "Yes, now."

Miss Parmeter's body had been moved to her bedroom, where it was about to be washed and dressed by the two respectably aged women sent by the firm Agnes Taylor had employed to make the funeral arrangements. They had got as far as laying out bowls, towels and a shroud. Dan told them to wait outside.

Sarah, averting her eyes from the figure lying on the bed and the paraphernalia surrounding it, opened a drawer in the dressing table and took out the key to a box decorated with Chinese scenes that stood on top of the table. Dan unlocked the casket. Inside, amongst what he assumed were her least valuable trinkets, lay a large key which he guessed fitted the garden gate. He pocketed it and he and Sarah left the room. Dan signalled to the women that they could return to their work.

"What are your plans now, Miss Dean?" asked Dan.

"Many women envied Miss Parmeter's style and believe that if they employ her maid, they will be able to match it. I shall have to choose my next situation carefully. Even I cannot perform miracles."

He thanked her and let her go.

Dan returned to the butler's room. The questioning went on with the cook, two footmen, two housemaids (one of them Mr Parkes's capable Miss Evans), and a scullery maid. They all had tales of Louise Parmeter's generosity and kindness: help in time of sickness; an apprenticeship for a younger brother or sister; a pension for an aged relative. At the end of it all, Dan had a complicated schedule of alibis that put each of the servants in view of one or more of their colleagues between 9 a.m., when Louise Parmeter went into her study, and shortly after midday, when her body was discovered. No one had seen her during that time and her standing instructions were that she was not to be disturbed while she was working. From time to time one or other of the servants had crossed the hall as they went about their business, but none had heard any sounds coming from her room.

Dan shuffled his notes together and put them in his pocket. The constables reported back from their canvass of the lane, which, apart from the stables, was occupied by small businesses serving the great houses in the square. No one had seen or heard anything. When Dan had dismissed them, he decided there should be enough daylight left to take a look outside. He went back up to the study.

He opened the door into the garden, checked the ground inside and out for footprints and found none. Three steps from the terrace led down to a gravel path. Dan walked along it, past the wide flowerbed which lay between the path and the high outer wall. The garden looked bleak and empty, but here and there tightly furled buds gave early signs of spring.

The garden ended in a small patch of woodland. It was dim and damp under the branches, the soil promisingly bare. Unfortunately, Townsend and the constables had already trampled the area around the gate, which was now locked. Dan tried Louise's key and confirmed that it fitted.

The wall was topped by broken glass, but that did not make it impossible for a determined person to scale. With the trees as cover, they would stand a good chance of not being seen from the house as they dropped down. Risky though, and they could not fail to attract attention in the busy lane on the other side. Townsend's conclusion that someone in the house had let the killer in seemed the likeliest explanation at the moment.

Dan heard a light tread on his right. There was someone creeping through the trees. He peered into the gloom, could just make out a shape drawing near. He stepped behind a trunk and waited.

Chapter Eight

A woman's figure became more distinct as she moved through the dappled shade, head bent, a white handkerchief fluttering in her hand. Dan stepped forward and took off his hat.

"Good afternoon, Miss Taylor."

"Mr Foster! I didn't know you were there."

She wiped her face, made a brave attempt to stop crying, failed. "Oh dear, forgive me, it has all been so awful."

He held out his arm. "Why don't you come and sit down? I saw a bench over there."

"Yes, the rustic seat." She placed her hand on his sleeve, let him guide her to the tiny glade with its carefully fashioned rough arbour. Dan settled her on the bench and sat down next to her.

"You are so kind. It's just that I don't know what's to become of me now Miss Parmeter has gone. I know I shouldn't be thinking of myself, but I don't know where I shall go, what I shall do."

"There, Miss Taylor, it's natural you should be worried about your future. There isn't a servant in the house who doesn't feel the same way."

She stiffened. "I'm not a servant."

"I know. You're Miss Parmeter's protégée. Which means what, exactly?"

"She has been my guide and mentor, and has helped me to make good the deficiencies of my education. As if it could have been anything but deficient, when I was constrained to devote all my energies to the sordid business of obtaining the necessities of life. Sometimes, Mr Foster, I have thought the Muses must be very cruel to visit someone in my position."

"What was your position?"

"I worked in my mother's millinery business. She had no choice but to go into trade after Father died. Of course, this meant I had less time to dedicate to my literary studies and I had all but given up hope of ever joining the pantheon of poets until one day Mother told me to bring some hats to Miss Parmeter. Mother, of course, had no idea who she was, but I had read all her work. I brought the hats, and I brought one of my poems with them. A pastoral… *The shining hill where Flora springs, / Where wafts the southern breeze, / The woodland grove where warblers sing, / Where sigh the ancient trees—*"

"Very pretty," Dan said, wondering how anyone could stand such stuff. The only verses he ever read were those printed in *The Sporting Magazine*, with refrains such as *"A boxing we will go, will go."*

She smiled. "Do you think so?"

She was not so plain as her blotched face had suggested. She was not dazzling, but pretty enough in an unassuming way. Perhaps if her dress were more flattering, she would even be a beauty.

"Imagine my feelings, Mr Foster, when I was shown into Miss Parmeter's boudoir – and she was not there! She had entrusted Miss Dean with making a selection for her. Mother had instructed me, as usual, not to leave until a purchase had been made. You will be surprised how often we have left goods on approval, never to see them again, even at houses of the most respectable appearance."

Dan was not surprised, but let her continue.

"I told Miss Dean that I would call for the hats on the morrow, and before leaving I slipped my poem into one of the boxes. Mother's scolding was nothing to the suspenseful terrors I endured that night! In the morning, pale-visaged, trembling, I got into the cab. I was scarcely able to breathe by the time the driver pulled up in the square. I tottered to the door – was admitted – after a short wait I was shown to the drawing room. Miss Parmeter was sitting on a sofa, surrounded by the boxes. I durst not raise mine eyes to her face, but fixed my gaze on the floor as I curtseyed."

"And she told you she liked your verses?" Dan said, hoping to bring her tale to a close before the moon came up.

She ignored his prompt. "'So you are the milliner's daughter who writes verse?' said Miss Parmeter. 'Madame,' I answered, blushing at my temerity, 'I am.' 'And what was your education?' 'My father was a clerk in a law firm, an honest if not an elevated calling. He taught me to read, tutored me as if I was a son. But he died, and for the rest I was left to myself, reading whenever I could steal an hour from my labours.' 'Have you read Shakespeare?' 'Oh, yes, madame, and the Bible, and poetry, and Eliza Hayward, and—' 'Have you read Dryden?' At this I felt my heart sink within me. 'No,' I stammered, 'I have not heard of Dryden.'

"She was silent for so long a time I ventured to raise my eyes and look into that intelligent face on which Genius had left its unmistakable mark. 'Very well,' she said. 'Bring me some more of your verses tomorrow at three.' With that, she rose and rang the bell. 'And I'll take them all,' she added, waving her hand at the boxes. 'Yes, madame,' I gasped, and, almost sinking, fled from the room."

She paused to draw breath. Dan seized the chance to bring her narrative to an end. "And so she became your patron and you came to live here. When was that?"

"Eighteen months ago." She sighed. "It is a year since my *Poems on Several Occasions* took their first tremulous steps into the world. Miss Parmeter found nearly five hundred subscribers – many of them peers of the realm – and arranged for her own publisher, Mr Johnson of St Paul's Churchyard, to publish them in a handsome volume. They have been described as 'works of native genius', 'full of noble sentiments', possessed of a 'fine imagination', and exhibiting a 'prodigious variety of poetic expression'. They ran into three editions. And the fountain of inspiration continues to flow, Mr Foster."

"Does it?" said Dan. "But it's getting cold, Miss Taylor. You should go indoors."

He escorted her back into the house through a side door near the kitchen garden. They parted in the hall, she to climb wearily to her room. Their conversation had clarified one thing for him. The first suspect in a murder case was often the person who found the body. In this instance, there was no reason to suspect Agnes Taylor, who had nothing to gain by Miss Parmeter's death. At one stroke, she had been deprived of patronage and place, was faced with the prospect of having to go back to a hard, obscure life. Why would she kill the woman who offered her a chance to rise in the world?

The study door shot open.

"Where the hell have you been, Foster?" John Townsend demanded. "I'm waiting for your report."

Dan followed him into the room. "There's not much to say. None of the people the constables spoke to saw or heard anything. As for the servants, there's not one of them who didn't have a good word for their mistress. Not one who doesn't have an alibi either. I did discover that she had her own key to the gate and would sometimes admit visitors who didn't want to be seen, though no one can suggest anyone she may have been meeting this morning."

"Which means there was no one: no one ever kept a secret from their servants. And it doesn't mean one of them couldn't have slipped away to open the garden gate."

"They would have had to lift the key first. Miss Parmeter kept hers in a locked jewellery box in her bedroom." Dan took the key from his pocket. "This is hers. Mr Parkes has the only other one."

Townsend brushed the key aside. "And it didn't occur to you that anyone in the house could have found an opportunity to get hold of one of them and have another copy made? Damn me, Foster, you've got us nowhere. You might as well have spent the afternoon dozing in an armchair for all the good you've done here. That only leaves one option. We'll have to search the servants' quarters."

He pulled the bell cord by the fireplace.

"But we've no evidence to suspect them. We've no warrant for a search either."

"Warrant? Pho! This is a matter that concerns the Prince of Wales. And I'd like to know when lacking a warrant ever stopped you doing your duty." The door opened and Parkes came in. "We're going to search the servants' rooms, Mr Parkes," Townsend said. "You will escort us, if you please."

"Search our rooms? Why? What for?"

"Why, to catch a killer. If you please, Mr Parkes."

"But this is an outrage!" Parkes rounded on Dan. "I told you, none of us would have done anything to hurt Miss Parmeter. Why should we be treated like common criminals? We have worked for her well and faithfully for years. To be suspected of having something to do with her death—"

Townsend rapped his cane on the floor. "Come along, Foster."

The butler's protests accompanied them as they worked through the rooms at the top of the house. Townsend scattered clothes, upended beds and chairs, tipped over boxes. By the time they reached the last apartment, which the footmen shared, Parkes had run out of things to say. Townsend tore off the bedsheets, threw over the mattresses, rattled his cane under the bed and brought forth ringing sounds from the chamber pot. Finally, he swept brushes, razors and soap off the dressing table.

"Are these all the rooms?"

"There's Pickering's lodgings over the stables," Parkes said.

"Who's Pickering?"

"Head groom, and coachman when required. There are a couple of grooms under him, but they live out."

"You didn't mention him," Townsend said to Dan.

"I didn't question him."

Townsend tutted. "We'd better go and take a look." He thrust his cane under his arm and stumped irritably out of the room.

Dan picked his way over the mess and, with an apologetic shrug at Parkes, followed Townsend down the wooden staircase and through the servants' door on to the carpeted second floor corridor. They went out through the study. Outside, Dan unlocked the garden gate and secured it again when they had passed through to the lane.

They faced a row of workshops and houses of varying shapes and sizes. A chair mender worked in a dim clutter of discarded chairs, tables and cupboards which he had patched together for sale to those who had not much money to spare. Behind a barred gate, two or three dairy cows were tethered to feed troughs. A muck-spattered milkmaid leaned on the gate and amused herself by winking at Dan as he and Townsend passed. The wide double doors of a cavernous building stood open, revealing vats of steaming water where soaked laundrymaids struggled to paddle, lift and wring unwieldy tangles of sopping linen. All was noise, hurry and ripe smells.

The stables were next to the laundry near the Mount Street end of the lane. The wide gates opened on to a well-swept yard with a muck heap in one corner, a water pump in the middle, and a sleeping dog which leapt up to bark at them. There was a coach house next to the stable block. A row of horses' heads hung over the stall doors, benignly eyeing the visitors. Through the open harness room door Dan caught snatches of a mournful rendition of *Over the Hills and Far Away*.

The melancholy notes stopped and a man in his shirtsleeves appeared in the doorway. He was taller than Dan, who put him at around six foot four. Dan, noticing the scarring on his knuckles, recognised a fellow pugilist. It was common for the wealthy to hire fighting men to take them about, for even the residents of Berkeley Square were not safe from footpads and highwaymen late at night.

Townsend, straightening his shoulders and giving a jaunty swing of his cane, saw only a potential suspect.

"You're the Bow Street men, I take it," Pickering said. "The lads and I have already spoken to your constables."

"Then you can speak to me, Snowball," said Townsend, stepping uninvited into the harness room.

Pickering acknowledged the insult with a twitch of his eyebrows and went in after him. He sat down at the table where he had been cleaning some metalwork, a mug of ale at his elbow. He made a show of working calmly at his polishing while Townsend made a show of searching the room.

Townsend rattled the row of harnesses hanging neatly along the wall with his cane. "Where were you this morning?"

"Like I told the constable, I was working here in the stables. There are plenty of stable hands who can vouch for me. Then I went to Lord Stanhope's in Conduit Street to look over a pair of bays he wanted to sell. Miss Parmeter had a fancy for them."

Townsend scattered a pile of folded horse blankets. "What time did you go out?"

"About half past eleven."

"And you have no idea who went into the house?"

"How would I? I wasn't here."

"Nor ever saw anybody hanging around?" Townsend asked, pulling a toolbox out from under the workbench and emptying its contents on top.

"No."

Townsend abandoned his scrutiny of a bottle of linseed oil and said, "You can come with us. We're going to have a look around your rooms."

"Why do you want to search my rooms?"

"Hiding something, are you?"

Pickering made no answer. He reached for the coat hanging on the back of his chair, but Townsend hustled him out. "Search his pockets," he snapped at Dan.

The coat yielded a comb, a pocket book, a handkerchief, a ring of keys, a nail from a horseshoe, and a handful of oats. Dan took it with him and went after the other two up the outside staircase to the living rooms which were over the stables. The coachman must have been as used to living with the smell of horses, straw and embrocation as Dan had been to the sweat, spirits and liniment when he was brought up in Noah's gymnasium.

"Find any keys, Foster?" Townsend asked when Dan got upstairs.

"Yes."

"Hand 'em over." Townsend thrust them at Pickering. "And where might these be for?"

Pickering counted them off. "The stables, feed bins, medicine cupboard, these rooms."

"Key to the gate?"

"No."

"What, and you just a few steps away from the shortest way into the house?"

"I go in by the area steps."

Townsend indicated that he should return the keys to Dan. "Go and check."

Dan took the bunch, handed Pickering his jacket and went back down the wooden stairs. None of the keys matched the key in his possession. For good measure he tried the ones that most nearly resembled it in the garden gate. None fitted.

When he got back to Pickering's room, Townsend was emptying drawers and pulling furniture about. Two pairs of best-quality boots lay where he had thrown them, the high polish scuffed by the impact. Pickering leaned against the wall, his arms folded, outwardly unruffled though his eyes followed Townsend's every move. The coachman had put his jacket on.

It was a good fit; the dark blue fabric over the striped waistcoat and black top boots suited him.

"Got a lot of fancy togs," Townsend said, flinging them on to the rumpled bed.

"Most of it is livery," Pickering answered.

"Odd, ain't it, for a man like you to know about horses? Not the usual line of business for your kind."

"No, I suppose employers are afraid that we'll roast and eat the horses. Or roast and eat the employers."

Townsend had his head in a cupboard and did not hear this. Dan hid his grin as Townsend emerged with a tin of rattling coin. He poured the contents on to the table. Pickering clenched and unclenched his fists, but said nothing. Dan guessed that staying silent was the only way he could keep his temper. The man had discipline as well as a fine form. Stood light on his feet too, with a good sense of balance.

"Where'd you get all this?"

"I saved it."

"What for? Trying to get passage back home?"

"What, to Vauxhall?"

Dan's smile broke out in full, was curbed before Townsend saw it.

"To Africa," Townsend said.

"Not me. Lambeth born and bred."

Townsend grunted. "Got a girl, though? Wanting to get married?"

"More than one, and no plans to make any of 'em permanent."

Townsend turned away from the cupboard and stood in the middle of the room, looking about him. There was nowhere else left to rifle. He prodded Pickering in the chest with his cane.

"I'm looking at you, Mungo. And I'm warning you not to go anywhere without telling me first. Got the constables here to keep an eye on you. So just you be careful."

Townsend jerked his head at Dan. The two officers went down to the yard. The sun was setting, the reddened sky grimy with chimney smoke. Clouds of soap-scented steam gusted from the laundry.

"It's mighty convenient that he was out of the way just as the murder was taking place," Townsend said.

"But we don't know for certain what time the murder was committed," Dan said. "It could have been at any time during the morning."

"Try and pay attention, Foster. I have already established that the killer was still in the study when Miss Taylor knocked on the door."

"That was just one possibility."

"That was my deduction based on the evidence."

"Even if the killer was disturbed before he could take all the jewels, it was not necessarily by Miss Taylor. He might have heard someone in the hall before that, panicked and been long gone by the time she arrived."

"You could go on making up ifs and buts for ever. I prefer to rely on the facts before me. The murder took place just before twelve, and Pickering made himself scarce at around the same time. He could have opened the garden gate before he went out."

"We didn't find any key."

"Use your head, Foster. There are a thousand and one ways he could have got rid of it by now."

"And a thousand and one ways he could have run by now."

"And drawn attention to himself? No, he's a cunning beggar, that one. On his own admission he was in and out of the main house. He'd have had a chance to get hold of the key. He could have given a copy to his accomplice beforehand just so we wouldn't find it on him. No, we're on to something here." Townsend put his hand in his pocket and pulled out a sheaf of papers. "Drawings and description of the jewels. Tomorrow I want you to take them round the higher-class pawnbrokers and jewellers. A haul like this is likely to have caused a stir and someone might have heard something. And get copies into Bow Street for circulation further afield. I'm going to check the coachman's story."

Townsend straightened his yellow waistcoat and fixed his cane under his arm before stepping around the corner into the square. He strutted along, head high, looking neither to the left nor the right. The crowd fell back and watched his impressive progress in awe. What could it all mean, they wondered, but that Principal Officer John Townsend was on the verge of solving another baffling crime?

Chapter Nine

Walking home through busy streets brightened by street lamps, the light of shop displays, and the glow from tavern windows, Dan recalled Miss Taylor's woeful face. Louise Parmeter's death had come hard to her: the loss of a patron was no small thing. Her life had something in common with his own. They had both come from poor backgrounds: she from a hard and uncongenial business, he from running wild on the streets. For both of them there had been a scarce believable rise from the depths of misery and poverty.

And then came the fall.

The fear of it was always there, a beast creeping in the shadows. He had glimpses of it in the sight of a starving child slinking barefoot in a filth-filled court, the lurch of a cripple, the milky eyes of a blind man, the stagger of a drunk in rags swarming with lice. The people who were still where he had once been. Where he could be again.

He passed the top of an alley, caught a blast of the foul stench from the dank darkness. A movement caught his eye. He peered into the gloom, saw the hunched shape of a rat snuffling in the rubbish. As he turned his head, he noticed a tall man in a long grey coat on the crowded pavement behind him. Before he was even sure the man was there, the figure darted into the alley, leaving behind only the impression of the tilt of a hat, the flick of a hem, the lift of a heel. A shadow skittering into the shadows.

Dan came up to the queue outside the doors of the Panorama in Leicester Fields, pushed his way through. They were waiting for admission into the circular building where they would marvel at three-hundred-and-sixty-degree views of London, Brighton, or the fleet at the Nore. Dan had seen that one himself and been impressed: he had felt as if he was standing on the shore looking out across the crowded anchorage. He would have to bring Alex when he was old enough.

In a few minutes he would be home with his family: his son, his wife, his mother-in-law. He was doing well, had earned a good reward on his last case, with any luck would do well out of this one. The Prince of Wales was not renowned for being close with his money. Dan could keep all of them fed, clothed and housed, and he was putting money by.

He would not fall. He shook off his dismal fancies and strode on.

Late in the afternoon of the following day, Dan decided he had talked to enough jewellers and went back to the Bow Street office. There was a note from Townsend summoning him to Berkeley Square. He turned round and went straight out again.

The square was full of carriages, their occupants flocking to visit friends in the hope of discovering some gossip about Louise Parmeter's murder. Plebeian sensation-seekers milled in the street around the house, thrilling to the sight of so many gorgeously dressed men and women, so many high-bred horses and liveried footmen, so many gleaming carriages with ornate insignia. A hackney coach drew up as Dan forced his way into the house.

The hall was crowded with servants, the men shouting and shaking their fists, the women wailing and weeping. Parkes's voice rose above the rest: "This is an outrage!" Miss Taylor, probably overcome by her sensibility, swooned in a chair while the scullery maid fanned her with a greasy apron. Sarah Dean stood quietly by, her haughty contempt more damning than all the noisy protests.

Pickering stood at the centre of the commotion, his hands cuffed behind him, his arms in the grip of two constables. One of the officers sported a red mark around his eye that in a few hours would turn into an impressive shiner. He was getting his own back on the prisoner by attempting to shove him along with vicious punches in the back. Pickering refused to budge.

Townsend, struggling to hold the servants back with his cane, called, "Foster! Don't just stand there. Get him into the hackney."

"Why have you arrested Mr Pickering?"

"That's police business. Not to be discussed in front of all and sundry."

All and sundry sent up a furious howl.

For the sake of showing a united front, Dan saved his questions for later. He shouldered the vengeful constable out of the way. "That's enough. Mr Pickering, you're with me."

Pickering allowed Dan to lead him off. Dan opened the front door. There was an "ooh!" of delighted surprise, then a surge of voices. "It's the Negro!" "Look at him, the murdering devil!" "They should have been cleared out of the city years ago!"

Dan got Pickering down the steps and into the hackney. Townsend stepped out behind him to cheers and applause. He acknowledged the adulation with a regal wave, descended, and pushed Dan aside.

"You can meet me at Bow Street."

"Mr Townsend," Dan said in a low voice, "this is surely over-hasty. There are other suspects."

"I think you'll find there's no need for your other suspects."

"But what have you got on Pickering?"

"Irrefutable evidence, that's what."

He stepped into the cab. Dan shut the door and waved on the coachman. He watched the vehicle rattle off, then glanced back at the house. The servants crowded around the front door, Parkes at their head. The door swung shut, blocking out their distressed faces.

A crowd had already gathered outside the Bow Street Magistrates' Office when Dan arrived. It was always a mystery how news got out so quickly. There were reporters there too, shouting questions and supplying their own answers when none were forthcoming from the police.

Pickering was still at the front desk, where the gaoler was recording his details. Full name: Ignatius Pickering; age: twenty-seven; occupation: coachman. Townsend stood by, agreeing placidly with his fellow officers that yes, it had been a good, quick arrest.

"Intuition and intelligence," he said, "that's what did it."

When Pickering had been booked in, Townsend ordered two men to take him into a side room. They pushed the prisoner into a seat and tied his ankles to the chair legs.

"Come with me, Foster," Townsend said. "You might just learn something."

Dan followed him into the room. He leaned against the wall, folded his arms, and waited for the lesson to begin.

Townsend paced around the prisoner two or three times before coming to a halt in front of him. "You know why you're under arrest?"

"A mistress is murdered. It must be one of the servants. One of them is black. It must be him."

Townsend clipped Pickering on the ear. "Don't be clever with me. You're here because you lied about your whereabouts. Your stable hands confirmed that you were in the yard all morning and went out at half past eleven yesterday morning, like you said. But when I checked with Lord Stanhope's head stableman, he told me you didn't get there till nearly one o'clock. It doesn't take an hour and a half to get from Berkeley Square to Conduit Street."

"What difference does that make? I was there, wasn't I?"

"With over an hour unaccounted for. And that hour fits in with the time Miss Parmeter was murdered, which was shortly before midday, when Agnes Taylor knocked on the study door."

He glanced at Dan. "As I have determined."

Dan made no comment. This was not the time to dispute the point again.

Townsend, satisfied that the argument had been conceded, continued, "Where were you and what were you doing?"

"Why should I have been doing anything particular? I dawdled over an errand. What servant doesn't?"

"That's a lot of dawdling for a ten-minute walk. What time did you get to Lord Stanhope's?"

"Why would I remember the exact time I got there?"

Another cuff. "You've got a fancy watch in that smart weskit."

"Doesn't mean I'm looking at it every five minutes."

"Were you keeping out of the way while your accomplice broke in and murdered Miss Parmeter? Or maybe you were doing the deed yourself?"

"Never! I would never harm her."

"So you got someone else to do it for you. Or was it an accident? Maybe he overstepped the mark, went further than you'd agreed? In which case don't you want to see him pay for it?"

"I had nothing to do with it."

"But you're the one who's going to hang unless you tell me where I can find him."

"I know nothing about it. And I don't see how you can pin it on me when I wasn't there."

"So where were you? Waiting somewhere for him to come and divvy up the spoils?"

"If I was in possession of a fortune why would I have stuck around mucking out stables?"

Townsend rapped the top of Pickering's head with his cane. "How do I know what goes on in that woolly head of yours?" He leaned down, put his face close to Pickering's. "Tell me who your accomplice is or I'll have you dancing at the end of a rope."

They went on like this for another hour, with Townsend delivering sly little raps and slaps and knocks. None of them were major blows in themselves, but cumulatively they were irritating and humiliating. Pickering's temper finally snapped.

"I tell you, I know nothing about it, you damned dog!"

Townsend bunched his fist, drove it into the side of Pickering's head. He tipped to the side and the chair toppled to the ground. Townsend raised his cane, but before he could strike the fallen man, Dan stepped in front of him.

"I think we've been at this long enough to see he's not going to change his answer," he said, righting the man and chair.

"He'll sing a different tune by the time I've finished with him," Townsend retorted.

"Do you want to spend the whole night in here with him? I say we should lock him up and leave him to think over his options. That should soften him up now he knows what to expect."

Pickering, his cheek seeping blood, opened his mouth to shout his defiance, but Dan, his hands grasping the prisoner's coat collar as he settled him in the seat, gave a warning shake of his head.

Townsend clicked his tongue. "It is getting late." He straightened his coat, tucked his cane under his arm, put on his hat. "Very well. Take him over to the Brown Bear."

When he had gone, Dan untied Pickering's legs and helped him to his feet. "You know," he said, "Townsend does have a point. That missing hour looks bad. It would be a lot better for you if you told us where you were."

"What's this? One does the beating, the other's my best friend?"

"Why don't you tell us? Are you protecting someone? Someone you're willing to hang for?"

"I've got nothing to say to you."

"Suit yourself."

Dan led Pickering across the street to the Brown Bear where the landlord provided cells for the use of the Bow Street officers. Dan shackled Pickering to the bed and re-cuffed his hands in front of him. Then he placed a pitcher of water and a hunk of bread within his reach, and left him a handkerchief so he could clean himself up.

Chapter Ten

"I never wanted him here in the first place." Caroline banged a dinner plate on the table. Mrs Harper stood by making soothing noises that only increased her daughter's irritation. "He's lazy, and he answers back, and he's always missing when I want him to do something. Why you ever thought he should live with us I don't know."

Dan, who had hardly had time to take off his hat and coat before Caroline launched into her complaint, said, "If you remember, when I offered Nick a home, you and I were not living together."

He was treading on dangerous ground bringing that up. He and Caroline had lived apart for a while after the discovery that he had fathered a son. Dan had kept Alex with him, employed a nurse to look after him, and offered Nick his keep in return for helping about the house. When Dan moved back to Russell Street he had insisted on keeping his promise to the boy.

"Come now, Caro, he's not a bad lad," Mrs Harper said. "He does his best."

"Does his best for himself, you mean."

"You still haven't told me what he's done," said Dan.

"He helped himself to the pie meant for tonight's supper. The greedy little pig ate the lot!"

"There's no harm done, lovey," Mrs Harper said. "I've been and got another pie."

"That's not the point, Mother. Oh, now look what you've done."

Caroline rushed across the room and lifted a bawling Alex out of his cradle. Angrily she jiggled him up and down. He gazed up into her face, puckered his forehead and cried louder than ever. Mrs Harper hovered around her daughter, trying to take the child from her. Irritably, Caroline snatched him away from her flapping hands.

"Nick ate a pie?" Dan said. "Is that it?"

"Isn't it enough?"

"Did you tell him he couldn't eat it?"

"Why should I have to do that? He shouldn't help himself to things."

"Caroline, you have to give the boy a chance. Just as Noah gave me a chance when I was his age."

She opened her mouth to make a sharp retort, thought better of it and said, "You were different."

"I wasn't. Here, give him to me."

Rescued from his mother's anger, Alex calmed down and nestled quietly in Dan's arms. Mrs Harper pottered around the table and finished laying up. Caroline joined her, fidgeted with one of the plates.

"I'll have a word with Nick," Dan said. "Where is he?"

"How should I know? He took off an hour ago."

"You didn't throw him out?"

"No. He ran away."

"He hasn't got anywhere to go."

At least she had the grace to look ashamed of herself. Dan put Alex back in his cradle. "I'm going to look for him."

He retrieved his hat and coat and stepped out into Russell Street, headed towards the lights and noise of the Piazza. The shops in the surrounding streets were still open, the coffee houses and taverns full. A few of the market stalls were trading, though most stallholders had packed up and gone home.

Dan made his way through the bawling traders and voluble pedestrians, many of whom nodded a greeting at him, for this was his home patch. Nick could be anywhere by now. He might have gone back to Southwark, where Dan first met him, to hook up with one of the gangs of street children. It was what Dan had done when he found himself alone in the world. He had left his mother huddled on a bundle of rags on the floorboards of their filthy room, reeking of gin, vomit and the last man to lie with her. The parish had come to take her away for burial. From his hiding place in the alley, he had seen them haul her out like a sack of rubbish. Then he had run. Not long after, he had been recruited into Weaver's child-troop of thieves, whores and pickpockets. That old devil must be long dead by now. If he wasn't, he soon would be if Dan ever came across him again.

Maybe Nick had not gone so far. Covent Garden was a good place for getting food and somewhere to sleep. There were plenty of stalls to snatch your dinner from, and when the shopkeepers had cleared the goods from the shelves outside their shops for the night, you could sleep snug in the space beneath. Dan leaned against one of the columns on the Piazza and scanned the bustling scene. After a moment he located a small figure standing in the shadows by a bread stall, watching the baker pack his unsold goods.

Dan stepped out from the colonnade and edged around the square. If it had not been Nick, he would have taken no notice: arresting a child for stealing a stale pastry did not appeal to him. He collared the boy as he reached out his hand, yanked him away from the table before the baker knew anything about it.

"Not coming home for supper, Nick?"

"Go to 'ell! I ain't coming."

"You are." Dan dragged him back to the colonnade, shoved him down on to the steps and sat next to him. "What do you think you were doing?"

"Wot's it look like?"

"Don't cheek me, Nick. Answer the question."

"Making a living."

"You don't need to make a living."

"She threw me out."

"If you mean Mrs Foster, no, she didn't."

"She wanted to."

"It's not surprising, is it, if you're giving her a hard time?"

"She's always on my back. *Call that clean? What do you think that is? Were you born stupid or are you doing it on purpose?* And now I suppose you are going to thrash me. Well I ain't staying for it."

He jumped up. Dan pulled him down again, held him in place while he wriggled and squirmed to break free.

"I remember," Dan said, "how at first it was like a miracle. Suddenly you've got enough to eat, somewhere to sleep. Someone to notice whether you're alive or dead. Then the difficulties set in. All the rules you have to learn: wearing shoes, reading and writing, plates and forks, washing – you always seem to have your head in a bucket. And all the ordinary things are no go all at once. Helping yourself to something from a market stall. Diving into a pocket. A drop of daffy. Dad caught me with a pint of gin once. He went mad, took it off me, said I'd be no good if I went that way. I never drank the stuff again."

Nick stopped struggling. "Did he beat you?"

Dan let go of his arm. "No, he didn't. And I'm not going to beat you. But you've got to do better, Nick, if you're going to be any help to me."

"Help? With your work, do you mean? Like when I watched them body snatchers for you?"

"I wasn't thinking of that, but if it's what you want later, when you've had a bit of schooling, then I don't see why not. I'm thinking of now. I didn't take you in to make things more difficult at home. I need you to pull your weight, help me out there."

"I was helping you out," Nick wailed. "I took him the pie like you said. And she said I was a thief, and when I tried to tell her she wouldn't listen."

"Like I said? What are you talking about?"

"Your pal. The one who asked me for something to eat."

"Someone told you I said you should give him a pie?"

"Just something to eat. But the pie was handy, so I give him that."

"What did he say his name was?"

"He didn't. Just said he'd left you not ten minutes ago and you'd sent him round to get some food. You don't mean it was a take-in?"

"What do you think? Did he come to the door, this pal of mine?"

"No. I'd just come out to go and get some candles and he stopped me, said he didn't want to knock on the door and trouble the missus. He waited in the street while I went back to the house for the food. You could knock me down with a feather. He was down on his luck, but he didn't look like a canter, not at all."

Dan laughed. "Looks like I took you off the streets just in time, if you're so easily fooled."

"But he wasn't on the cheating lay, I'm sure of it. Are you going to arrest him?"

"He'll be long gone by now. Besides, what's he done? Tricked someone into giving him a pie. I should think he'd have a shock if he found out he'd picked on a Bow Street officer's house."

Nick shook his head. "It don't make no sense. I could have swore he weren't shamming."

"Call it a lesson learned and be less ready to give away my household goods in future. What's more important is that you owe Mrs Foster an explanation."

"But I tried to explain. She wouldn't listen."

"You survived for years on the streets of London, and now you run away from a woman's sharp tongue? You can do better than that." Dan stood up. "And I'm ready for my supper. You coming, or do you prefer some rotten leftovers from the market?"

Nick grinned, fell in beside him. "Not me."

"And about that schooling."

Nick groaned.

"If I can do it, you can. I can find someone to teach you two or three mornings a week. If I do, will you go?"

Nick scuffed a bruised apple into the gutter. "All right… Mr Foster?"

"Yes?"

"You call Mr Noah 'Dad'. But he's not your dad. Mrs Harper told me."

"No, he's not."

"And you're not my dad."

Dan glanced down at the boy. He had his hands in his pockets, his head bent in thought. Dan frowned. This was going somewhere he had never intended. He already had a son, had never led Nick to believe that was a place he could occupy.

"No," he said, carefully. "But that was different. Noah didn't have children of his own."

There was a pause before Nick answered, "But you do."

"Yes. I'm Alex's dad." Was that spelling it out too bluntly?

They turned into Russell Street, walked on in silence. When Dan next looked at Nick, he had turned his face away, was staring into the road.

"Here we are," Dan said, rapping on the front door.

It was opened by Mrs Harper.

"Nick, there you are! Come along in, lovey, out of the cold. Why you didn't take your coat I don't know. No scarf either." She put her arm around his shoulders and guided him into the kitchen.

Nick sniffed. It's just the cold air, Dan told himself. He'll be fine once he's had a bit of supper and warmed himself by the fire.

When they had finished eating, Nick helped Mrs Harper tidy up. Alex was already in bed. Caroline flounced into a chair by the fire and opened a novel. It was one of Louise Parmeter's. She had been lucky to get it. Since the murder, the booksellers were running out of copies of her books.

Caroline was still smarting from being proved wrong about Nick's thieving, although Dan had broken the truth to her as gently as possible. Tact had not won her over and Dan foresaw an uncomfortable evening ahead. A good time to go to the Feathers in Holborn, see if he could gather anything useful about the murder of the girl in the blue dress.

"I have to go out," he said. "I'll be late back."

Caroline did not look up from her book. "When are you ever anything else?"

Chapter Eleven

Dan was at Noah's gymnasium early the next morning, working off his frustration with the lack of progress in both his cases. He had learned nothing useful at the Feathers last evening, and faced the prospect of wasting another day in the Louise Parmeter investigation while Townsend tried to bully a confession out of Pickering. Though he had to admit, as he sat sweating in the steam bath next door to the gym after his exercises, that Pickering's refusal to account for his whereabouts was damning.

Things started to look up when he was greeted at Bow Street by the news that John Townsend had been summoned to Windsor. One of the officers on permanent duty there had been called away and Townsend was to take his place at the King's side until tomorrow. That gave Dan an opportunity to follow his own leads.

He still had no idea why Townsend had asked for him only to charge ahead and arrest the first person that suited him without looking at the evidence Dan had gathered. The recently jilted young Cruft and the spiteful Lord Hawkhurst both merited further investigation. Sarah Dean had mentioned that Lord Hawkhurst's persecution of Louise Parmeter ended some months earlier. Randolph Cruft's resentment, on the other hand, was still raw. It made sense to start with Cruft.

First, Dan checked on Pickering. The door to the Brown Bear stood open and there were already porters, hackney coachmen and market traders inside enjoying their first ale of the day. There were one or two fellow officers too, waiting for work to come in from the magistrate, or a member of the public to rush in with a beating, robbery or, with any luck, murder to report.

Dan ordered some coffee and rolls and went upstairs. He asked the man on watch to unlock the door. A serving boy arrived with the tray of food and Dan carried it inside. Pickering lay on the bed. He sat up and swung his feet on to the floor.

Dan set down the tray and poured out the drinks. "Not the best in town, but it'll do. Here."

Pickering hesitated, took the mug. "Smells good," he conceded. He bit into one of the sugary rolls. "So are you taking me before the beak this morning?"

"I'll leave that to Mr Townsend, and as he's been called away, you'll have to wait." Dan took a bite of the roll, set it aside. Too sweet. "Why won't you tell us where you were on Monday morning?"

"I did tell you. I went to Lord Stanhope's stables."

"It didn't take you more than an hour to get from Berkeley Square to Conduit Street. You must have stopped somewhere on the way."

"I didn't."

Dan emptied his cup and stood up.

"That's it?" Pickering said.

"No point to keep asking you if you won't change your answer." Dan rapped on the door, waited for the gaoler to open it. "Maybe you'll answer me this. Do you know Randolph Cruft?"

"I know of him. Mr Parkes did a very good imitation of him. Sarah – Miss Dean – said he'd proposed to Miss Parmeter, but I know nothing about that."

"Did you ever see him going in at the garden gate, or passing through the mews?"

"No. Why, you don't think he had anything to do with her murder?"

"Maybe I do, but you're the favourite suspect at the moment. So if you do remember where you were on Monday morning, it might be worth letting me know."

As usual the Piccadilly road was jammed with coaches and the pavement crowded with shoppers. Hairdressers and chemists, hatters and greengrocers, jewellers and booksellers plied their trades out of the tall, inconvenient buildings of the previous century. Here a woman made and sold artificial flowers; there a man with less delicacy made and sold water closets. Yet it was not all commerce. The Green Park end was given over to mansions, the grandest of which was Devonshire House, set back behind high walls and ornate gates. The Crufts' residence was in Bolton Street close by.

It was some minutes before the door opened to Dan's ring at the bell. A lofty footman stared down at him. "The tradesman's entrance is via the area steps," he said, beginning a stately retreat.

Dan put his shoulder against the door. "Nice for the tradesmen, but I'm from Bow Street Magistrates' Office. Principal Officer Foster."

The man seemed inclined to insist that a Bow Street Runner belonged with the tradesmen, but after a second's hesitation said, "Walk in. I will tell Mr Cruft you are here."

He took Dan's hat and coat and left Dan in the hall to count his own reflections in the silver, glass and marble. The footman returned and with frigid politeness showed Dan up the stairs to a library. Its windows overlooked a formal garden with a large glasshouse at the end, its panes opaque with the steam exhaled by exotic plants. The library was magnificent, which was all Dan could have said about it afterwards. One magnificent library looked much like another: gleaming wood, ticking clock, periodicals scattered on small round tables, rows of leather-bound books with gilt titles.

Mr Cruft rose from behind his large desk. As he was

a short man, he was obliged to walk around it to shake hands.

"Good day, Mr Foster, good day. I think it is not taking too great a risk to say I know why you are here. Have a seat, have a seat. Can I offer you anything? Tea? Coffee? Wine? Madeira?"

"No, thank you," Dan said, taking the offered seat.

Cruft dismissed the footman with a nod and went back to his chair. He sat down and fiddled with a heavy gold watch chain that hung across his silk waistcoat.

"I was hoping to speak to Mr Randolph Cruft," Dan said.

"My son is not in London at present. His absence is, however, connected with your visit."

Dan took out his notebook. "Where is your son?"

"I sent him to Childwick Hall, my Hertfordshire estate. The boy is not yet of age. He is far too young to invest his future happiness in any female, and certainly not one of Miss Parmeter's type."

"You sent him away to remove him from her influence?"

"Correct. You must understand, Mr Foster, that Randolph has something of a deficit in the brain vault. This may seem like a harsh assessment of one's own flesh and blood, but it pays in this, as in all other matters, to take realistic stock of things. Of course, I don't deny that the woman was possessed of considerable assets, and not only in the fiscal department. What man would not be tempted to spend his leisure hours with such a creature? But she could not be regarded as a serious venture. However, it was clear to me as soon as I met her that she had something more long-term in view."

"It was my understanding that she turned down your son's offer of marriage."

"A transparent negotiating tool, designed to persuade my son to make a larger nuptial settlement. Youth does not like to hear the voice of experience, but I have been in business many years. I recognise a bubble when I see one."

"You say you met her. Where and when was that?"

Cruft flicked back through the pages of his engagement book. "I called on her at her home three weeks ago."

"And you asked her to stay away from your son?"

"I did more than that. I made two very generous offers, both of which she refused."

"Which were?"

"My opening bid was a proposal that I take over my son's role in the transaction, which would have ensured that she suffered no loss. At the same time, it would have undeceived my son as to the nature of her attachment to him. This was my preferred option. She, however, denied any intention to involve herself with any man on a business footing. I had no choice but to have recourse to my next strategy, which was to provide a cash settlement. This she also refused. She put on an impressive performance of affronted dignity, but we men of commerce know a thing or two about double dealing. The only real question at issue was what the final balance would be. That is where our negotiations stood at the time of her death."

"How much did she ask for?"

"She had not stipulated an amount."

"But you were expecting a demand, and that it would be high?"

"Most certainly."

"Must have been quite a worry."

"Not at all. One does not rely solely on the offers on the table. If absolutely necessary, I would have cast off my son without a shilling, which would rather reduce his market value, don't you think?"

"So her death is convenient for you."

"It has certainly saved me money and trouble. But I did not kill her, Mr Foster. That would have been a quite unnecessary risk."

"When did your son go to Hertfordshire?"

"He left the day after I spoke to Miss Parmeter."

"And how do you know he hasn't defied you and come back to London?"

"The steward has instructions to write to me every day giving details of my son's movements, and Randolph is required to countersign each letter. My steward has worked with me for many years; he is not susceptible to bribery. In any case, now the danger is removed there is no reason why Randolph cannot return. I have written to him to that effect."

Dan thought there were other motives besides money that might prompt someone to show sympathy to a young, lovesick man with such a father. And if young Cruft had any spirit at all, he would not abandon his love simply on a parent's say-so. With that in mind, his father might have taken more direct steps to remove the threat. If the elder Cruft's was not the hand that dealt the killing blow, it might be the hand that paid someone else to do it for him.

"When do you expect him back?"

"By the end of the week."

"I'll need to have a word with him." Dan put away his book. "Thank you for your time, Mr Cruft."

"Not at all." Cruft rang a bell on his desk. "Give my regards to Sir William, won't you?"

Meaning Cruft and Chief Magistrate Sir William Addington were friends and Dan had better watch his step.

Chapter Twelve

At Bow Street, a passenger who had just arrived on the Bath coach at the Angel in the Strand to find that his luggage had not arrived with him was complaining to the clerk. Behind him, a growing queue grumbled to one another about the wait. A pale woman sat on the crowded wooden bench behind the hubbub, her hands folded in her lap. She wore a dark cloak over a smart, plain dress and well-made leather shoes decorated with buckles. The clerk caught her eye over the enraged traveller's shoulder and nodded at Dan. She stood up and timidly approached him.

"If it's to report a crime, you'll have to speak to the desk clerk," Dan said.

"Are you the officer who arrested Mr Pickering?"

He stopped. "I am. Do you have information for me?"

"Is there somewhere private we can talk?"

She was softly spoken; he had to stoop to catch what she said.

"There's somewhere quieter." He led her into the office, found an empty desk under the curious stare of Inky Tom, the junior clerk. "So, what is it you want to tell me?"

"Mr Pickering could not have had anything to do with Miss Parmeter's murder." She looked down, tears trembling on her lashes. "He was with me at the Apple Tree Tavern at St James's Market on Monday morning. He won't tell you because he is trying to protect me. My husband has a violent temper."

"Do you and Mr Pickering often meet at the tavern?"

She wiped her eyes. "Sometimes. I told *him* I was visiting my mother. He was at work. We have a shoe shop near Fleet Street. I won't have to go to court, will I? If he finds out—"

"Not unless Pickering goes to trial, and if you're telling the truth, I can't see any reason he should. I'll have to check, Mrs...?"

"Mrs Martin." She raised her head, directed an appealing look at him. "Will you check straight away?"

"I could go now, but you'll have to wait here while I'm gone."

"I can wait."

He beckoned to Inky Tom. "Keep an eye on her. She's not to leave before I get back."

St James's Market with its mouldering market house had not kept up with the district's more recently established grocers, butchers, fishmongers, confectioners and other provisioners of royalty. Meat and fish were still to be bought there, but haughty servants looking for delicacies for their masters' tables were rarely seen in its precincts. The Tun and St Alban's taverns, the Charles Street card rooms, and the chocolate rooms in St Alban's Street continued to attract the rich and fashionable. Beyond them was a web of close, crumbling streets best avoided by gentlemen who valued their watches and bank notes. It was here Dan found the Apple Tree Tavern, a small house separated from its tumble-down neighbour by wooden supporting beams slung between the two properties.

Inside, the smell of coffee, ale and woodsmoke mingled to create a homely atmosphere. The wooden floor had been sanded, the tables polished, and the glasses on the shelves behind the bar gleamed. A large map of Africa hung on one of the walls. Half a dozen newspapers were folded over wooden ladder rails beneath it. Next to the map was a print of an author holding an open copy of the Bible. The wording identified the picture as the frontispiece to a book: *The Interesting Narrative of the Life of Olaudah Equiano, or Gustavus Vassa, the African*. The artist had captured the look of a man with much to tell; his very image seemed about to break into speech.

A man with straggling white hair, his clothes faded and

frayed, sat at one of the tables. He had a gin and hot water in front of him and was filling out a lottery ticket. On a settle by the fire two workers from the market, one wearing a bloodstained butcher's apron, chatted over their porter.

The man behind the counter hung up a clean tankard and wiped his hands on his blue apron. "Good day. What can I get you?"

"Nothing." Dan took his tipstaff from his pocket. "Foster of Bow Street Magistrates' Office. Mr...?"

The lottery player looked up from his writing. The butcher lowered his glass. His companion paused in the act of tamping the tobacco in his pipe. The welcome drained from the publican's face.

"Trinder. How can I help?"

"Do you know a coachman named Pickering?"

"I know him."

"Was he in here on Monday morning?"

"Yes."

"Was he alone?"

"Came in with his lady friend."

"What time?"

Trinder tapped his finger on his chin. "About – let me see now – quarter to twelve so far as I recall."

"That sounds right," said a voice from the fireside. "They were already here when I came in at midday."

Dan turned round to face the butcher.

"I wasn't long after you, if you remember," said his friend. "They were sitting over there." He pointed to a table in the corner with the stem of his pipe. The four men all turned and gazed solemnly at the table.

"Do they often meet in here?"

"Mr Pickering is a regular," answered Trinder. "I'd seen the woman with him once or twice before. Don't know who she is."

"What did she look like?"

The man with the pipe leaned towards the blaze and lit a spill, put it to the clay bowl, puffed at the stem, and said, "She was white. A trim little thing."

The butcher nodded. "That's her all right."

"When did they leave?" asked Dan.

Three pairs of eyes swivelled round to look at Trinder. He said, "I was busy serving. As far as I remember, about an hour later."

"That's it exactly, Mr Trinder," said the lottery player. "It was quarter to one."

The smoker said, "So it was. I remember because I was just thinking it was time to go and get some oysters. Always have oysters on a Monday."

"That's right," said the butcher. "Oysters on a Monday."

"He drank coffee as usual," said the lottery player. He leered. "Pickering says it's good for the stamina."

"So all of you saw Pickering in here with a woman on Monday morning?"

There was a chorus of "ayes". Dan took out his book and made a note of their names.

Pickering rose to face Dan. A flicker of apprehension passed over his face, and his body tensed. Silently, he waited for whatever fate had to throw at him. In all probability, a charge of murder.

"Mrs Martin called at the office. She left a few moments ago."

Whatever Pickering had been expecting, it wasn't that. Far from being pleased to hear she had come forward, he greeted the news with a dismayed, "No! She shouldn't have done that."

"That's why you wouldn't tell us where you were on Monday," Dan continued. "To protect her from her husband."

"I – I – did she say that?"

"And took a risk to come and tell it from all appearances. Do you know where she says you were?"

"Has she told you?" Pickering was hedging, trying to work out how much Dan knew, how much he should disclose.

"She has. And now I want you to tell me."

"The Apple Tree Tavern?"

"You tell me."

"It was the Apple Tree."

"What time did you get there?"

Pickering had recovered his poise, seemed more sure of himself. "About quarter to twelve."

"Do you remember who else was there apart from you and Mrs Martin?"

"George Trinder, the landlord. And Jack Hazard – that's what we call him anyway, I don't know his real name – doing his lottery."

"No one else?"

"Two or three men came in after us. I didn't really notice."

That settled it. Pickering had been at the Apple Tree with Mrs Martin at midday on Monday, and there were four witnesses to confirm it. Dan banged on the door and called to the gaoler.

"This man is free to go."

Pickering held out his hands. The gaoler unlocked the handcuffs and left the door open when he went out. Pickering took up his hat and moved towards the landing.

"Tell me," Dan said. The coachman halted. "Were you really willing to hang to save her a beating?"

"I don't have to worry about it now, do I?"

Dan listened to Pickering's footsteps pass along the hall and down the stairs, to be lost in the comforting murmur of voices from the bar. John Townsend had demanded an alibi for the time he believed the murder had been committed and now Pickering had one. Since there was nothing else to connect him to Louise Parmeter's death, there was no reason to keep him in custody. It was the result Dan had wanted. Surely now he could get Townsend to move the case on, start considering some of the other possibilities.

Yet there was something odd about this. Mrs Martin had surprised Pickering, no doubt of it. He had not expected her, or even, judging from the look on his face, wanted her, to put herself at risk. A man who was prepared to go to the scaffold for a woman who withheld the words that could save him must be a very devoted lover. Why then had he shown no anxiety on learning that she had put herself in danger from her violent husband to save him?

It was curious, perhaps nothing more, most likely had no bearing on the case. But it was a puzzle, and Dan preferred puzzles with solutions. He gave Pickering long enough to get outside then followed him.

Pickering headed towards the Strand. Mrs Martin joined him on Bridges Street. She was not crying now. Perhaps that was not remarkable since she was about to be reunited with her lover. What was remarkable was that there was a man with her, a slight figure with intense blue eyes in a thin face. He shook hands with Pickering, said something which Pickering brushed aside, a trifle peevishly it seemed to Dan. Mrs Martin slipped her arm through the stranger's and the three of them continued along the Strand towards Fleet Street. Pickering was doing most of the talking, Dan noticed.

Dan followed them to Wine Office Court, a narrow lane between Fleet Street and Gough Square. They stopped at a small house with a bow window displaying shoes for men, women and children. The name over the door was 'Martin'. So this was the husband Mrs Martin was so afraid of. Martin unlocked the door. The three wished one another good evening, then the couple went into the shop, closed and locked the door.

Whatever there was between Mrs Martin and Pickering, it was not a love affair. What, then, had been the purpose of their meeting on Monday morning? And did it have any connection with Louise Parmeter's murder? Doubtless that would be Townsend's conclusion, and Dan wouldn't entirely blame him for it. There was something unsatisfactory about Pickering's alibi, and if Townsend got wind of it the case would get no further forward after all.

Pickering was on the move again. He hunched into his coat collar and turned away from the shop. Dan set off after him.

Chapter Thirteen

Dan followed Pickering back to the stables. The great gates across the yard had been fastened. Pickering took a key from his pocket and let himself in through the wicket, leaving it ajar behind him. From the lane Dan watched him cross the yard and knock on the harness room door, where the dog inside was already barking.

"Jacko, it's me," Pickering called.

The door was opened by a short, slender lad holding a lantern. It was hard to tell who was more pleased to see his master: the dog circling around him with its tail wagging, or the stable boy with his grin a mile wide.

"All well with the horses?"

"Yes, sir," Jacko answered.

"Have they been exercised?"

"Yes. We took them out today."

"Let's take a look, shall we?"

Jacko went back and pulled on his jacket, came out with a bunch of keys which he handed to Pickering. The coachman opened the stable door. They went inside, the dog trailing happily behind. The light from the lantern scattered shadows around the interior. Dan listened to the murmur of their voices, the rap of the disturbed horses' hooves, their soft whinnies. The sounds mingled with the slosh of water, clatter of tubs and rumble of mangles from the laundry.

Pickering, Jacko and the terrier came out of the stables.

"You've done well," the coachman said. "I'm pleased. Get some sleep now."

Pickering locked the stable door and gave Jacko the key. Smiling proudly, the boy returned to his pallet bed in the harness room, the terrier following. Pickering waited until Jacko had bolted the door before running up the wooden stairs to his own rooms. A couple of minutes later a light appeared, moved about inside, became stationary. Nothing happened for several minutes and Dan was beginning to wonder if Pickering had settled down for the night when the light went out. The coachman emerged dressed in a smart hat and coat, a bundle slung over his shoulder. He passed through the wicket gate, locked it behind him and set off along the lane.

"So they've realised their mistake, then?"

The speaker was a brawny-armed woman somewhere in her fifties who stood, arms akimbo, on the threshold of the laundry.

"They have, Mrs Watson. I'm as innocent as a newborn babe."

She chuckled. "I wouldn't go that far, Mr Pickering. But the idea that a gentleman such as yourself would strike down a lady like that."

"It's because I'm a gentleman such as myself that they got that idea."

She tut-tutted. "Never known an officer of the law with the brains he was born with. It's never what's right with them, but what's easy."

"You have reason there, Mrs Watson."

"Will you come in for a dram to celebrate?"

"Perhaps another evening? I've something arranged for tonight."

Mrs Watson winked. "Another sort of celebration, I daresay? Well, I don't blame you for having something better to do than share a toddy with an old neighbour."

"But yours is always such a fine mixture. I shall partake at the first opportunity, if I may."

"I look forward to it, Mr Pickering. And I'm glad to see you back amongst us. There, I had better get on."

"You're working late again."

"Yes. I'm short two pair of hands tonight. Julia's still laid up with her leg, and that daft Welsh Charity School girl took it in her head to run off yesterday. If it's not one thing, it's another."

"It's always the way," Pickering sympathised. "I'll hold you to the promise of that toddy."

The neighbours parted and Pickering set off towards Regent Street. From there he went through Soho and on to Seven Dials, where he turned into a narrow lane off Monmouth Street. Most of the shops were shuttered and lights glowed from the upstairs windows. Pickering went to an open door between a cheap furniture warehouse and a second-hand-clothes shop. Inside, a steep flight of wooden stairs led up to a drinking club from where came pulsing music and the babble of voices. A number of men and women hung about in the lane, taking a break from the heat and the din.

The doorway was blocked by a man built like a lumper. Pickering wished him good evening and would have hurried by but was detained by the doorman's grip on his hand. Several bone-shaking pats on the back accompanied his booming commiserations on Pickering's arrest and congratulations on his release. Pickering freed himself from the bruising goodwill at last and ran upstairs.

Dan waited nearly half an hour for an opportunity to follow. It came when a group of loud drunks lurched into view. He staggered after them up the ill-lit stairs. The air grew hotter and noisier as they climbed, hit Dan like a gust of steam from the laundry when one of the drunks opened the door at the top. They stumbled into a room that ran the length of the furniture store beneath. Two low chandeliers swayed smokily from the ceiling. There were tables and chairs around the walls, lit by candles in wax-encrusted bottles. The room was crowded with people drinking, playing cards or dice, shouting into one another's ears. Groups of young men and women stood about gulping beer and eyeing each other; couples embraced in corners; solitary drinkers propped up the bar.

The music came from three musicians on a low platform opposite the bar. Two played fiddles, the third balanced a pair of drums between his knees which he struck with his bare hands. The centre of the room had been left clear for dancers whose antics bowed the floorboards up and down to such an extent Dan wondered the ceiling below did not collapse. One or two couples, heedless of the tempo, swayed dreamily together. A woman with a pipe in her mouth, skirts hitched to her knees, jigged contentedly on her own.

Dan made his way over to the counter and ordered a soda water. He sipped, and scrutinised the room. A bit of gambling, a bit of whoring, a bit of furtive selling of stolen watches. Nothing to get too excited about. No sign of Pickering.

A long rectangle of light appeared at the right of the band's platform. A door Dan had not previously noticed had suddenly opened, emitting a blare of noise to compete with the music. Dan caught sight of the chamber within through the whirling dancers. It was enough to see what was going on in there.

He got rid of his glass and circled the dance floor. He reached the door as it began to swing shut and shoved his boot against it. A lined face on a long, wrinkled neck thrust itself into the gap.

"Invite only," said the face, its thin lips revealing a mouth as toothless as a turtle's.

"I'm with Pickering," Dan said.

The man eyed Dan for a few seconds, then stepped back and let him in. Dan squeezed into a shadowy spot near the door, peered through the heat haze and smoke to the boxing ring in the middle of the room where two indistinct figures slogged it out. For one of them the fight was nearly over. He stumbled around the ring, head lolling, hands flapping.

His opponent brought the bout to an end with a rush at the

dazed man. He caught him by the thighs, lifted him into the air and flung him on to the boards, knocking the breath out of him. The cheers set the shuttered windows rattling. The ring filled with trainers, seconds and two of the loser's friends who rolled him through the ropes and carried him off.

The tense atmosphere relaxed as the audience milled around delivering its verdict on the bout, collecting its winnings, paying its debts. In the confusion Dan glimpsed the winner's smooth, straight back. He was sitting on his trainer's knee, the man almost buckling under the weight though he had the build of an ex-pugilist himself. The boxer wiped his face with a towel, drank some of the water offered him by his second, and spat most of it into a bucket in a bloody stream. He jumped to his feet, pranced from foot to foot, aiming blows at the air to howls of delight from the company. Dan could see why he was their champion: his form and poise were magnificent.

He skipped around the ring. "Anyone else?" he roared.

Dan had found Pickering.

The drunks Dan had followed into the club had pushed their way to the front of the audience. One of them took off his hat and threw it into the ring, revealing a close-cropped skull. He had a labourer's build: broad, muscular shoulders, thick arms, tough hands, massive legs, a lowering face under thick black brows. He stripped off his neckcloth, coat and shirt while his companions shouted encouragement.

"Give Blackie what for!"

"Teach him who's master."

"Show the Negro what a British man can do."

Pickering looked down at them, his eyes glinting coldly. Suddenly he laughed, snapped his fingers. "I accept the challenge."

The man climbed into the ring. He fixed his eyes on Pickering, only half attended to the referee warning them to stick to Broughton's Rules. No hitting a man when he was down, or grabbing him by the hair or breeches, and a fallen man who failed to come back up to the line within thirty seconds to be the loser.

As soon as the bell rang, the challenger powered out of his corner and swung a hammer blow at Pickering. Pickering dodged it, got in a light hit on his face. The other man laughed it off and went after him again. Pickering ducked and deflected, edged back towards the ropes. He was nearly on them when his opponent swung back his arm. It would have been a tremendous blow had it landed home, but Pickering dodged and slipped away. Doggedly, the bulky man turned after him, but was prevented from following by the bell.

Pickering led his opponent the same dance throughout the second round until the sweat poured down the man's hairy back. Seconds before the end of the round, Pickering got one in under his left eye. Blood streaming from the cut, he staggered to his corner. His second soaked a sponge in cold water and applied it to the wound. He pushed it away, let out a stream of curses.

"The bugger won't stand still, damn him. I'll have the black hide off his back, so help me."

The two set to again. Pickering kept his hand in front of his eyes, hunched up defensively, parried blows. His cringing attitude gave the other man confidence to drive home his attack. His blows grew wilder, became careless. Pickering's supporters exchanged delighted grins and the crowd began to murmur excitedly. They knew was what coming. The stranger was too reliant on force without speed or strategy to anticipate it.

Pickering shot a stinging backhander into his opponent's temple with his right, immediately crunched into his chin with his left. Off guard, the man instinctively raised his hands to his face and Pickering got him in the chest, the blow sounding like a drum beat in the sudden silence. Pickering drove him against the corner post, where they exchanged blows, hard and fast. Pickering put his all into the last swing of the round, and as the bell went, the outclassed pugilist slid to the ground, his arms stretched along the rope.

The challenger lumbered out for the next round, breathing hard, and clumsy with fatigue. Three minutes in, Pickering levelled him with a hit under his ear. The man went out cold and did not make it to the line.

His friends booed and grumbled.

"Call yourself a referee?"

"You want to do something about these lights. They give the advantage to a man used to the African sun, but are too bright for a Briton."

"There's a trick in it somewhere. The black must have had weights in his hands."

"Give it a rest, mates," called one of their neighbours. "Your man could never have beaten Pickering. He's too slow."

"No science," put in another.

"Pickering had the upper hand from the first round," someone else added.

The man who had complained about the lights shoved the last speaker in the chest. He shoved back. The insults became more personal and fists began to fly. The disturbance spread, but it did not take the defeated man's crew long to realise that they were outnumbered. Throwing out curses and threats, they gathered up their semi-conscious hero and left.

Pickering, meanwhile, had collected his winnings, donned his shirt and coat, shaken hands with his male admirers, kissed his female fans, and good-naturedly refused offers of drinks and suppers. The fighting was over for the evening and the satisfied audience drifted back to the main room.

Chapter Fourteen

Pickering, his greatcoat fastened tight against the cold, led Dan towards the lights on Monmouth Street. A few moments later, they were on Oxford Street. Pickering crossed the busy road and went into the galleried building near the corner of Tottenham Court Road. Dan knew the place: the Boar and Castle Coffee House, its yard a constant coming and going of mail coaches. It was not the cheapest establishment, claiming to serve the best wines in town, though as Dan did not drink them he did not know how accurate the claim was. The coffee was good though. Pickering must be planning a stylish celebration with his winnings.

The coffee room was full, with one or two large, boisterous parties adding to the clatter of pans and jugs, the clink of cup and glass. Waiters scurried in and out. The scent of roasting coffee was rich and warming. Pickering hesitated on the threshold and scanned the high-backed booths along the side of the room. He recognised someone, made his way over, shrugged off his coat and sat down. Dan moved after him and hung up his hat and coat on a nearby row of coat hooks. While he eavesdropped he made a show of looking through the pockets as if he had lost something.

Pickering's companion was a small, stout man, plainly though prosperously dressed. He had an open bottle of wine in front of him and a spare glass.

"Nice drop of claret this. Or d'you prefer coffee?" His accent placed him from somewhere in the East End of town.

"Wine for me, Mr Rule."

Rule poured the drink. With a pained expression, he watched Pickering swallow it in one gulp. The coachman pushed his empty glass towards Rule and he refilled it. While Pickering swigged that, Rule waved to a waiter, held up the empty bottle. The waiter nodded and hurried off to fetch some more.

"Must bring my lady friends here," Pickering said. "Sort of fancy place that would appeal."

"Did the Runners give you that?"

Pickering raised his hand to a graze on his face. He laughed. "I'd like to see the whoresons try. Wasting time with me when Miss Parmeter's killer's out there."

Reinforcements arrived and Rule filled their glasses again. "Things will be more difficult without her."

Pickering reached into a breast pocket, took out the purse of winnings and passed it across the table. "I got this."

Rule picked it up and weighed it in his palm. "How?"

"Fighting."

"You can't always get money that way."

"Can't I? There's no one to match me."

"We need a steady supply. This will be enough for tonight's shipload. After that—" Rule shrugged, spread out stubby fingers.

"Then we'll shift what we've got and manage as well as we can when the next lot comes in. You haven't heard of anything else yet?"

"Nothing doing at the moment. Do you want something to eat?"

Pickering emptied his glass, stood up. "Have to get back. The stable boy's on his own. Could do with some sleep in any case. See you at the Martins' on Saturday night?"

Rule agreed. He rose and they shook hands. Pickering snatched up his coat and left. Dan decided there was no point following him just to watch while he slept. Far more useful to find out who Rule was and what Pickering had paid him for. It must be something important for a man to give away every penny of a hard-won prize.

Rule settled the bill and left. In Oxford Street he stopped at a hackney stand. Dan moved close enough to hear him say "Tower Hill" and see him step into the carriage. He ran up to the next in line, held up his tipstaff to the driver hunched dozing in his seat.

"Bow Street Officer. Keep that vehicle in sight."

The driver jerked awake. "Is it murder?"

"Might be."

Astonishing how the merest hint of being caught up in a murder case thrilled people. Useful, too. It got the driver on his side. The coachman, the cold tedium of waiting for humdrum fares forgotten, gleefully raised his whip over his pair of horses.

It was an old vehicle, damp and dirty inside, the floor covered with stale straw. Dan opened the window as they rattled away. Gradually they left the lights and lively crowds of the West End of town behind. Before long they were in a district of warehouses, shops, modest houses and shipping offices, interspersed with mansions and grand office buildings. They were close to the water, and above the jumble of rooftops, ships' masts rose against a troubled sky where clouds loomed. The occasional cart or dray rumbled about the wharves; clusters of lanterns gathered around the steps leading down to the watermen's boats; hazy light and noise clouded around the taverns. The wet-beast smell of the mudbanks, slimy stone, rot and decay of the rubbish that ended up in the Thames filled the carriage. Tar, coal smoke, the sickly smells and bitter fumes of industrial processes in shipyards, workshops and distilleries drifted in with it.

They drove down Little Tower Hill to the waterside and passed St Catherine's stairs, beneath which the passenger boats had been moored for the night. The driver pulled up on the north side of the road. Dan leaned out of the window.

"He's stopped." The cabman pointed with his whip.

Rule got out of his carriage, waited while the driver consulted his list of prices by the light of the carriage lamp.

Rule paid him, then let himself into one of the buildings facing the river. It was dark on the ground floor, but lights showed in the living rooms above.

Dan got out. "Wait for me here."

The driver nodded, jumped down clutching a couple of blankets and flung them over the horses. The street was damp underfoot, the cobbles slippery. Mist swirled around Dan's knees. There were still people about: sailors, women, porters, dockers, press gang officers, other more furtive folk slinking about their nefarious business. Dan caught snatches of foreign words, a blare of lines from a song, a woman's cackling laugh. Somewhere a glass broke. Further off, a dog howled.

The building the man had entered was a large one that ran some way back from the road. Two windows on either side of the front door were closely shuttered, but the nature of the business carried on here was signalled by the wooden figure above the door. Fixed to a small platform, a blue-coated midshipman holding an octant looked out across the water. It was a ship's chandlery, a substantial and prosperous one from the look of it. Its clientele was less likely to be the individual sailor buying his own instruments and supplies, but masters fitting out an entire ship, stocking up on oils and tar, cordage, tools, salt meat and ship's biscuit. The name above the door was George Rule.

Was Pickering planning a voyage? Was that what the money was for? And what had the Martins to do with it? It seemed that Rule was their confederate, but in what? Were they involved in some sort of smuggling operation? Or were they more interested in lifting the cargo from vessels moored in the Thames, the ships' loads to which Rule had referred? And how had Louise Parmeter been involved?

What could a wealthy courtesan, a shoemaker and his wife, a ship's chandler, and a coachman have in common?

Chapter Fifteen

"You did what?" said John Townsend. He was wearing his highest-collared coat, his yellowest waistcoat, whitest cravat, and carrying his heaviest silver-topped cane.

"I released Pickering yesterday. He does have an alibi. He was only lying to protect a woman. But Mrs Martin has come forward and there are four witnesses who confirm they saw them together in the Apple Tree in St James's Market."

"You could have four and forty witnesses and it wouldn't make any difference. His sort stick together, see."

Dan and Townsend were in Louise Parmeter's study on the day of her funeral. She had been a regular attender at St George's Church in Hanover Square: it was where all the people of fashion went to be seen on a Sunday. The church's burial ground lay just beyond the stables in the lane, but it was so full that human bones had been known to appear on the surface after heavy rain. She was to be buried at the new ground near Tyburn.

Dan said, "Pickering's account was consistent with Mrs Martin's."

The door was closed, but mindful that the mourners gathered in the hall might be able to hear him and that some of those people were the cream of the ton, Townsend lowered his voice. "God's Blood, Foster, why the hell would you believe a Negress?"

"Mrs Martin is white."

"The kind of white woman who lies with an African."

"I had no reason not to believe her. And it explains why Pickering lied."

"Whether it explains anything or not, it is not your place to go releasing suspects on your own authority."

"I have as much authority as do you."

"In any other case, perhaps. But this concerns the Prince of Wales, and he is my responsibility. I've a good mind to have you taken off the case."

"Then do that."

"Aye, and see how well it goes down with Sir William Addington. You'll be finished."

"Maybe I would, if I'd let the killer go free. As it stands, I don't think we've come close to catching whoever did it. But if you're so convinced Pickering is involved, why don't you arrest him again? He's standing just outside the door."

"Laughing out the other side of his face, thanks to you. And even if he has an alibi, it does not alter the case. The fact remains that he went out of his way to be away from the house when the murder took place."

"But we can't be certain what time it happened," Dan insisted.

"Very well, Foster, let's say you're right – though I don't think you are, mind. What difference does that make except that instead of sitting in the Apple Tree Tavern with his mistress, Pickering was working in the stable yard? Coolly going about his business while just across the lane his partner was letting himself in at the garden gate and robbing and killing Miss Parmeter."

"You could say the same of any of the servants."

"True, but he's the one we caught out in a lie."

Dan could not deny it. He also knew that Pickering's alibi was not as straightforward as it seemed. There was the puzzle of his cordial relations with the jealous husband, as well as the mysterious meeting with the ship's chandler, Rule. Having heard Pickering and Rule say Louise Parmeter's death made things difficult for them, Dan did not think it was something they had sought. He doubted he could convince Townsend of it though, and if Townsend knew all the circumstances,

Pickering would be back in gaol within the hour. But Pickering behind bars could not lead him to the discovery of what he and his friends were up to, or if it was in any way connected with the murder. But there was no point trying to explain that to Townsend.

"Howsomever, it makes no odds," Townsend said. "Miss Parmeter was killed just before twelve and Pickering's the only one who was away from the house at the time. That in itself strikes me as peculiar, and it should strike you the same way. But now you've gone to the trouble of releasing him, we're going to need more on him before we can take him back. I say it will pay to keep an eye on Pickering, and as I'm in charge of the case that's what we'll do."

"Thus far I agree with you," Dan said. "All I am asking is that we don't focus solely on Pickering. We know no reason for him to want Miss Parmeter dead." Before Townsend could argue, he added, "Apart from the diamonds, and he doesn't have them. But they are not the only possible motive. I think she may have been killed by a former lover. One of them took to sending her pointed gifts such as mourning gloves and a coffin plate engraved 'Here Lies a Whore'. If that's not a threat, I don't know what is. More recently, a young man had offered to kill himself for love of her and she had merely laughed at him. I doubt the attempt was serious, but the humiliation could easily have turned to anger. We already know that she had her own key to the gate and was in the habit of receiving visitors privately in her study." Townsend did not look too sure about the last point. "I told you on Monday."

"I'm not in my dotage, Foster. Get to the point."

"Both of these men could have known when she'd be in her room and how to get into the house without being seen."

"What men? Do you have any names?"

"Lord Hawkhurst sent the gifts. The other is Randolph Cruft, the banker's son."

Townsend stared at Dan for a moment. "Lord Hawkhurst

and Randolph Cruft? Don't you know Cruft is the Prince's banker, and Lord Hawkhurst the Prince's friend? Do you really think people of their rank are likely to break into a house and commit robbery and murder?"

"There's no evidence that anyone did break into the house. You said yourself that whoever did it was admitted by someone inside. Besides, there are the memoirs. A common thief wouldn't have been interested in them. Both these men are in a position to be embarrassed if they are made public. And the Prince did ask us to find them."

"So he did. But I don't think we are going to find them in the possession of Randolph Cruft or Lord Hawkhurst. No, Foster. You've had your fun. Time to get back to the real world." At risk to the buttons on his waistcoat, Townsend gave a belly laugh. "Lord Hawkhurst sent the gifts, did he? That's just like him. The man has a rapier wit."

"I don't think Louise Parmeter found them very funny."

"Pho, Foster, don't be such an old Square Toes. You've made a mess of things and no mistake, letting the black go. The thing is, what are you going to do about it?"

"I'm going to talk to Randolph Cruft when he gets back to London."

"Gets back from where?"

"His father sent him to their Hertfordshire estate to keep him away from Louise Parmeter. It's only twenty miles away. The question is, was he there on Monday morning?"

"How do you know all this?"

"I spoke to Cruft senior yesterday."

"What? You went to see Mr Cruft? You haven't visited Lord Hawkhurst, have you?"

"No, not yet."

"Not yet? Lord give me strength. I will not have you calling on His Lordship until—" He broke off.

"Until what?"

"Eh? Until nothing. Until I can come with you."

"Does that mean you do think we should speak to him?"

"Speak to him? About a murder? Why not? It's as good as anything. Yes, Foster, we'll speak to him. But you will not call on him without me, d'ye hear? You are not accustomed to dealing with men in his rank of life. I'll fix a time to take you and let you know." The clock on the mantelpiece chimed the quarter hour. "Time to be moving off. You can come and pay your respects. No need to follow the cortège."

"And Cruft?"

Townsend was already moving towards the door and either did not hear or chose not to answer. Dan decided to take his silence for agreement to continued investigation of the histrionic young man. He followed Townsend into the hall and stood to attention with his hat under his arm while the undertakers carried the coffin downstairs. The servants were drawn up in two lines, the scullions and boot boys scuffling at the back, the cook pinching the kitchen maids until they shut their mouths and stood up straight. Parkes was to follow the procession with Pickering and the two footmen in their smartest liveries.

Of all the mourners, it was Agnes Taylor who took it the hardest. Judging from her swollen face and red eyes, she had been crying for hours, and was not done yet. Sarah Dean, from time to time applying a dainty lace handkerchief to her eyes, glared at the poetic protégée in contempt whenever she vented another noisy sob.

Dan wondered how many of the aristocrats in the hall, who were eyeing one another with varying degrees of hostility, had reason to think they might be in Louise's memoirs. Townsend knew most of them, but the only people Dan recognised were a few of Louise Parmeter's Drury Lane friends. Sir William Addington stood beside the theatre manager, Richard Sheridan, whispering eagerly into his ear. Sheridan listened with a restless air: boredom, or the agitation of a man in need of a drink. Dan supposed the chief magistrate was there to ingratiate himself with the Prince. It must have been a disappointment for him that George, perhaps considering his parents' feelings for once, had not come.

In the street a line of constables held back the crowd, who gasped in admiration at the funeral carriage with its gleaming glass and paintwork and glossy black horses, plumed and rosetted in black. The sleek undertakers, prospering in the service of Death, stood by in their long coats and high hats trailing silk ribbons. The bearers manoeuvred the black-draped coffin into the carriage and the procession slowly set off. When it was out of sight, the housekeeper ushered the servants back to their work. Dan put on his hat and loped down the steps into the street. Most of the crowd had dispersed, but a few hung around to wait for the next bit of excitement.

While Townsend was busy bowing and shaking hands with the great ones, Dan took the opportunity to go to the Feathers to meet Jones the carrier. He took up position on the opposite side of Holborn, from where he had a good view of the entrance. He was not the only one waiting for the Tewkesbury wagon. A small group of people stood in the yard.

Before long a covered wagon drawn by a team of eight plodded into view. The driver was a stocky, ill-kempt man wearing heavy corduroy breeches, a sagging, stained hat, and a thick green coat. He turned his team out of the stream of traffic into the inn yard. Dan crossed the road and entered the shadows under the brick arch.

The wagoner applied the brake, stowed the whip on the side of his seat, and jumped down. He went round to the back of the wagon, where the curtain was already twitching, and said gruffly, "Lunnon."

Four passengers, stiff and bleary-eyed, climbed out, some to be met by friends, others to shoulder their bundles and make their solitary way into the streets. Jones clambered inside the wagon and began to stack the parcels, cheeses and baskets of game ready for unloading. A young man fussed around reading labels until he found one addressed to himself, shouldered the box and carried it off.

The boy, Thomas, meanwhile, ran out of the stable to help with the horses and gabble news of the events of the last few days. The carrier, without pausing in his work, glanced at the outhouse where the woman's body had lain.

"The Runner wants to speak to me, does he?"

"He said so," the boy replied. "He's a knowing one, Mr Jones. Looks at you as if he can tell exactly what you're thinking."

"Knowing, is he?"

The boy nudged Jones's arm and said reverentially, "He's here."

Dan emerged from the archway.

Jones grunted and turned back to his unloading. "What do you want of me?"

"Last Friday you set off from here for Tewkesbury as usual," Dan said. "Shortly after you'd gone a woman's body was found."

"If I'd done for her, I'm hardly likely to have come back here, am I?"

"Maybe not. But you might have seen or heard something last Thursday night."

"Like what?"

"Anything unusual. Someone hanging around the yard. Sounds of a struggle."

"Not from Cripplegate, I wouldn't."

"What do you mean?"

"Always stay with my sister and her husband in Cripplegate on Thursdays. You can go and ask her if you like."

"What's the address?"

"Chiswell Street, opposite the Finsbury Eating House."

"I will check your story, Jones. And if I find out you're lying to me, I'll make a point of meeting your wagon here every Thursday."

"Please yourself. You won't find anything on me."

Dan nudged a butter barrel with his toe, eliciting a sloshing sound. "What, not even the odd drop of French brandy that's found its way up the Severn?"

"You are a knowing one, be'nt you?" Jones glanced about him and lowered his voice. "If you'd like to take some home. On the house, of course."

"Not for me."

Dan turned on his heel and strode back to the din and whirl of Holborn. In the spot he had recently occupied stood a tall man in a greatcoat and broad-brimmed hat. Like Dan, he was watching the entrance to the Feathers. His stealthy manner made Dan connect him with the carrier's illicit trade. He was there for the brandy, had seen Dan talking to Jones and was waiting for him to leave. Even if Dan was minded to hang around to see if he was right, they were such small operators it would hardly be worth the effort. And he would have to explain to Sir William what he had been doing at the Feathers when he was supposed to be working the Parmeter case.

A crested carriage flashed past. When Dan looked again, the man had gone. Cautious fellow. Today, though, he and Jones would be left to get on with their business without Dan's interference. He went straight to Chiswell Street, where he got confirmation that Jones had been in Cripplegate on the night of the murder at the Feathers. He could be crossed off the list of suspects. It might have felt like progress, except that his was the only name on it.

Chapter Sixteen

"Lord Hawkhurst is expecting us, Harry."

"Of course, Mr Townsend."

Townsend had made quick work of setting up the meeting with Hawkhurst: it was only yesterday that he had agreed to the interview. Harry, the footman who let them into the Cavendish Square house, would have been a fine-looking young man if he had taken more care with his dress, combed his hair and lost his paunch. Handing over his hat and coat, Dan caught the sour whiff of drink on his breath.

Dan had seen his fair share of opulent halls in the last few days and this one was no exception. It was, however, battered and neglected. There were muddy boot marks on the floor, a jumble of riding whips, cricket balls and boxing gloves on the marble-topped table, and the bust of some worthy ancestor had been used for pistol-shooting practice.

"This way."

Harry, their coats over his arm, slopped towards a door with chipped paintwork. It opened before they reached it. A young woman emerged, propelled by the sound of male laughter. She was wearing a sprigged dress which made her look younger and prettier than when Dan had last seen her, but her face was flushed and she swayed when she came to a stop.

Inside the room someone kicked the door shut. Dan stepped forward and took her arm. "Miss Taylor? Are you ill?"

She turned unfocussed eyes on him, hiccupped and said, "Mis' Foster...sho kind...overtaken by faintness...my excessive sensibil'ties—"

He led her to one of the hall chairs, swept off the crumpled silk jacket on the seat, and lowered her into it.

"Call a hackney for the lady," he said over his shoulder to the grinning footman.

"Call one yourself," Harry retorted.

"Do it now, or I'll kick you downstairs."

The flunkey shrank back in alarm. He glanced uncertainly at Townsend, who nodded. Muttering, Harry dumped their coats on the table and went out into the street. Dan would have liked to ask Agnes Taylor what she was doing here, but she seemed to have fallen asleep. Harry returned to say the carriage was outside.

"Did she have a cloak?" Dan asked.

Grudgingly, Harry fetched it from the cloakroom at the side of the hall. He leaned one hand against the wall, the other on his hip, and watched Dan help Agnes Taylor out of the house.

"Be quick, Foster," Townsend called after him. "His Lordship mustn't be kept waiting."

Dan handed Agnes her cloak and settled her into the coach. He gave the driver the Berkeley Square address and some money for the fare. When he got back to the hall, Harry was spluttering indignantly at Townsend. He tapped his temple with his finger, hastily dropped his hand when he saw Dan. Townsend looked at Dan and pursed his lips, but before he could pass comment the door opened again. A long, thin face thrust itself into the gap.

Behind the face, someone called, "Who is it, Bredon?"

"The deuce," Bredon cried, "it is the Townsend!"

The men inside the room cheered. "The Townsend! The Townsend!"

Harry winked and slouched off. Bredon flung open the door and with a flourish stepped aside. Townsend strutted over the threshold and Dan followed him into a large drawing room. There were half a dozen men inside, though the noise they made suggested four times as many. Bredon held up his hand and the chanting trailed off.

A line of tall windows let in a drizzly grey light. The only furniture was an assortment of chairs and tables around the walls, the dusty tables given over to collections of glasses and bottles. Two swordsmen in protective doublets stood on a long strip of carpet in the centre of the scuffed floor. One was doubled over with his hands on his knees, panting and sweating. The other was hardly out of breath. He was older than his opponent by at least a decade, but less flabby, tall and lean with dark curly hair, a full mouth, the regular features of a man who could be described as handsome. His looks were marred by the humour in his eyes, for it was an ill-natured, cynical one. This, Dan guessed, was Lord Hawkhurst.

Lord Hawkhurst threw his foil aside. It spun across the floor and came to rest against the wall. He unbuttoned his doublet, strolled to one of the tables, filled a large glass with wine, then flung himself down across a couple of chairs. Bredon sidled over to join him. The two men were contemporaries, and Bredon's claim of the place at Hawkhurst's side suggested long familiarity. Yet while Hawkhurst seemed indifferent to his companion, Bredon was slyly attentive of him.

The five younger men clustered around Townsend as if he was their favourite uncle, all speaking at once.

"Why, Townsend, you missed a delicious frolic." This from a barefooted man with untidy hair and unshaven chin who was dressed in breeches and shirt that looked as if he had slept in them. "A woman came here seeking subscriptions to a book of euley-lol-lologies."

A strapping young buck pressed a hand to his chest and said mincingly, "Simple and pathetic stanzas from my feeble pen, but drawn from a wellspring of earnest feeling."

The others chimed in, each shouting to be heard above his fellows.

"And she was appealing for the support of poor dear Miss Parmeter's friends."

"Who she knew would wish to include their names in a little volume of touching and mournful lines penned in memory of the unfortunate lady, so cruelly slain."

"With a good deal besides of epitaphs and monumental inscriptions and melancholy reflections."

"Let us not forget the melancholy reflections!" yelled the man who had been fencing with Hawkhurst, stabbing at the curtains.

"And Hawkhurst said, 'I wouldn't piss on that damned whore if she was on fire.'"

"And the lady started to flutter."

"And Hawkhurst ordered the footman to bring in some water."

"And when she wasn't looking, he poured brandy into it."

"She drank near half a pint before she noticed," roared a rosy-faced Irishman with the chins and stomach of an habitual over-eater.

"And Hawkhurst said, 'Drink up, my dear, 'tis nothing but a little cordial to restore your strength.'"

"And then he offered her some more and she said, 'Don't mind if I do!'"

"And swigged it down like a good 'un!"

This was too much for the youths, who collapsed into one another's arms, braying with laughter. Lord Hawkhurst, the instigator of the frolic, listened to all this with a discontented expression, Bredon watching him all the time.

"A damned poetry book by a damned woman," Hawkhurst growled. "Teaching a pig to count has more sense to it. Poets! I'd see the whole tribe in hell."

The man who had been fencing with him stopped swishing his blade at an imaginary foe and cried, "Why, Fotheringham, don't you write verses?"

Fotheringham, a pale, pimply undergraduate, reddened. "One poem, once. Haven't touched the stuff since."

At this they laughed all the louder. Hawkhurst grimaced

and slumped deeper into his chair. Bredon jumped to his feet and snapped his fingers.

"So, Townsend, what have you brought us?"

Townsend addressed Lord Hawkhurst. "This is the man I told you about, Lord Hawkhurst. Dan Foster."

Hawkhurst came back to life. "The boxing cove?"

"No, My Lord," Dan said with an irate glance at Townsend. "A principal officer of Bow Street investigating the murder of Louise Parmeter."

Lord Hawkhurst raised one eyebrow. "So this is the fellow who's so eager to find Louise's murderer amongst her ex-lovers? Must be any number of suspects."

His tagtails guffawed. Bredon handed Townsend a glass of wine. Dan shook his head when a glass came his way.

"What's this, what's this, what's this?" Bredon squeaked. "You've brought us a bloody Quaker?"

Townsend took an appreciative sip of his drink. "No accounting for taste."

Hawkhurst rose and sauntered over to Dan, slowly circled him. He came to a halt in front of him and slapped him on the arm. "Keeps himself in training, I see. Well toned too. Excellent. Well done, Townsend."

Dan, who could not understand what Hawkhurst meant by crediting Townsend for his muscles, attempted to take control of the situation. "Perhaps you would prefer it if we conducted our interview in private?"

"No, no, here will do. Bredon?"

Bredon gave an eager bow and hurried out of the room. The others were silent, their eyes flickering from Dan to Hawkhurst. Something was going on here: but what? Dan looked at Townsend, who was contemplating the bottom of his glass with a nonchalant air. The sound of Bredon's footsteps in the hall, the opening of a door, and the rumble of distant voices fell into the expectant silence.

Dan refused to be distracted. "It's been suggested," he said to Lord Hawkhurst, "that you were in the habit of sending Miss Parmeter objects intended to threaten and intimidate."

"And I know who did the suggesting," Hawkhurst said. "That tight-arsed lady's maid."

"Is it true?" Dan persisted.

Hawkhurst walked to the table, refilled his glass, rubbed his chin. "What do you think, Officer?"

"I think it would be better if you answered the question."

Hawkhurst laughed. "Ain't he direct?"

The door swung open and Bredon reappeared, ushering in another man like a stage manager presenting a new act. The newcomer's appearance made a sharp contrast with Bredon's weedy body, shrivelled muscles and drink-pickled face. The muscles rippled on his shoulders, torso, arms and legs. He was dressed in breeches and soft pumps, bare to the waist, his face, hands and neck darkened by outdoor labour. He had short hair, cut like a pudding bowl, keen eyes, the naïve look of a young working man who thinks his fortune is about to be made. Confused by the drunk, eager faces, he looked uncertainly around the room.

"Foster, meet Tom Hart," said Hawkhurst. "I'll tell you anything you want to know. I'll tell you things that will make your hair turn grey. I'll confess to deeds my closest friends don't know about. I won't keep a secret from you. All that, and all you have to do is beat him."

"Beat him?" Dan repeated. "You mean fight him?"

"But of course I mean fight him. Why else are you here? Townsend, don't say you didn't tell him!"

Dan sought out Townsend, who stood smirking by the table. He knew. The whoreson knew. He had arranged the whole thing in advance. That was why he had changed his mind about questioning Hawkhurst, just so he could play this stupid prank.

Tom Hart smiled, his confidence returning as his gaze settled on Dan. The comparison was in his own favour: the match was even at most. Dan could see it in his eyes. Hart thought this was his chance to shine.

"I'll not fight anyone," Dan said.

He moved towards the door. He refused to look at Hart, to give the slightest excuse for Hart to think he was ready to meet his challenge. Hawkhurst jerked his head. The pugilist stepped forward. His bunched fist hurtled towards Dan's face.

Chapter Seventeen

It was instinct that saved Dan. He parried Hart's blow with his left arm and backed away, found his way to the door blocked by the young men. He tried to swerve round them, but they joined ranks and shuffled across his path. Hart was behind him but Dan would not face him. He tried to force his way through the bawling drunkards, saw in their gleeful faces that Hart was coming after him, and had to spin round and deflect another attack. Hart was a powerful if unsubtle fighter, and now he was doing what he did best, his nervousness was forgotten.

Dan held out his hands, struggled to make himself heard above the din. "Hart, I did not come here to fight you."

Hart grinned, his crooked teeth making him look boyish. In a broad Yorkshire accent, he said, "I knew you'd say that. You don't fool me."

"I'm not trying to trick you. I don't want to fight you. They're just playing games with us."

The other man shook his head. "Suit yours'en."

He aimed another blow. Dan ducked, heard the satisfying 'smack' as Hart's fist connected with Fotheringham's erupting face. The poet fell back, howling. His friends yelped with delight.

Hart swung back to challenge again, but Dan had had enough. There was only one way to end this and he took it. As he defended himself from the next punch, he drove his right fist into Hart's face. The man's eyes widened in surprise. He staggered back, swayed and toppled.

The disappointed groans died to an uneasy silence. Dan looked down at Hart. The young fighter would have a dreadful awakening. Whatever promises Hawkhurst had made him would always have been liable to disappointment, dependent as they were on the whim of a wastrel lord. After this, all was over before it had begun. Hart would be left to make his way back to whatever farm or cotton mill he had been plucked from, his dreams of pugilistic glory ended. All to provide entertainment for Hawkhurst and his friends.

Dan moved towards the door. This time no one tried to stop him.

"Foster, wait!" Hawkhurst called. "Will you accept my challenge?"

"My Lord!" Townsend exclaimed. "I must counsel you against such a move."

"Keep out of it, Townsend. Foster, will you go a few rounds with me?"

Townsend's face was the colour of clay. The fight with Hart was one thing, but a Runner fighting a lord, and a lord who was a friend of the Prince's! It should not – could not – happen. It was overstepping a mark. Worse, there'd be questions asked about his part in it. He met Dan's eye, gave a warning shake of the head.

"Yes," Dan said.

At once the atmosphere was taut, excitement snapping in the air. No mill between low pugs this, but a serious stand-up match between two cool-headed men who knew what they were doing. Dan had seen the mufflers in the hall, knew that Hawkhurst was a sporting man. That he was a confident fighter was obvious from the self-assured way he stripped off his fencing doublet and pulled his shirt over his head, revealing a wiry body. Quickly his orders were given: Harry the footman was sent for to act as his second, the Irishman allocated to Dan, a couple of servants summoned to carry off Hart.

Dan's second held out his plump hand. "Ormond."

Dan hesitated. He would rather manage alone than put up with a loutish drunk for an assistant. But Ormond's appointment had sobered him: sport like this was too serious a business for a fuddled head. Dan took the proffered hand. Ormond regarded him with the awkward sympathy of one who looks on a doomed fellow creature.

Dan took off his necktie, jacket and shirt, draped them over a chair, sat down and pulled off his boots. He and Hawkhurst were of a similar size and build; a brand-new pair of pumps was offered to him from the lord's store. They were a good fit, good quality too.

Fotheringham, his spotty chin turning from red to blue, had sufficiently recovered from his injury to fix his attention on an escapade that was destined to be the talk of the London clubs. The barefooted man chalked a far from straight line on the carpet. Hendbury, Hawkhurst's fencing adversary, was chosen as referee, with the spark who had mimicked Agnes acting as umpire in case of dispute.

While all this was going on, Ormond whispered to Dan, "It might not be too late to stop this. I could speak to Hawkhurst on your behalf."

Dan made no reply. Ormond sighed and accepted the towel, bucket and sponge Harry handed him.

The circle was formed, a quieter one now, its bets placed – not so much on who would win, but on how many rounds it would take Hawkhurst. Dan and Hawkhurst stepped up to the line. Hawkhurst's fencing friend decreed "Broughton's Rules". The fighters shook hands and went back to their makeshift corners. Harry's face leered at Dan over Hawkhurst's shoulder: he was going to enjoy seeing the Bow Street man beaten to a mush.

Fotheringham rang a hand bell and the fighters came out to meet one another. They circled in the silence, footsteps alternately muffled by the strip of carpet or tapping on the wooden floor. Their breathing became louder. Grunting softly, they loosed experimental punches, none of which hit home.

The round ended and the combatants retired to their corners. Dan let Ormond wipe him down while he considered what he'd learned. Hawkhurst moved well; moved quickly, too. He was used to drinking enough to floor the average man without feeling the ill-effects of it. The damage would show as he aged, but that gave Dan no advantage now. What was more promising was the stiffness of Hawkhurst's style. It was too disciplined, too classical, over-reliant on well-learned and practised moves. It was a style that would work well if he was up against another gentleman boxer.

Dan was no gentleman.

In the second round, he complemented Hawkhurst's precise style by throwing some wild swings and letting himself be wrong-footed once or twice. When he got a punch in, he acted as if he'd just won the champion's belt. When he took one, he played baffled, as if he hadn't known where it came from. They went at a good pace, the speed of the contest enough to thrill the audience, show both fighters to advantage.

In his corner, Hawkhurst lapped up his friends' encouragement, not all of which failed to reach Dan's ears. *He knows a few moves, but you've been tutored by the best. All he's had is some washed-up fighter in a backstreet gym. He's no match for your science.*

Dan winced as Ormond wiped blood off his lip. "You keep going like this, you'll tire him," the Irishman said.

It was true, but it was not how Dan was planning to end the fight.

Ormond narrowed his eyes. "You're up to something."

Dan took the cup of water from the Irishman's pudgy fingers, swigged, spat into the bucket. The referee called them up to the mark. By now Townsend was looking more relaxed. The world would remain the right way up: Dan wouldn't be knocking down Hawkhurst any time soon. Hawkhurst had the same thought. He came out with an arrogant swing, a superior smile as his fist glanced over Dan's cheek. Dan faltered, shook his head, wiped his forehead with the back of his hand. Hawkhurst's eyes glinted. He stepped after Dan, feet perfectly placed, arms at the perfect angle. He might as well have announced in the press that he was about to land a killing right.

Time for a change of mood. Dan drew back his left fist and hammered it into Hawkhurst's face, followed it up with the right, powered forward, driving the man back with the sheer strength of his blows. A snarl and a hit, a snarl and a hit, on and on, unstoppable, blind to the dismay on Hawkhurst's face, deaf to the shocked yells and screams of Hawkhurst's friends. He didn't stop until science was on its knees, its white fingers scrabbling on the rug.

Dan sprang away, rolled his shoulders, prowled around the kneeling man while Hendbury counted the seconds. Hawkhurst, the blood running from his mouth, got one foot on the floor and tried to rise on trembling legs. He didn't make it and sank down, shaking the sweat out of his eyes. He tried again, but it was too late. The half minute was over.

His friends rushed forward, helped him to his feet and on to a chair, all fussing and talking at once. Harry sponged his wounds, but he pushed the man's hand away, croaked, "Brandy." Someone thrust a glass into his hand.

Ormond threw a towel over Dan's shoulders. "You're the real go, all right, Foster, and no one can deny it. Backstreet gym, be damned! Who taught—"

He was interrupted by Townsend jabbing his cane into Dan's chest. "You bloody animal, look what you've done!"

"You wanted me to fight," Dan said. "So I did."

"Not like this! You're in a gentleman's drawing room, not on some street corner. You could have killed him. Attempted murder, that's what it is, and I'll see you strung up for it!"

He grabbed Dan's arm. He might as well have grabbed a wild cat. Dan, still wrought to fighting pitch, knocked Townsend's hand away and put up his fists. Ormond sprang between them, held out his arms, kept the two men apart.

"It was a fair fight, and there's no one here to say otherwise," Ormond cried. "Not one foul called, isn't that right?" he demanded of the referee.

The swordsman opened his mouth to speak, quickly shut it and looked to Hawkhurst for guidance. The vanquished lord sat with his head in his hand, clutching his empty glass, paying no attention to the altercation.

"It was nowhere near fair," Bredon said. "Foster should be thrashed – and I'm the man to do it!"

He went for Dan. The referee clutched Bredon's jacket and dragged him back. Bredon whirled round and the two fell to blows. Fotheringham leapt in and attempted to pull them apart. The barefooted man caught hold of Fotheringham's hair, but only maintained his grip for a few seconds before he screamed and tumbled to the ground, where he rolled about massaging his bruised toes. Townsend swung his cane at Dan, the swings blocked by Ormond. The others dithered on the edge of the melee and made feeble attempts to disentangle it. Harry took advantage of the confusion to help himself to some generous swigs from a wine bottle.

A glass flew over the brawling heads and smashed to pieces on the door. "Enough!" Hawkhurst roared. "Be quiet, the lot of you!"

They froze into a dishevelled, battered tableau.

"My Lord." Townsend broke the silence. "Please accept my apologies. I had no idea Foster lacked all sense of propriety. He has disgraced the office I am proud to represent, and I will see to it that Sir William is informed immediately."

"Shut up, Townsend," said Hawkhurst. "Why haven't I got a bloody drink?"

His young followers tumbled over themselves to get to the table. Bredon stalked in front of them, poured a brandy and carried it over to Hawkhurst. He took up an attentive stance beside his chair.

"Propriety be damned," Hawkhurst said. "What's the use of

that to a man in the ring? He's everything you said he was, and more. He'll more than do." He glared at the young men. "And what's the matter with you, you damned puppies? If you're so afraid of laying out a bit of rhino, you don't belong here." He put his fingers to his jaw, experimentally opened and closed it. "Since Foster's such a talent for dissembling, I know exactly who to match him against."

"What do you mean, match me against?" demanded Dan.

"What do you think?" retorted Hawkhurst. "For a fight by royal command in the presence of His Royal Highness, the Prince of Wales."

"I'm not fighting anyone, royal command or not."

Hawkhurst laughed. "No one refuses a royal command. Not even me." He rose to his feet. "I'm going to Vauxhall. I need some cunny."

He strode towards the door, grabbing a bottle of wine on the way, Bredon following. The rest of the company, their differences forgotten, huzzahed, scrambled about looking for shoes, waistcoats, jackets, hats and coats, and scurried after him. When the front door had slammed shut and the strains of the ragged chorus of "*A boxing we will go!*" had died away, Harry tucked two unopened bottles under his arms and staggered off to enjoy them in peace.

Dan was left standing in the midst of a wreckage of empty bottles, spilled wine, broken glass, foils, fencing doublets, discarded towels and sponges. In the silence, he became aware of a puffing sound. He looked round. Townsend had slumped into one of the chairs, where he sat breathing heavily and mopping his brow with a large spotted handkerchief.

"I thought I was sunk then, to be sure!" he said.

"*You* were sunk? What the hell were you thinking?"

"Come on, Foster, don't be so missish. You're a boxer, ain't you? All you had to do was box."

Dan took his shirt from the back of the chair and pulled it on. "You've ruined a promising fighter just to impress your friends."

"That booby Hart? It's the way things fall and the lad has to learn it. Either he's got what it takes or he hasn't. Hawkhurst thinks you've got what it takes, and that being so, the Prince will think it too."

"I'm not here to fight, but to solve a case."

"Pho! Do you think I sent for you for your detective skills? The Prince still likes to follow the science though he doesn't go to public matches now, on account of his vow not to. He happened to mention recently he'd like to see a good, well-regulated bout if such could be arranged without attracting too much attention. Then along comes the case, and with it a way to bring you up to scratch."

"So that's why you told him I'm a pugilist."

"Well, ain't you? The great Dan Foster who never loses."

"I've never said that."

"No, you only think it. You should have let Hart win if you feel so strongly about it. No, the truth is, Foster, you are a fighter. Put you in the ring and you can't help yourself. The Prince asked Hawkhurst to cast an eye over you, and if he thought you were up to it, fix the thing privately." Townsend chuckled. "There was I racking my brains to find a way of getting you in front of him, and then you said you thought he was a suspect. It's the one time when one of your ideas has come in handy."

"His Lordship can fix what he likes. I will not fight."

"There'll be a handsome reward for all involved. As I see it, everyone wins. You. Me. The Prince."

"You and I will do nothing like."

Townsend rested his cane on the floor, twirled it between his fingers. "Are you seriously telling me you'd turn down the chance of the prize of a lifetime? Other men would give their right arm for a go. Or aren't you man enough for the challenge?"

"I don't fight for money."

"Oh, ho, above all that, are you? I wager you wouldn't hand the purse back if it came your way. But if you're looking for something more noble, what about loyalty to your Prince? Or are you above humouring the most generous royal gentleman in the world?"

"It's got nothing to do with loyalty."

"Go ahead, then. Refuse the Prince. What good do you think that will do your career?"

Dan pulled on his jacket and moved towards the door. "Townsend, so help me, if I spend another minute in your company, I'll knock your head off."

Townsend laughed. "You could. Like I said, you're a fighter."

"I tell you, I will not fight."

Chapter Eighteen

"You will fight," said Sir William Addington. He stood by the window, a sheaf of papers in his hand. Not a lawyer's brief, Dan noticed, but what looked like the script of a play.

Sir William moved back to his chair and sat down.

"The honour of the service is at stake. Refuse and you make us a laughing stock. Worse still, you will give the men of Bow Street a reputation for cowardice. Besides, what's the difficulty?"

"Townsend had no right to put me forward."

"Townsend may have done you a great favour. Even the loser's purse will be a tidy sum. Not that I think you will lose," Sir William added. "Come, Foster. This is unmanly and I didn't expect it from you. Surely you aren't afraid?"

"No, I'm not afraid. But I did not choose to be put in this position."

"Few of us do choose to be put in our positions. You need to face realities. As I told you, the Home Secretary does not want relations between himself and the Prince to get any worse. All it will take is a whisper of the royal displeasure in his ear and he won't think twice about casting you off." Addington gave a solemn shake of his jowls. "I won't be able to save you."

No, Dan thought, you'll be too busy protecting your own job.

"Come, man, it's one fight. If you win it, you could make a fortune. Think of your family."

"And the honour of the service?"

*

"A fight in front of the Prince of Wales? All the lords and ladies there to see my husband? Oh, Danny, I'm so proud of you!"

Caroline circled her arms around Dan's neck, plastered his face with kisses. Dan, who had just arrived home, clasped her around the waist and drew her to him, gazed over her head, let her think he shared her joy.

"Do you hear that, Mother? Just wait till I tell Nell!"

Mrs Harper smiled at the embracing couple. "Our Dan! Who'd have thought it?"

"Why not our Dan?" Caroline laughed. "He's the handsomest, cleverest, most wonderful man in the world."

Alex stood gripping the seat of a chair which he had used to pull himself upright on his wobbly legs. Caroline ran to him and, much to his surprise, scooped him up.

"That's your daddy, Alex! He's going to fight for the Prince of Wales!" She danced around the room, singing nonsensically to Alex, who gurgled gleefully in her arms.

"The Prince of Wales! The Prince of Wales!" Abruptly she stopped. "Dan, what shall I wear?"

"It's going to be a private occasion," Dan said. "The Prince and a few friends."

She pouted. "Men only, do you mean?"

"I don't have any say over who will be invited. I just have to turn up and fight."

"Is it really so, Mr Foster?" asked Nick. "When is it to be? Who will you fight? Can I come wiv you when you go training?"

"As long as it doesn't make you late for lessons. It's to be in two weeks' time. As for who I'm to fight, I don't yet know."

"Oh, who cares about that?" Caroline said, the prospect of a bright future overcoming her disappointment at not being there to see it. "It's your big chance, Dan. I always knew you were meant for great things, and now the Prince of Wales says so too. Dan Foster, champion of England! Do you think we will be able to afford a bigger house? And some new furniture to put in it?"

"Don't go dreaming about money we haven't got."

"But we will have, when you're rich and famous."

"I'm not going to be rich and famous from one fight."

"A fight in front of the Prince of Wales! Mother, we'll look at some catalogues at the Exchange tomorrow. Red curtains. I've always wanted red curtains. And a kitchen range."

"Caroline, it's just one fight."

But she was not listening.

"Caroline's thrilled," Dan said.

"It's only to be expected," Noah answered. "She's always wanted you to be a boxer."

"I can't get her to understand that this is a one-off. That I didn't want it. That it doesn't mean I'm going to make a career of it."

Noah rose from his armchair and stirred the fire with the poker. "She was never a great listener."

Dan fell silent, unwilling to pursue the point. Noah had never stood in the way of his marriage, but nor had he made a secret of his opinion that Dan had married too young and that Caroline was not the right one for him. Dan frowned into his coffee. He knew that now, when it was too late.

He had vowed to make an effort with Caroline, to patch things up between them, and she had agreed to bring up his son. At the least, he owed her his loyalty, had an obligation to defend her from criticism, even that of his father. He wondered how she would bear it when she realised he meant what he said.

"Who will they put you up against?" Paul took a swig of his toddy. He was the only one of the three who drank spirits. Every evening, the old soldier treated himself to a steaming glass of gin, hot water, sugar and lemon. A well-earned treat at the end of a long working day, when everything in the gymnasium was neat and clean, and all ready for the training sessions in the morning.

"They haven't told me. I think that's part of the entertainment. For them anyway."

"Makes no difference," Noah said. "You're in good condition and will be in better still when I've done with you."

"Damn them all to hell!" Dan said. "And John Townsend above all. The man means me no good, of that I'm certain. Hopes to see me fall. Why should I give him the satisfaction? Why should I fight?"

"Because you can go out there and win and prove that you're a better man than any of them." Noah leaned forward, rested his hand on Dan's knee. "And tell me true, son. Don't you like winning? And won't you like the money that comes with it when you do?"

Dan looked into Noah's smiling face, the crinkled eyes that willed him to be his best. As they had since that day Noah had picked him up, a wild, ragged street boy full of guile and hate. Noah had seen something in him, had given him dignity and honour. Had taught him they were things worth fighting for.

He laughed softly. "You're right, you wily old man."

Paul smacked his lips happily over his drink. "That's right, that's right. You need to put your heart into it, boy. Half measures don't win. So you'd better be in here bright and early tomorrow because there's a lot of training to get in and not much time to do it."

There was a loud pounding on the door.

Paul put down his glass. "Who's that at this time of night?"

"Leave it," Noah said. "We're closed. They'll go away in a moment."

The knocking went on, louder than ever.

Paul stood up. "I'll go."

He took up a candle from the table and went out into the gym, shading the flame with his hand. The light drew his shadowy figure through the dark space where ropes and punch bags swung eerily in the gloom. His footsteps echoed on the bare boards. He opened the creaking door at the top of the landing and went down the stairs, dragging the dim light with him.

Noah stood up and raked out the last of the fire ready for the night. Dan watched him, both of them still aware of the sounds from downstairs. The bolts drawn back, Paul's querying voice, a mumbled reply. A scuffle, Paul's cry.

Noah and Dan were already on their feet. They pelted across the gym and down the stairs. The front door was open. Paul lay across the threshold. The extinguished candle had rolled away, smoking and dripping wax on the tiles. Paul's eyes were closed and there was a bloody gash on his forehead where he had hit the doorstep.

Noah dropped to his knees, turned the unconscious man over. "Go. I'll see to Paul."

Without a word, Dan leapt over the prostrate form and into the street. On his right, it sloped up to the busy, well-lit Strand. To his left, steam issued from the door of the Turkish baths and swirled in the light over the door. Lights burned in neighbouring dwelling houses, but the offices and warehouses at the wharf end were unlit. The street ran down to a darkness webbed by the masts of river barges and the scaffolds of cranes.

He glimpsed a figure in a long coat pass from the light into the gloom and raced after him. Their footsteps echoed between the houses, burst out more clearly when they reached the open quayside. Dan paused to listen, started in the direction of the receding footsteps. The river was a sheet of slithering blackness with broken lines of light reflected along its banks. The ropes and blocks on the flat-bottomed vessels rattled in the cold night breeze. There were sinister splashes and gurgles from water lapping against the dank stone.

He stumbled over a rope, righted himself. His feet crunched over nuggets of coal that had tumbled from a heap in a stall at the water's edge. Beyond the stall, the path lay between a warehouse wall on his left, the drop to the river on his right.

A figure appeared, its face turned towards him, flickering pale in the intermittent moonlight under the scudding clouds. He flung out his arms and Dan's path was blocked by an avalanche of crates. They crashed down, some breaking into shards and splinters Dan had to jump back to avoid.

Dan sprang on to the pile, but it was not stable enough to climb, sent him skidding back to the ground. Some fragments of wood slid into the river, spraying him with droplets of water. He did not want to go the same way. He scrambled away from the water's edge, got to his feet. He could no longer hear the sound of running.

Cursing, he turned and sprinted back to the gymnasium. He hammered on the door.

"Dad, it's me!"

After a moment, Noah drew back the bolts. He had placed his lantern on the stairs and armed himself with a pistol.

"Didn't get him," Dan said.

Noah locked the door and the two men went back upstairs. Paul sat by the fire, a second glass of spirits in his hand. Under normal circumstances he never drank more than one.

"What happened?" Dan asked.

The old soldier shook his head. "I hardly know. I opened the door, asked him what he wanted, and next thing I knew, he hit me."

"What did he say?"

"Nothing."

"We heard his voice."

Paul knitted his brows. "I have it! He said, 'Foster?' I said, 'Who's asking?' And then he hit me."

"Did you get a look at him?"

"He was tall. That was all I saw. Couldn't see his face."

"Dad, have you had any trouble with anyone lately?"

"None I recall."

"Do you owe anyone money?"

"You don't have to ask."

Dan would have been surprised if the answer had been yes. Noah was strict in matters of business.

"Has anything out of the ordinary happened in the gym? An argument? A complaint?"

Noah rubbed his chin thoughtfully. "Nothing like that. Perhaps he meant to rob me."

"There are easier places to target," Dan said. "It's not as if you'd come to the door carrying your cash box. And he said your name. It looks personal to me."

"Yes, but which Foster do you think he wanted?" Noah asked.

"You think he was after me?"

"He just said Foster, isn't that right, Paul?"

"Yes," the old soldier answered. "I'm sure of it."

"Then most likely it's some criminal you've crossed," said Noah.

Dan shook his head. "He might mistake Paul for you, but he couldn't mistake him for me."

"The lamp Paul was carrying would have dazzled a man looking in from the dark street. All he'd have seen was a figure behind a blaze of light half-hidden behind a door."

"It's possible, I suppose. But are you sure you can't think of anyone who has a grudge against you? Someone you've had a falling-out with?"

"No one comes to mind," Noah said.

"If you think of anything, let me know." Dan stood up, drew on his coat and hat. He reached down and took his old friend's hand. "How are you faring, Paul?"

"I'll be all right. You just make sure you're here in good time for training tomorrow."

"I will. You get some rest. And you be careful, Dad."

Noah held up his pistol. "Let him try again. I'll be ready for him. And I'd say the same to you. Watch your back on the way home."

Noah followed Dan downstairs. Dan stood in the street until he had heard Noah draw the bolts, then he turned right and walked up to the Strand. He felt for the gun in his pocket. Like his father, he would be ready.

It would help if he knew what he was supposed to be ready for.

Chapter Nineteen

Dan stood in the drawing room at Berkeley Square in front of a painting of a young Louise Parmeter dressed in something pale and gauzy. She sat on a stone bench and gazed dreamily into a distance of trees and fields. She certainly had been a beautiful woman, but he thought there was something ruthless in the set of her mouth. Perhaps it was a look possessed by everyone who had clawed themselves up to independence from poverty. Perhaps he had it himself. Next to her portrait, lest anyone should forget that she had once been loved by royalty, hung a print of a younger, thinner Prince of Wales.

The door opened and Sarah Dean came into the room. "Miss Taylor will be down in a moment."

He had called to ask how Agnes Taylor was. He was also curious to hear her version of the encounter at Cavendish Square yesterday, and in particular why she had thought it worth asking Lord Hawkhurst for a subscription towards a book of poetry commemorating a woman he had loathed.

Sarah moved to his side and looked at the painting. "It's by Gainsborough. They all queued up to paint her: Reynolds, Romney, the Cosways, Lawrence. Even now you can buy prints of her when she was at the height of her fame. She was still getting requests, but she wouldn't sit for any of them."

"Was she always in the news?"

"Wherever she went, whoever she was with, whatever she wore. There were hundreds of satirical prints, countless obscene ones too. But she was a leader of fashion. I shall never forget the effect it had on me when I read about the new shades of blue and grey she brought back from Paris ten years ago. They shook the world. I knew then I had to work for her."

Blue and grey did not sound such great discoveries to Dan.

"How did you manage it?" he asked.

"I was working for the Duchess of Deavor, and I asked her to introduce me."

"A very obliging employer."

Sarah smiled. "Duchesses have their secrets. And I am the best. Miss Parmeter knew it." She turned back to the portrait. "I was going to dress her in the blue and grey on the first night of her return to the stage."

"She was planning to go back to the theatre?"

"Yes. She'd been talking to Mr Sheridan about it for weeks. The silly man wanted her to take on older roles: Mrs Hardcastle, Mrs Rich, Lady Oldham. As if I should dress old wives and matrons! Still, he didn't have much choice in the matter. He owed her such vast sums of money."

"Mr Sheridan owed Miss Parmeter money?"

"Mr Sheridan owes everyone money." She sighed. "It would have been her greatest triumph." She shook herself out of her melancholy, said briskly, "I shall leave you to your tête-à-tête with Miss Taylor."

"It's hardly that."

She looked at him with a shrewd eye. "I will tell you one thing, Mr Foster. You would do well not to waste too much sympathy on Miss Taylor."

"What do you know against her?"

"Is it true that she was at Lord Hawkhurst's yesterday afternoon?"

"She went to ask him to subscribe to a book of poems about Miss Parmeter. He and his friends tricked her into drinking strong spirits."

"I doubt much trickery was needed. And only a fool would put herself in such a situation with such a man."

"I own I was surprised to see her there. She must have known what he was like, especially after Miss Parmeter's affair ended."

"Miss Taylor has an inflated opinion of her power to influence men."

"You think she hoped to influence Lord Hawkhurst?"

"I really couldn't say what she hoped. But she will have few opportunities to find a rich husband when she leaves this house."

"Miss Taylor wants to marry Lord Hawkhurst?"

"I think she wants to make a good marriage. How else is she to continue living in the manner to which she's become accustomed? But Agnes Taylor is no Louise Parmeter. She will never be able to manage a man like Lord Hawkhurst."

The door opened and Agnes came in. She stalked past Sarah without acknowledging her. Sarah smirked at Dan, curtsied pertly and left.

Agnes sat down. She was pale, but seemed otherwise unharmed by yesterday's adventure. Dan took a seat opposite her.

"I called to see how you are feeling," he said.

"That's very kind of you, Mr Foster. I am sorry you were put to so much trouble."

"If you don't mind me saying so, it wasn't very wise of you calling on Lord Hawkhurst like that."

"I had only ever seen him in company with Miss Parmeter and her friends. I had no idea a man of breeding could so far lower himself as to keep company with drunkards, Irishmen and pugilists. Thank heavens that you were there to rescue me from my tormentors."

Dan wondered what she would think if he told her how he had come by the bruises on his face. "You saw the pugilist, did you?"

"The brute was in the room when I arrived. To a woman of my sensibilities, Mr Foster, the mere sight of the savage was quite overpowering. I have been languishing on my feverish couch ever since."

It was one way to describe the effects of drink, Dan supposed.

"Yet strength returns to my quivering limbs," she continued, "and vitality to my o'er-tried heart. The Muses have poured their blessings on me. I am no longer at the mercy of patrons and subscribers."

"Something has happened?"

"I have today received a missive from Messrs Cadell and Davies offering to publish my next book of poems. The verses in question have been seen by no other mortal, not even dear, lamented Miss Parmeter. They have been judged on the merit of their natural genius."

"I congratulate you. I hope this means that your future is assured?"

She glanced at the door through which Miss Dean had lately passed and raised her voice. "I shall be that rare thing, Mr Foster. A woman who lives by her pen."

Dan left Agnes to the enjoyment of her new prospects and walked to the Cruft mansion. Randolph Cruft had not yet returned, had sent a letter to say he intended to stay in the country a few days longer. Now why, Dan wondered, could that be? The young man had not wanted to leave London, yet offered the chance to return, he did not take it. Perhaps he was consumed by grief for his dead mistress. Perhaps he had found someone else to comfort him. Or perhaps he was keeping out of the way until interest in the case had died down.

Dan considered his options. Whatever he decided, he intended to avoid John Townsend as much as possible. A trip to Hertfordshire to find out what Cruft was up to would achieve that aim nicely. However, it would mean missing the meeting at the Martins' house, and with it a chance to find out what Pickering, Rule and the Martins were involved in.

He was also interested in what Sarah had said about the dispute between Sheridan and Louise Parmeter. Faced with a debt he could not repay and the prospect of giving an actress roles he did not want her to have – surely an unusual situation for a theatre manager – it was possible their argument had become acrimonious. And there was still Hawkhurst, who had not yet answered any of Dan's questions.

Dan decided that Hertfordshire could wait.

Chapter Twenty

Drury Lane Theatre rang with the sound of hammering, creaking ropes and crashing scenery. Stagehands, costumiers, prompters and writers scurried back and forth, shouting at one another. Women shuffled about the house, clanking pails and beating dust from curtains and cushions. The jangling, whining and squeaking of the musicians tuning their instruments rose up from the orchestra pit. It was a mystery to Dan how any play could appear out of such chaos.

The central figure in all this, drawing the eye by some unaccountable air or charisma, was Richard Brinsley Sheridan, a robust man with a raddled face. He stood in the pit with one of his business managers. He held a newspaper in one hand which he slapped loudly with the other while he railed against its contents to the soothing nods and murmurs of his companion. Soothed, however, he was not.

Drawing nearer, Dan discovered the cause of his grievance.

"Borrowed it? Borrowed it? If I did, it was from none other than myself. *Think not, my Love* is my song. I wrote it when I was courting the first Mrs Sheridan. Who does this self-styled 'Lover of Truth' think he is? And Schick's translation of *The Stranger* 'published by Mr Dilly in the Poultry is by far a more correct translation of Mr Kotzebue's comedy' than mine? Was there ever such a blockhead? Such a poor contemptible booby? Such a swaggering puppy?"

Usually Sheridan, who made a point of being polite to the Bow Street men, greeted Dan with an affable nod. Now he rolled up the newspaper and brandished it at him.

"What now? Another of his dreadful scripts? Haven't I got enough to do without having to wade through a host of Matchless Orindas, Sir Foppesly-Fops and Lady Tumbles? Well, why not? What else am I here for?"

"Mr Sheridan, sir," Dan said. "I—"

Sheridan gestured at one of the benches. "Leave it there! I'll neglect my business – stay away from the House of Commons – take no food or drink until I've conned it. The honour is all mine."

Sheridan's companion cleared his throat. "I do not think, Mr Sheridan, that Officer Foster is here to deliver a script."

"Is he not one of Sir William Addington's men?"

"I am, sir," Dan said. "I'm here about a case I'm investigating."

"You haven't brought me another of Sir William's plays?"

"No, sir."

"You're sure? You aren't hiding it in that greatcoat of yours?"

"Indeed, no, sir. I didn't know that Sir William was in the habit of sending you plays."

"Then you must be one of Bow Street's least observant officers."

"An officer doesn't like to pry, sir."

Sheridan laughed. "Oh, don't you, Officer Nosey? Well, well, Mr Foster, forgive my temper. These play-writing magistrates are the very devil. Though I'll say one thing for Sir William: he doesn't give up. It must be twenty years since Garrick rejected his scribbling. Now it's my turn. If there's one thing worse than thwarted ambition, it's renewed thwarted ambition. What should have put the dramatical maggot in Sir William's head again is beyond me. Still, since you do not come bearing a comedy in five acts, I think a celebratory drink is in order. Fetch a bottle, Thompson."

At least one puzzle has been cleared up, Dan thought. He now knew why he had heard Sir William declaiming to himself in his office lately. The chief magistrate had been trying out his speeches.

Thompson was gone and back with bottle and glasses within two minutes. Sheridan sat down, and motioned to Dan to join him on the bench. Dan shook his head when Thompson offered wine to him. Thompson moved away, taking the spare glass with him.

"What's your business, Officer?"

"I'm working on the Louise Parmeter murder."

"Poor Louise! A dreadful loss. I still remember her Jacintha in *The Suspicious Husband*. Damned fine legs. A brilliant wit, too. Sir William could learn a thing or two from her plays and novels."

"I gather that Miss Parmeter was considering a return to the stage."

"Yes, she was. And we'd have been lucky to have her."

"In the right parts."

"How do you mean?"

"I understand you had a disagreement over what parts Miss Parmeter should take."

"That's true, we did. Nothing unusual in that, Mr Foster. Actors and actresses are apt to misjudge their talents. I've known tragedians who itched to be comedians and hadn't the faintest notion of comedy, comedians who longed to play tragic roles who hadn't the least idea how to die well."

It was an unfortunate turn of phrase, which Sheridan seemed not to notice. He took a long draught of his wine.

"But how do you think this connects with Louise's murder? It was merely a difference of artistic opinion. You surely don't think we'd substitute real daggers for our theatrical sparring, eh?"

"I think it's possible where money is concerned."

"Come, come, Officer. Get to the point. What are you trying to say?"

"Only that I'm informed you owed Miss Parmeter a great

deal of money and she was using that to compel you to give in to her demands."

Understanding flashed across Sheridan's face, closely followed by laughter. "You have a thing or two to teach Sir William Addington about drama yourself, Mr Foster. It's an ingenious plot. However, it won't hold up." Sheridan looked for Thompson, who was going through a sheaf of figures with the head carpenter, who glumly shook his head whenever the bookkeeper struck another item off his list. "Mr Thompson, here a moment, if you please!"

Thompson nodded at the carpenter and hurried back to Sheridan.

"How much money do I owe Miss Louise Parmeter?"

"Nothing, Mr Sheridan. That debt was repaid two weeks ago."

"There you are, Mr Foster. All paid up, fair and square."

"Only because you borrowed £200 from the upholsterer – to whom you still, by the by, owe £350," said Thompson.

Sheridan waved his hand. "Thank you and be gone, Master Robert Shallow."

Thompson rolled his eyes. "I don't see why you always have to bring Sir John Falstaff into it whenever I bring up the question of your debts."

"Because, my dear Thompson, there is not one trait in human nature which Shakespeare does not penetrate. Now, be gone." Sheridan drained his glass and stood up. "I hope I have satisfactorily answered your questions?"

"You have, thank you," Dan answered. "I hope you understand I had to ask them."

"I bear no ill will, Officer. Louise's killer must be caught. His Highness is quite distraught about the matter. What, still here, Thompson?"

"There is that business we need to discuss."

Sheridan held up a silencing hand and asked Dan, "Is there a Mrs Foster?"

"There is."

"Then I'm sure you'd like tickets for tonight's performance. Thompson here will make the arrangements."

Thompson clicked his tongue. "There won't be a performance if you don't come and talk to the actors. I've done all I can. They're threatening to strike unless they get some wages."

"Very well, I'm coming. I'll have the tickets sent round, Mr Foster."

Dan's glimpses of loud, strutting, over-dressed actors when he was on duty had more than satisfied what little interest he had in the stage. Luckily, he was able to say, "It's very kind of you, but I have work to do tonight."

"Come on Monday then. Much better. We're doing *The Stranger* for Mrs Siddons. And you will have the delight of hearing my original epilogue to my Semiramis. *'Dishevelled still, like Asia's bleeding queen / Shall I with jests deride the tragic scene?'*" Sheridan spotted the look on Dan's face. "Hum. You may prefer *The Devil to Pay* afterwards. It's an operatic farce."

"It's very generous of you, but—"

"Nonsense. Thompson, a box for Mr and Mrs Foster. And make sure it is plentifully supplied with supper." Sheridan held out his hand. "Good luck, Mr Foster."

They shook hands and Dan watched him make his way across the theatre, scattering greetings to musicians, stagehands and cleaning ladies as he went. A box with supper! He would never be able to look Caroline in the eye again if he turned the offer down. A night at the theatre it was then. He sighed, put on his hat and made his way towards the exit.

It was late afternoon by the time he reached Lord Hawkhurst's house. The footman, Harry, made some effort to smooth his tousled hair and rub the sleep out of his bloodshot eyes before stomping upstairs to tell Lord Hawkhurst he had a visitor. Dan waited in the hall for a quarter of an hour before Harry came back and announced that His Lordship would see Dan.

Dan followed him upstairs. Harry knocked and opened the door of Lord Hawkhurst's bedchamber. "Officer Foster, My Lord."

Hawkhurst's voice, hoarse with too much wine and lack of sleep, issued irritably from inside the room. "Show him in. And bring some coffee."

Harry opened the door and smirked Dan inside.

The curtains had been opened to let in the dust-betraying daylight. The room was untidy, the bed rumpled and occupied by a young woman with her hair loose about her shoulders who wore nothing but a simpering smile. Another woman some two or three years older stood beside the bed, lacing herself into her bodice.

Hawkhurst sat by the fire, his back to his company. He was unshaven, but his hair had been combed and his shirt and breeches were fresh.

"There ought to be an assize of whores like an assize of bread," he said without any greeting and addressing himself to the flames. "Here's one adulterated by false teeth, padded bosom, and fake hair. There's another engrossed wholesale and regrated from market to market at vast profit." He twisted in his chair. "Get out, ye trulls. Now."

The woman in the bed seemed inclined to pout and protest, but her companion seized a heap of clothes and dropped them on the coverlet. It should have been hint enough, but still she hesitated. Hawkhurst seized a boot from the floor and flung it at the bed. It missed by a wide margin. With a squeal of alarm, the girl leapt out of bed and, clutching her garments in front of her, pattered barefoot after her colleague. The door closed behind them as the boot's partner thudded against the boards.

Hawkhurst leaned back into his chair. "Where's Townsend?"

"Officer Townsend isn't coming. It's just me, My Lord," Dan said.

"Come to cry off the fight, have you?"

"No. I've come about the investigation, My Lord."

"What have I to do with your investigation?"

The door opened and Harry came in. He set down a tray with pot and cup and poured out Hawkhurst's drink.

"Where's the brandy?" demanded Hawkhurst.

"You didn't ask for any, milud," Harry said.

"Then go and get some. Simpleton."

Harry, looking none too pleased, hurried off. Hawkhurst sipped the reviving liquid and gave a long sigh.

"What did you say you wanted?"

"I've come about the investigation," Dan repeated. "I won fair and square yesterday and I claim my prize. Your answers to my questions."

"You were supposed to fight the other fellow – what's his name?"

"Hart. And I did fight him. Knocked him out anyway."

"And?"

"And nothing, My Lord."

"Too polite to mention that you beat me as well, eh?"

"I didn't think it my place to draw attention, My Lord."

"Oh, didn't you? And you can drop the My Lords. I can see it sticks in your craw."

Dan said nothing to this. Hawkhurst refilled his cup and took another draught. "I didn't deny I sent those things to Louise. I don't see what else you can have to ask me."

"They looked very like threats. Were you threatening her?"

"God knows what I was doing. I must have been drunk indeed if I thought they would frighten her."

"What did you think?"

"I don't know. That they'd make her as angry as I was." Hawkhurst stretched out his bare feet, crossed them at the ankles. "I daresay she simply smiled that maddening smile of hers."

"Did you know she was writing her memoirs?"

"Who didn't?"

"You weren't worried that she might have written something about you?"

"She could write what she damned well liked. And if she only wrote half the truth, she's had none to better me. But what are you now? A literary critic?"

"The memoirs were taken by whoever killed her."

"You think she was killed to prevent their publication? Interesting idea. Townsend didn't tell me you had ideas."

"It happens sometimes."

"More than you let on, I'll wager. You want to know if I killed her and took the memoirs. I didn't."

"Do you mind telling me where you were on Monday morning?"

"I haven't seen a Monday morning, or any other morning for that matter, for a long time. I go to bed about four and don't usually get up until two or three in the afternoon. Isn't that right, Harry?"

"What's that, milud?" said the footman, entering with the brandy.

"The officer wants to know where I was on Monday morning."

"You brought your charming guests home at about four o'clock, milud."

"And after that?"

"After that?" Harry repeated, as if he had never heard of an 'after that'. "You were here, of course. Mr Bredon has returned home, milud. He is with his valet and says he will be ready for you when he has finished changing."

"Charles?" Hawkhurst squinted into his brandy. "What pleasures does he have lined up for me today?"

"He didn't say."

Hawkhurst drained his glass. "Better prepare to face them. Draw me a bath and find me some clothes... I'm grateful to you for a new experience, Officer Foster. Two new experiences. I've never been interrogated by a Bow Street Runner before, and certainly never been bested by one at fisticuffs. But now I've had enough of your questions. I hope you're in training?"

"I am at the gymnasium at five most mornings, My Lord."

Hawkhurst said nothing to this, but his eyes flickered up to Dan's, and Dan thought there was something like envy in them. Dan glanced around the stale, messy room. Harry turned away from the closet where he had been rattling about and brought over a suit of clothes for Hawkhurst's approval, which was given with a weary nod.

Dan bowed and took his leave. He knew that he had as much information as he was going to get. Hawkhurst's entire household would doubtless corroborate his story. Whether it was true or not was another matter.

Chapter Twenty-One

Dan crossed Berkeley Square with its brightly illumined windows and rows of lamp-lit carriages. Foot and coachmen clustered together chatting and smoking, eyes fixed on the doors from which their masters and mistresses could emerge at any time and snap them to attention. The sound of dance music drifted from one of the houses. Shadowed figures swirled against the blinds.

When Dan entered the lane behind Louise Parmeter's house, he could have been in a different city. Here there were no lamps and the only light came from the open doors of the laundry. Inside, stooping women, dragging skirts heavy with water, toiled over the vats. Milky-coloured washing water gurgled along the gutter and spilled between the cobblestones. The air was thick with the smell of starch and soap, mixed with the smell of cow dung from the dairy. Further along, the stable gates were shut and no lights showed.

Dan was aware of the other man's presence even before his eyes had fully adjusted to the gloom. The curving lines of his back and head against the garden wall gave him away. There was just enough moonlight for Dan to recognise Grimes, one of the night patrolmen who worked out of Bow Street. Dan had been a member of the patrol himself before his promotion to principal officer four years ago. He had been expecting to see someone there, had guessed that Townsend would set a watch on his favourite suspect.

"Evening, Grimes."

"Mr Foster? I wasn't expecting you. Mr Townsend never said you was coming."

"Is Pickering inside?"

"Hasn't been out all evening."

"I can take it from here."

"I don't know. Mr Townsend said I should stay all night. He was very particular."

"It doesn't need two of us. You get off home."

Still Grimes hesitated.

"You can put in a claim for the full night's work. I'll cover it."

Grimes grinned. "You're a gent, Mr Foster."

He moved off noiselessly and Dan took his place. Ten minutes later footsteps crossed the stable yard and a key rattled in the lock of the wicket gate. Pickering came out and relocked the door. He crossed the lane and crept through the shadows opposite the laundry to avoid being seen. Dan did the same and followed him to Fleet Street.

Pickering hurried past the shops and businesses crammed into Wine Office Court and knocked a distinctive '*rat-a-tat-tat*' on the front door of the Martins' shoe shop. The door of a room at the back of the shop opened, framing Martin in a rectangle of light. Martin had muffled the shop bell; wordlessly he let Pickering inside. The men passed through the shop and the inner door closed, leaving the premises once again in darkness.

Dan found himself a doorway on the other side of the court and watched as another half-dozen men arrived, all using the same '*rat-a-tat-tat*'. The ship's chandler, George Rule, was the last to turn into the alley from Fleet Street. When Martin had let him in, he poked his head outside to take a look around before he stepped back inside and shot home the bolt.

It was an hour and a half before the meeting ended. The men came out one at a time, left their host with silent handshakes and walked away with quiet footsteps. Rule was second to last. Five minutes later Pickering appeared. He and Martin exchanged a few words on the threshold, their voices low and tense. Martin went back inside. Pickering turned right on to Fleet Street and set off towards the Strand. He carried a bag which he had not had when he arrived. It was long, looked like the sort of canvas satchel a carpenter might carry tools in.

From the Strand, Pickering led Dan into Drury Lane. The taverns and coffee houses around the theatre were packed, giving out the sounds of raucous voices, popular songs, stamping jigs. After a while Pickering and Dan left these disreputable streets and passed into quieter, more refined regions where the quality enjoyed their expensive recreations. In the end, though, Dan thought, it came down to the same things: drink and sex.

After half an hour's walking, they left London's livelier streets behind. On the far side of a wall on the right lay the shadowy gardens of the British Museum in Montagu House. The Frenchified roofs and turrets rose above the height of the rustling lime trees. Pickering continued past Bedford Square, where all lay in respectable silence dimly lit by lamps over the doors. He entered Gower Street and stopped outside a house in a terrace which backed on to open ground behind Montagu House.

Dan remembered Gower Street before the houses had been built. Once these fields had been a favourite spot of duellists; now new properties were steadily encroaching on the land. To the north, the road ran away into dark fields, but already it was flanked by a line of construction sites. During daylight it was a noisy, muddy region of brick carts, labouring men and hasty contractors.

The upper rooms of the house were in darkness. A glow of light lay like a pool at the foot of the area steps. Pickering slowed down. Was he paying a call on one of the servants? Dan glanced down into the kitchen. The buzz of servants' gossip mingled with the faint clatter of pots and pans. Some were clearing up from the last meal; others already chopping, measuring and mixing food for the next.

Pickering moved forward. He walked to the end of the terrace and turned down a muddy track which led round to the rear. In spite of the darkness and the uneven ground, he knew where he was going. He stopped at a stretch of garden wall not much taller than himself. He slung the bag across his back, the contents clinking, and poised to spring up, grab the parapet and haul himself over.

Before his feet left the ground, Dan caught him in an armlock. He kicked back, tried to jab his elbows into his assailant, but Dan had the advantage of surprise and forced him to his knees, one arm twisted behind him. With a deft movement, Dan slipped a pair of cuffs on to him.

"Right, Pickering, you're under arrest."

Chapter Twenty-Two

Pickering twisted his head round. "Foster! Let me go. It's not what you think."

"No?" Dan held on to the cuffs with one hand, kicked open the bag, rummaged inside with his free hand. "A jemmy. Picklocks. Wrench. Pliers. Looks like burglary to me."

"I'm no thief."

"You can tell that to the magistrate, you and your accomplices."

"They're not my accomplices. Simpson, the man who owns this house, is the thief. Worse than thief, for what he takes is a person's liberty."

Dan fastened the bag and hauled Pickering to his feet.

"No, wait! You have to listen to me. I'm not here to rob him, but to rescue the boy he's got locked up in there."

"What boy?"

"A lad called Joseph. Simpson's going to transport him to Jamaica, where he'll spend the rest of his days slaving on his plantation. That's kidnapping, and it's illegal."

"So is burglary."

"This isn't burglary. I've come for the boy."

"If the boy's been kidnapped, why don't you go to the magistrates and get a writ for his release?"

"Because it's expensive, and anyway we don't have much time. Rule says Simpson has a ship already fitted out down at Rotherhithe. The boy will be long gone by the time we've got a habeas corpus. I have to get him out tonight."

"If you're lying to me, Pickering, I'll know soon enough. Come on."

"Where are you going?"

"To the house."

"You can't. If you go in there, Simpson will say the boy's a thief and produce witnesses to back him. Joseph won't stand a chance. He might as well be shipped to the plantations if all you can offer him is the noose."

Dan could not pretend Pickering's fear was not justified. Masters and mistresses often took their revenge on out-of-favour servants by accusing them of stealing, and money bought the testimony they needed to prove it.

"Then what do you suggest we do?"

Pickering jerked his head at the wall. "I already have a plan."

"Oh, no. You don't think I'm going to help you break in?"

"What else can we do?"

Dan felt the weight of the bag in his hand. There was every tool he could need in there; more than he was used to. And time was running out.

He put down the bag, reached the key to the cuffs from his pocket, felt for his gun at the same time. "I warn you, I'm armed. Try to escape and I will shoot you down."

"I'm not going to escape."

Dan released the cuffs, thrust the bag into Pickering's arms. "You can carry this. Go on."

Pickering took the bag and swung himself up and over the wall. Dan followed. They crouched on the other side.

"What's your plan?" Dan whispered.

"To jemmy open one of the windows."

Dan pointed at a glass door into the garden. "What's wrong with the door?"

"I thought a window would be easier."

"Jemmying a window is noisier. We'll try the door first. You lead."

"But—"

"This is no time to have a debate. Go on."

They stooped down, zigzagged across the dark lawn and halted by the door.

"Hurry up then," Dan said.

Pickering opened the bag, hesitated, then took out the bunch of picklocks. Dan, his back against the wall, scanned the garden. He had noticed a path around the side of the house; if anyone heard them and came out, they would have to come that way. But all was dark and still.

The picklocks scratched and scraped. Pickering cursed. Dan turned an exasperated eye on his fumbling efforts.

"For God's sake, give them to me."

Crestfallen, Pickering handed them over. Seconds later the lock clicked.

"What kind of police officer are you?"

Dan ignored Pickering's question. As he had hoped, the door was not bolted, but it took some effort to push it open because of the heavy curtains that hung in front of it. Dan approved; they were good for muffling sound. The two men stepped inside.

They were in a room with a long, gleaming table with half a dozen chairs around it. There was a sideboard laden with dishes, silverware and a pair of candelabra. In the middle of the table, a vase of hothouse flowers gave off a sickly scent. Two places had been laid with gleaming cutlery and fine china, but the fire was unlit. Over the hearth hung a map of the Jamaican plantations.

"The breakfast room," Pickering said. "This way."

"You know where we are?"

"I've some idea. If my information is correct, Joseph is in his master's dressing room."

He opened the door a few inches. They looked out on to a hall and a flight of stairs. From somewhere beneath them came voices and gusts of laughter. They crept up the stairs to the first floor with its carpeted landing and row of closed doors. Pickering confidently made his way to one of the doors and swung it open to reveal, in the soft glow from the fire, a lady's bedchamber.

"Blast. I thought it was this one," he muttered.

"Take your time about it."

"I'm not used to this, you know," Pickering retorted.

"I can see that. What about in here?"

Dan opened another door. The room looked more promising. Here again, a fire had been lit ready for its occupant's return. The brushes on the dressing table were a man's, and a man's robe hung on the door. A door near the head of the four-poster bed led to the dressing room. Pickering hurried across and opened it.

The only light came through the window from the street lamps. It was enough for the two men to make out a large wardrobe, a boot stand, wash stand, and towel rail. There was a small fireplace with a narrow mantelpiece over it, but no fire. Against the opposite wall stood a small iron bed with no sheets, blankets or pillows. A huddled shape lay on top of the mattress. It started up and let out a whimper of alarm. There was another sound: the chink of metal.

Pickering knelt beside the bed and clasped the boy's hand. "Joseph, we've come to take you away from here."

The boy's teeth chattered, with cold, with fright. "But he'll be back soon – Mr Simpson."

Dan turned back into the bedroom, grabbed a candle from the bedside table, lit it at the fire and took it back to the dressing room. Joseph's face turned towards Dan, his eyes wide, blinking in the light. His face crumpled.

"You've come to take me to the ship!"

"Quiet!" Pickering hissed. "Look at me. We're not here to take you to the ship. We're taking you out of this." He tried to sound reassuring, but he had caught sight of something on the boy's neck. He looked back at Dan with despair in his eyes.

Puzzled, Dan brought the candle closer. Joseph was wearing a metal collar. A chain led from it to the bed railings.

"Hell," he said.

"What are we going to do?" asked Pickering.

"Move aside. Give me the picklocks. Hold the candle."

Pickering did as he was told. Dan examined the fetters. The last link of the chain was attached by a padlock to a loop soldered on to the collar.

"I can't get the collar off, but I should be able to open the padlock."

"I've got tools to deal with the collar," Pickering said.

Dan told Joseph to hold still, but the boy could not stop shaking. The minutes passed and still the padlock had not opened. Joseph looked at Pickering over Dan's head. The coachman's face was grim. Tears began to spill out of Joseph's eyes. Dan felt the lock about to yield, then Joseph sobbed. The movement knocked Dan's hand, dislodged the picklock. Dan bit back a curse and started again.

This time he had it. He unhooked the padlock and let the chain fall on to the mattress. Pickering helped Joseph to his feet. He was a tall, handsome youth, aged about sixteen. He wore crumpled breeches, shirt and jacket, and his legs and feet were bare.

"Where are your shoes?" asked Pickering.

"He took them away."

"Never mind. I can get you some. Come on."

"This isn't right," said Dan. "Simpson shouldn't get away with it. I should stay and arrest him."

"You can't. I told you. If you move against him, he'll have Joseph taken for a thief."

"But here's the evidence. I'm a witness. So are you and Joseph."

"A witness of what? That he had to restrain a thieving servant. He'll be able to prove it ten times over. Who will believe a boy who says he was kidnapped and threatened with slavery in a country that boasts it is free of slavery? I tell you, you force Joseph to testify and he's done for."

"I won't do it!" Joseph cried. "I won't!"

Pickering signalled to him to be quiet. "Foster, if you can guarantee that arresting Simpson will result in prosecution for him and freedom for Joseph, then go ahead. Look me in the eye and tell me that's how it's going to be. If you can't tell me that, then at least tell me that's how you believe it's going to turn out."

Chapter Twenty-Three

"Bring him in. Grace has some food ready. I—"

Martin, who stood at the open door with a lamp in his hand, broke off. "A police officer?"

"He's on our side," Pickering said, pushing the shop door open and pulling Joseph inside. Dan stepped in after them. Martin gazed at him in dismayed silence.

"Shut the door," Pickering said. "Get the boy into the back and douse the light, for heaven's sake."

Martin, still transfixed by the sight of Dan, said, "But what's he doing here?"

"I'll explain in a minute. Let's get into the back or we'll have the whole neighbourhood awake." Pickering guided Joseph through the shop.

"You'd better do as he says," Dan said to the bewildered shoemaker.

Mechanically, Martin bolted the door and hurried after them. The parlour behind the shop was simply but comfortably furnished. A fire burned in the hearth, a vase of flowers stood on the table, there was an open workbasket near the fire. On the chair next to it lay the shirt Grace Martin had been mending when Pickering rapped his 'rat-a-tat-tat'. On the seat opposite was the Bible her husband had been reading. The warm, savoury smell of bread and soup drifted from the kitchen.

Pickering guided the boy to the fireside and helped him into a seat. The door behind him opened and Grace Martin emerged from the passageway. Her gaze went straight to the boy huddled in the chair, his eyes heavy, his head nodding over his chest.

"Why, he looks perished! Pass my shawl, John. And he has no shoes! We must find—" She caught sight of Dan and all sign of welcome left her face. "You!"

"And John is the wife beater, I suppose," Dan returned.

Her eyes flickered to her husband. She turned pale and said, "You will at least let me give the boy something to eat before you drag him back to the monster who calls himself his master."

"No one's dragging him back anywhere," Pickering said, taking off his hat and coat and draping them over one of the dining chairs by the table. "We owe a debt of thanks to Mr Foster. If it wasn't for him, Joseph would still be chained to his bed."

"Chained?" she repeated. She looked at Joseph. He had lifted his head and the firelight glinted on the collar around his neck. "Oh, you poor boy!" she cried.

"Can't get it off until I fetch some tools from the stables," Pickering said. "Mr Foster here picked the padlock. It was Mr Foster who broke into the house too. He's a mighty handy fellow, for a Bow Street Runner."

"That's enough, Pickering," Dan said. "Unless you want me to arrest you all here and now, I want some explanations."

"And so do I," said John Martin. He turned to Grace. "But first, let's get some food into the lad."

"I'm famished too," Pickering said. "Hungry work, breaking and entering, eh, Mr Foster?"

Dan glared at him. The coachman laughed.

John, reminded of his duties as a host, gestured towards the table. "Of course, please sit down." Nervously, he added, "Mr Foster?"

Dan hesitated. The food did smell good and he realised he was hungry. And after all, it was hardly eating with desperadoes – though he'd done that often enough. He took off his outdoor things and took the place indicated. It was a tight fit between the table and a small bookcase against the wall. He spotted several of Louise Parmeter's works: poetry, anti-slavery tracts, and a book entitled *An Address to the Men of Great Britain on Behalf of Women*. There was no copy of the book Caroline had been reading, or of any of the other novels. Presumably the Martins were too earnest to read romance.

Grace draped her shawl over Joseph's shoulders and went to the kitchen to fetch the meal. She brought in bread, knives, spoons, bowls, glasses, a jug of beer. She pursed her lips when Dan asked for water and stalked off to the kitchen to fetch it. Pickering laughed, picked up the bread knife and cut a slice of bread. "We'd better tell her what happened before she pours the water on your head," he said.

When she was back in the room and they had all settled at the table, Pickering recounted the events of the evening in between taking mouthfuls of food and beer. Dan mostly let him tell it his way, only uttering a warning growl when Pickering spoke too enthusiastically of his housebreaking skills. When he had finished speaking, John grasped Dan's hand and, almost moved to tears, shook it heartily.

"Will you forgive me for the untruths I told you, Mr Foster?" Grace asked. "It seemed the most obvious way to account for our being together in the Apple Tree."

"You thought it better to let me think you were having an affair than tell me you were planning a burglary," Dan said.

She felt the rebuke and blushed.

"My wife did tell the truth in its essential parts," John defended her. "She and Mr Pickering were in Trinder's tavern when they said they were."

"So why didn't you tell me from the start that the two of you were together?" Dan asked Pickering.

"Because I wanted to keep Mr and Mrs Martin out of it. I didn't want the Runners coming around here asking awkward questions. Not that it's worked out as I hoped, for here you are."

Dan scratched his chin. "Then why did you come to Bow Street, Mrs Martin?"

She glanced at Pickering. "John and I thought it the best course of action."

"If I'd had time to send a message direct to Trinder, it wouldn't have happened," Pickering said. "But there wasn't a chance to give Jacko a long explanation before your myrmidons grabbed me, so I just told him to bring word of my arrest here. I knew Mr and Mrs Martin would get me out of prison. I only had to keep quiet and sit it out. I thought they'd send Trinder, that he and the others could say I'd been at the Apple Tree without any need to mention Mrs Martin."

"That's why you were surprised when she showed up at the Brown Bear," Dan said.

"It was a simple misunderstanding," John said placatingly.

"It was an unjustifiable risk," Pickering retorted.

"I would have thought clambering over a wall with a bag full of burglar's tools was a risk for a man who wanted to avoid prison," Dan said. "But to get back to the point. How did you know Joseph was at Simpson's?"

"The milk woman was friendly with him," Pickering answered. "She hadn't seen him for a few days and asked after him at the kitchen door. One of the servants told her. Thought it was funny. The boy's been something of a pet of Simpson's. He'd let it go to his head and wasn't very popular with the rest of the household."

"And Simpson had grown tired of his pet?"

Pickering nodded. "It's not an unusual story. The boy's got older and suddenly the tricks of a child aren't so charming in a youth. As a servant he's grown tiresome; as a slave he's worth money."

"And this milk woman came to you?"

"She came to the Apple Tree. I got the message."

"What happens to him now?"

"We get him out of London," John said. "Somewhere he can start a new life."

"It still doesn't sit right," Dan said. "If the boy would only testify."

"You know he won't," said Pickering. "If he does, he will be done for. And so will we. You're a police officer and you think your word will be enough. But what about when the lawyers start saying we're all thieves together, you, me and the boy? That we went there to rob the place? That you're a thief taker turned thief? And let's face it, you know your way around a picklock."

Dan knew Pickering was right. It would be hard to free the boy from the snares his master had laid for him. Harder still to justify burglary. Did he regret his behaviour? He decided he did not. The thought of leaving the boy cold, half-starved and in chains for a moment longer than he had to was intolerable. Joseph had a split lip too, had been beaten at some point. And there was that collar, which had yet to be removed.

"And this is what you and your co-conspirators get up to," Dan said. "Rescuing slaves like Joseph."

"The law is vague on the question of whether or not Joseph and others like him, who were born on the plantations, are slaves when they are in this country," John answered.

"A slave traders' law," muttered Pickering.

"Indeed," John said, before continuing, "Being on English soil does not confer emancipation, and neither does the master lose his rights in what they are pleased to consider their property. On the other hand, the law is clear that kidnapping and sending a servant overseas against his will is illegal. As a result of this, cases like Joseph's are less frequent than they used to be. Most masters think it's more trouble than it's worth for the sake of one or two individuals."

"You mean they can't cope with servants who have legal rights, no matter how limited they are," said Pickering.

John accepted this second interruption with a patient nod. "Nowadays we spend more of our time working with captives in transit, kept chained in a hold or warehouse while the ship prepares for the onward leg of its voyage. Or it might be a sailor who's worked a passage over here expecting to be paid off at the end of the voyage, but finds himself in irons and bound for the plantations instead."

"And Rule is well placed to keep you informed about such men."

John nodded. "The masters are very secretive. Anyone who speaks out is likely to find himself out of work or set upon by bludgeon men. Rule has to pay to get the information."

"Which is what you gave him the fight money for, Pickering?"

"You know about that?"

"I saw you fight and followed you to the Boar and Castle afterwards."

"I had no idea."

"You wouldn't. Must cost a bit to get them away too. I assume you don't get all your money from fighting."

"No," said Grace. "We rely on the generosity of supporters."

"Was Miss Parmeter a supporter? Is that why Rule said things would be difficult without her?"

"I don't know why you're asking," Pickering said. "You seem to know everything already."

"So her death is a blow for you."

Pickering clenched his fist. "Not just for her money. There was no one like her. She would treat a man for what he was, be he the lowest beggar in the land or the highest prince. She was a thousand times better than the people who passed judgement on her, the ladies who wouldn't be in the same room with her, the gentlemen who sneered while they lusted after her."

"There's no need to take it like that. Fact is, it's in your favour. Means it's less likely one of you wanted to kill her."

"To kill her? If I had the man in front of me, I'd—"

Dan interrupted Pickering before the threat was uttered. "Did she know what you were doing?"

Pickering hesitated. "She never asked any questions."

"It was not only her money she gave," Grace said. "She wrote against slavery wherever she could, in tracts, in her novels and poems. She was a good friend. I hope you find whoever killed her."

"I'll do my best." To Pickering, Dan said, "You said Joseph's was a common fate. Was it yours? Is that how you and the Martins come to be working together?"

"Was it mine?" In a swift, angry gesture, Pickering tugged up his sleeve and thrust his right fist at Dan. "Is this skin a badge of slavery? Do you think that we are all slaves? Does the idea of a free black man strike you as so outlandish?"

"I meant no offence. But your sympathy for Joseph—"

"Was what any right-thinking man would have for someone in captivity."

"Come, come, Mr Pickering," John said. "Surely Mr Foster has demonstrated the same sympathy?"

"That's true." Pickering lowered his arm, hesitated, then said, "My father was born on a British slave ship out of West Africa. His father was already dead, and his mother died when he was two or thereabouts. They were on a plantation in Barbados then, but before long Father was sold on to a Jamaican estate. He knew no one there, no one knew him. The woman who brought him up was kind, but neither she nor anyone else could tell him where his parents came from, where he came from. There was no one to teach him even one word of his own language and if he had heard any from his mother, he soon forgot it.

"He grew to be a handsome, well-built boy. When his master's daughter married, her father gave him to them as a wedding present, along with a house servant called Betty. She and her husband took the pair back to England, where Father made a fine show sitting at the back of his new master's carriage. Then his master lost him in a game of cards, to an officer in the British army. The captain was a reckless, extravagant man. When his debts caught up with him, he speedily decamped to avoid a debtor's prison. Father was left to fend for himself. He seized the chance to break free, got a job in a livery stable and started dealing in animal feed. From small beginnings he built up a business of his own. When he had saved enough money, he went back to his old mistress and bought Betty's freedom. Betty is my mother and they live in Vauxhall, where he has his warehouse and office." Pickering took a drink of his beer, smiled ruefully at Dan. "Perhaps Joseph's plight did appeal to me because of Father's history, but the fact is there are many more like him, men and women who have no idea who their parents are or what their heritage is. That may seem hard for a man like you to understand, Mr Foster."

"Perhaps it might," Dan said. He knew as little about his own parents as Pickering's father knew about his, but was not here to share confidences. He put down his cup, pushed his chair away from the table and stood up. "You lot were lucky tonight. If the man Officer Townsend had sent to keep a watch on Pickering had been there instead of me, you'd be in prison by now. You're playing a dangerous game and next time you get caught it won't turn out so well. I'm warning you to watch your step. If you break the law again, you will have to pay for it."

"What law?" demanded Pickering. "The law that makes slaves of my kind?"

"If you want to call it that."

"Then let me tell you, Mr Bow Street Runner, I don't care a turd for your laws. We are not the criminals. You saw what they'd done to Joseph, know what they were planning for him."

"That doesn't alter anything. Townsend's man will be back. You need to be more careful. That's all."

Dan picked up his hat and moved towards the door.

"Don't tell me you don't recognise a bad law when you see one," the coachman called after him.

Dan did not answer. Martin jumped up to let him out. He paused at the front door.

"It is a slow and tortuous path to the emancipation of our Negro brothers, Mr Foster, with so many powerful interests ranged against us. We seldom meet allies along the way. I do sincerely thank you for what you have done tonight."

"Just mark what I said. And make sure Joseph is gone from here by Monday."

Chapter Twenty-Four

It was nearly three o'clock when Dan turned in to Russell Street. At the end of the street, dishevelled figures flitted against the bright lights of Covent Garden like carvings on a carousel, endlessly going around the same small circle with their fixed, painted grins and gaudy finery. Sunday morning would see many of them in the roundhouse, bilked, beaten, robbed or poxed. Or any combination of those.

He let himself into the house. It was too late to disturb Caroline; he would grab a couple of hours' sleep in the kitchen. He pushed open the door, was surprised to see the room lit by fire glow and candlelight. He heard Caroline's low breathing before he saw her. She was asleep in the chair by the fire, a rug over her knees.

Had something happened? Was it Alex? The thought made him catch his breath.

"Caroline?"

Her eyes shot open. "You're home then."

He smelt the wine on her breath before he saw the glass and empty bottle on the floor by the chair. Her voice oozed a rage that had not deserted her even while she dozed. He knew with a dismal certainty that she had been sitting there for hours, feeding her fury. He also knew that there was nothing he could do to avert it, no matter how carefully he picked his words or gentled his smile.

Still, there was nothing for it but to try. "I'm sorry I'm late. You didn't have to wait up for me."

"That's all right. I put your bastard child to bed."

The venom in her voice staggered him. "My what?"

"I put your bastard to bed while you were out making another one."

"Making another one? What are you talking about?"

"What do you think?"

"I have no idea."

"Then how do you explain that?" She nodded at the table.

He saw nothing but the cups and plates laid ready for the morning. Mrs Harper always left the kitchen tidy before she went up to bed.

"That."

He looked again, spotted a piece of paper. He went and fetched it, took it back to the candlelight and read the blotted scrawl:

Ask your husband about his fancy piece in King Street.

He turned the sheet over. It was written on the back of a bill of fare from Long's Tavern, near Long's Court in Orange Street, close to Leicester Fields.

"What the hell is this?"

"You tell me. Someone put it through the door this evening. You told me you were working."

"I was working. In Gower Street, nowhere near King Street. I don't know who sent this or why, but whoever it is, they're just trying to make trouble for me."

"Always about you, isn't it? What about me? The wife sitting at home while her husband's out fucking every whore in town?"

"For God's sake, Caroline."

"Don't you like hearing the truth? Fucking a whore. Fucking a whore. Fucking a whore."

This was not, he knew, the moment to say, "You're drunk." Instead, he pushed the paper in his pocket, dropped to his knees in front of her, caught her resisting hands in his.

"Listen to me. I made one mistake and I'm sorry for it. But now there's you, there's me, there's Alex. Do you think I'd do anything to risk that?" She made an impatient sound, tried to snatch her hands away. "You love the boy too. I know you do. You look after him as if he's your own. He is ours, Caroline. After everything that's happened, do you think I would do anything which meant we'd lose what we've got?"

She raised her brimming eyes to his face. "Is that what you really think, Danny?"

He touched his head to hers, felt the sour heat of her breath in the closeness. "It's what I really think. Come on, love. Don't let a spiteful trick sway you like this. I promise you I will find whoever wrote it, and for causing you this upset, I will shove the paper down his throat."

She smiled. "Will you?"

"I will." He hid his relief when she removed her clammy hands from his. "Better now?"

"Yes." She wiped her eyes, sniffed. "You never tell me about your work."

"It's not very exciting most of the time."

"Who were you seeing in Gower Street?"

"I followed a suspect there."

"Then what did you do?"

"Stood outside a house in the dark. Like I said, not very exciting. I'd rather have been here with you and Alex."

"Would you really?"

"Yes, really." He glanced at the clock. "It's late. We should go to bed."

"Yes, I'm tired."

She swayed to her feet, smiled at him as if none of her outrageous words had been spoken. That was how these episodes always ended. She forgot them as soon as they were over. Either her forgetting was a natural consequence of the drink, or she had found some way of hiding the memories from herself.

"I'll light the way," he said, taking up a candlestick. Best not to trust her with it.

She put her arm through his, let her head fall on his shoulder with a contented sigh. He did not recoil from her touch, would not let her suspect that he did not share her forgetting. The images of her like this, stumbling and raving, were hard to put from him.

With much blundering against the walls, he helped her upstairs and, following her giggling instructions about laces and pins, helped her undress. When she was down to her shift, he got her into bed. She curled up on her side, mumbled, "Aren't you comin' t'bed?", fell asleep.

He gazed down at her. What was the darkness in her? Where did it come from, this dreadful discontent, this angry misery? Her peace of mind was so fragile, liable to give way at the slightest thing. When it did, she turned to drink.

How much was he to blame? There was no point in trying to measure that. He had loved her once; now he didn't. But even before he had realised it, she had been like this. When they were courting, her abrupt changes of mood had been part of her allure. Now he knew that something dangerous lay behind them. Perhaps it was a kind of sickness, something she couldn't help. He pushed back a strand of her tousled hair from her face, pulled the covers over her.

He moved over to the cot. They planned to move Alex into Eleanor's room when he was a bit older, but for now he slept with them. Dan touched his son's cheek. Alex did not stir, his peace undisturbed by the unhappiness in the room. Dan picked up the candle and went downstairs.

Chapter Twenty-Five

In the grey light, the streets shared the worn, dishevelled look of the few people who still weaved about them. Orange Street, which had been built in the reign of King William and Queen Mary, reeked of old drains and stale air trapped in constricted courts and mean little buildings. Dan passed a disused carriage works, a derelict tennis court, a church no one worshipped at. There were a few small, shuttered shops. Long's Tavern was indistinguishable from these, its frontage consisting of a low door between two grimy bow windows.

Dan hammered on the door and shouted "Bow Street Officer!" for several minutes before footsteps shuffled along the passage. The bolts shot back. A tousled, unshaven man in breeches and hastily tucked-in nightshirt glared blearily at him.

"What the bloody hell does Bow Street want at this time?"

"A word," Dan said. He stooped and pushed his way inside.

The taproom smelt of old smoke, boiled cabbage and sour beer. The tables had been cleared and the chairs stacked on them, but last night's sand had not been swept from the floor. Used pipes, plates and dirty glasses littered the bar. A greasy, down-at-heel girl clattered listlessly at the hearth, scraping out the ashes. She shovelled the grey heaps into a bucket, releasing clouds of dust which made her snuffle and sneeze. The fine particles coated the salt cellars, vinegar jars and relishes on a nearby table.

The landlord went behind the bar and poured himself a glass of brandy. He was anything but a stout, merry host. He was tall and thin with sharp features that wore an expression of perpetual suspicion, as if he expected his customers to pocket a tankard or give him false coin.

"This your place?" asked Dan.

"Yes, this is my place. Your name Foster?"

"How did you know that?"

"Got something here for you."

The landlord put down his glass, rummaged about on a cluttered shelf at the back of the bar and handed Dan a letter.

"He said you'd be calling for it, but not that you'd be so bloody early."

Dan snatched the letter. It was sealed and his name, with no title, was written in capital letters on the cover.

"Who gave you this?"

"Didn't tell me his name."

"What did he look like?"

"Big man. Shaved head. Yellow face, all bone and eyes. Sat over there to have his meal, shivering in his greatcoat though there was a good fire going. Wouldn't let anyone else sit at his table, though we were busy. No one liked to argue with him. He asked for paper and such, wrote his note and left. And now you've got it, with Bow Street's leave, I'd like to get back to my bed."

"Did you notice anything else about him?"

"Just that he was a miserable cove. Are we finished?"

Outside Dan broke the rough wax seal and unfolded the letter. It was blank.

While he struggled to get his anger under control and decide what to do next, he refolded the note and put it in his pocket book with the scrawled message on the bill of fare. He had built up quite a collection of odd bits of paper. Alongside these, he still had the sketch he had made of the wound inflicted on the murdered woman at the Feathers. None of them had been much help in solving the mysteries that surrounded them.

He made up his mind and set off for Cecil Street.

*

"He was deliberately taunting you," Noah said, handing back the bill of fare.

"I think so."

"And you think there's a connection with the attack here the other night?" asked Paul.

Dan was sitting between Paul and Noah on one of the hard-backed chairs from the table. The old soldier sat low down in his sagging armchair, Noah on the best of the fireside chairs, though that looked the worse for several years' wear.

"It seems too much of a coincidence otherwise," Dan answered. "And there's more. The day I took on the Parmeter case, I had a feeling I was being followed when I left Berkeley Square. Thought I caught a glimpse of someone in Leicester Fields. At the time I dismissed it as my imagination. A day or two later, I saw a man watching the Feathers when I was talking to Jones the carrier. I thought he was part of the smuggling operation, so I ignored that as well. Now I wonder if I should have trusted my instinct."

"Always," Noah said. "As I've taught you in the ring, so in life. But if he is connected with the Parmeter murder, what does he expect to gain by following you around?"

"Maybe he hopes I'll lead him to the diamonds. Or the missing memoirs."

"If he wants you to lead him to the prize, where's the point of making his presence known?" Paul objected.

Dan reached behind him to put his cup down on the table. "No, it doesn't make sense. The last thing he would want is to draw attention to himself."

"But if he is connected with the case—"

"He could be the killer," Dan completed Noah's sentence. "I know. Risky putting himself in my way if so."

"He might want to put you out of his way," Noah said. "Thinks you're getting too close."

"What would be the point? Even if he succeeded, there'd

be others to carry on the investigation. The Prince of Wales is involved; this isn't one that's going to go away. And I'm not close, not close at all. Townsend is set on putting it on Pickering, the coachman. The only other suspects I have are a couple of disgruntled ex-lovers, and neither of them has any need to steal a lady's necklace. That suggests it was the memoirs they wanted. If I could only find out what's in that book that might be worth killing for. None of Louise Parmeter's friends can tell me anything about it. Though—" He broke off.

"What's that, son?"

"I just remembered something Mrs Martin said. That Louise was a good friend. I thought she meant a friend to their cause, but I wonder now if she meant something closer. It would be worth having another word with her."

Noah, who did not know who Mrs Martin was, knew better than to ask questions when Dan was thinking aloud like this. He got up, went over to a shelf and took down a pair of mufflers.

"You know," he said, "you have got two murder cases on the go."

Dan looked up. "You think it might be connected to the murder of the girl in the blue dress?"

"You started that about the same time as the Parmeter case, didn't you?"

"It would fit with seeing him at the Feathers," Dan said. "He'd be spying on the investigation. In any case, that's where I need to start. I'll talk to the carrier again, see if he knows anything about him. Problem is, he won't be back from Tewkesbury until Thursday and I don't want to sit around doing nothing. I'm going to Holborn. Maybe someone else has seen the man hanging around."

Noah threw the boxing gloves into Dan's lap. "Not yet, you aren't. You've got some training to put in."

"But—"

"It's early yet. And you've got a fight coming up. Whoever Lord Hawkhurst sends in against you, he'll not be a fighter to take lightly."

"That's right," said Paul, hauling himself eagerly out of his chair. "Time to do some work, my lad."

Chapter Twenty-Six

"Joseph has gone. You can come in and look if you like." John Martin stepped aside from the shop doorway to allow Dan inside.

It was Monday morning. Dan had spent yesterday trudging around Holborn. He had called at the Feathers first and spoken to the stable boy and the landlady. Neither had recalled seeing anyone matching the description of the man who had left the letter at Long's Tavern in or around the yard recently.

"And why would we?" the landlady had demanded. "This is an inn; people come and go all the time."

After that he had spent the day seeking information from the residents of Holborn. The shops and smaller taverns had been closed, and having to rouse people from their Sunday torpor had slowed down his enquiries. He had also called into the larger coaching inns which stayed open to cater for the travellers staying at them. In the streets he had questioned boot blacks, beggars, street vendors and loungers for whom Sunday was no different from any other day. All with no result.

"I'll take your word for it," Dan said. "I'm here on another matter. I'd like to speak to Mrs Martin."

"Of course. Go through." John ushered Dan into the parlour.

Grace sat at a small desk adding up figures and writing in a ledger. She put down her pen and stood up when the men came in.

"Checking up on us, Mr Foster? Mr Pickering collected Joseph not half an hour ago to put him on a coach to – well, let's just say, to put him on a coach."

"Let's just say that," Dan agreed, taking off his hat. "I want to talk to you about Louise Parmeter."

"Louise?" She sat down, smoothed her skirt, composed her features, gestured towards a chair. John remained standing by the open door, one eye on the shop.

"How well did you know her?" Dan asked when they were settled.

"We had known each other a very long time. Since we were girls. I met her when she first came to London. She and her mother lodged at my parents' house. She was the same age as me but so much more grown up. And so gay and bright! She always found something to laugh at in the midst of setbacks and hardships. Sometimes they didn't have money for food so we'd share our meals with them: my parents loved her almost as much as I did. When she had employment, the hours were long, the work tiring, the stage managers troublesome. But when her luck turned and she found fame and fortune, she didn't leave her old friends behind. In fact, I think we were all the more precious to her."

"Did you know about her memoirs?"

"I knew she was writing them, and forever threatening to publish them. I told her that she risked making enemies, but she wouldn't listen."

"Enemies of who?"

"She never mentioned any names."

"Did you ever read them?"

"No. I don't think she showed them to anyone."

The bell on the shop door rang and John left his station to go and greet his customer, an imperious lady who had brought her subdued daughter to be measured for new shoes. Grace listened with tilted head for half a moment. She caught Dan's eye and smiled ruefully: dealing with awkward customers was all part of the business.

"Why are you asking about the memoirs?"

"They were stolen by her killer."

"And you think that's why she was murdered? But we'd heard it was for her diamonds."

"Those as well. You said she never asked any questions about your abolition work. How much did she know? Did she, for example, know about the burglary?"

Grace hesitated. "Yes, she did, and considered it no wrongdoing. Louise loathed the vile trade. She was brought up in Bristol and saw at first hand how the city's merchants wrung their wealth from the pain and suffering of others."

"It's a grim business, that's for sure."

"Business! Sin, rather. We are all created in God's image, Mr Foster, and no man has the right to enslave God's creation."

"It's not a subject I know much about."

"Then you should. I will find you some literature to read." Grace sprang to her feet and went to the bookshelf.

Studying earnest abolitionist tracts was not what Dan had had in mind. "Maybe when I've got more time," he said, retrieving his hat and standing up.

Before he could escape, she thrust a handful of pamphlets into his hand. His heart sank when he saw that the topmost one was written in verse: "*Would that the hand of God had stayed the wind and waves / That sped the cruel vessel o'er the frightful seas, / Or delivered to the tempest its encargoed slaves, / Or to the deep consigned, in answer to their pleas, / Those commerced souls…*"

He expected to see Louise Parmeter's name on the title page; Grace had mentioned her anti-slavery writing. Instead, *The Afric's Lament* was by Agnes Taylor.

"Is Miss Taylor involved in your activities?" he asked.

"Not her. She only wrote that to impress Louise. And if the truth be told, it's probably more Louise's work than Agnes's. Louise told me Agnes's first book of poems needed a great deal of rewriting before it was fit to publish, and the poems for her second were in the same unpolished state. But Agnes thought she was ready to make a success on her own and refused to listen. When she managed to find a publisher to encourage her vanity, there was no reasoning with her. If I'd have been in Louise's place, I'd have let her get on with it and learn her lesson when the book fails, as it surely will."

"You already know about Miss Taylor's publishing agreement? But I thought she only learned about it herself a day or two ago."

"If you mean the agreement she made with Messrs Cadell and Davies behind Louise's back, Louise told me about it weeks ago. She warned Agnes that it would do her career no good to rush poor work into print. She only had Agnes's interests at heart, and look how she repaid her."

"What do you mean, repaid her?"

From the shop came sounds of the ladies' bustling departure, the rattle of the door opening and closing, the ting of the bell. John crossed the room and resumed his station in the doorway.

"The terrible things she accused her of." Grace glanced defiantly at her husband. "It's true. Louise knew that Agnes's poems were not ready for publication and refused to return them to her unless she agreed they would work on them together as they had planned. But Agnes wanted her manuscript back without any alteration. She accused Louise of stealing her work and attempting to sabotage her career out of envy."

"Harsh words said in the heat of the moment," John said. "I'm sure they would have come to an understanding if things had not turned out as they have."

Grace turned her indignant face to him. "She even suggested that Louise had deliberately sold her previous poems at a cheap rate to keep her in a lowly station."

Dan interrupted what was clearly a long-running contention between husband and wife. "Louise Parmeter was holding up the publishing deal by refusing to return Agnes's poems?"

"Yes," Grace said.

They had not found any poems in Louise Parmeter's study. Only an empty desk drawer – a desk that someone had gone out of their way to open. Dan had suspected from the outset that the diamonds had only been taken as an afterthought. He thought the real target of the robbery had been the memoirs, the murder the act of an enraged lover who couldn't bear the humiliation of being mocked in print, or someone who feared the revelation of some compromising secret. What if the real target had been an ambitious writer's manuscript, withheld by an overbearing patron?

Easy now to guess what had happened. Agnes had gone into Louise's office to plead, cajole, demand. Louise had refused to return the manuscript, dismissed her protégée, picked up her pen and calmly continued with her writing. The sight of her at her desk in her opulent study, complacently enjoying what Agnes desperately wanted for herself, had been too much for the unfortunate woman. She had grabbed the candlestick, brought it crashing down on the bent head with all the force of years of want and struggle and powerlessness behind it.

She knew where Louise kept the key to the drawer, had retrieved her poems, seen the memoirs and taken them too. Then on an impulse, she had undone the clasp of the necklace, snatched the earring from the right ear, clumsily tearing the lobe in the process. Perhaps she had been unable to face the thought of moving the bloodied head to get at the other jewel, or a noise had disturbed her. However it was, she had left it and fled.

When she had hidden the papers and jewels in her room, she had gone back downstairs, knocked on Louise's door and raised the alarm. No wonder she had fainted when Dan suggested that Louise knew her killer. She had pulled herself together though, and had given nothing away since.

If she had had the nerve to do all that, maybe the murder had not been done on the spur of the moment. Maybe it had been carefully planned, the weapon identified in advance, the scene set to make it look like robbery.

He handed the pamphlets to John. "I have to go."

Startled, Grace said, "But you can't think Agnes murdered Louise?"

"I think she needs to answer some questions."

"But I didn't mean to suggest – John, I didn't."

"I know," he said, though his eyes were reproachful.

Chapter Twenty-Seven

At Berkeley Square, the front door was open on a flurry of noisy, busy people who neither saw nor heard Dan when he went inside. The shelves and alcoves in the hall had been emptied of vases, plants and statues. All the doors stood open. Louise Parmeter's study had been stripped of paintings, ornaments and silver, and in the middle of the bare floorboards two men hammered lids on to crates.

He negotiated a path through wooden boxes and drifts of straw to reach Mr Parkes. The butler stood in the doorway of the drawing room with a bundle of inventories in his hand. Inside the room, the maids billowed sheets over the furniture. Parkes turned a harassed face to Dan.

"The solicitor sent orders to close up the house," he explained. "He's coming round later to pay our wages and collect the keys. Miss Parmeter has a brother, a merchant in Italy. The house is his now."

"I'll need everyone's addresses before you all disappear."

"I will collect them for you."

"Good. While I think about it, you'd better have Miss Parmeter's key to the garden gate back." When Parkes had taken it, Dan asked, "Is Miss Taylor still here?"

"She's in her room. I'll send one of the maids to tell her you are here."

"No need. Which is her room?"

"It's first on the left. But—"

Dan was already running up the stairs, taking them two at a time. Parkes gave up and went back to his work. Miss Taylor was not his mistress, her proprieties no concern of his.

Dan knocked on the door, went inside before Agnes had finished calling an irritable "Come in!" He noted the case on the bed filled with clothes, next to it a portmanteau of knick-knacks from the dressing table and wash stand. Agnes stood by a box on the floor, clutching a handful of books. She looked up in surprise.

"Wondering where to pack the diamonds, Miss Taylor?"

Her smile twisted into a panicked grimace. "I – I don't know what you mean." She managed to retrieve the smile. "An odd pleasantry, Mr Foster."

"You lied to me. You told me on Saturday that you'd only just heard about your publishing deal when you'd known about it for weeks – and been arguing about it for weeks with Miss Parmeter. I know she was keeping back your poems, stopping you from having what you wanted more than anything. That's a powerful reason to murder her."

"Murder her?" Her hands flew up to her face.

"Spare me the theatricals. She was getting in the way of your ambitions, and so you killed her and took back your manuscript, along with the diamonds and her memoirs."

She swayed, pressed one hand to her forehead.

"There'll be no more swooning. And unless you want me to rip your things apart, you'd better tell me where the diamonds are."

Her hands fell to her side. "I only took back what was mine. Louise had no right to keep my work from me. But I didn't kill her. She was already dead when I got there."

"You'll have to explain yourself."

"Isn't it clear enough? I knocked on her door. She did not answer so I went inside, found her weltering in blood. I was going to sound the alarm, but then I saw my chance to get my poems back."

"And the diamonds?"

"They'd already gone." She reached into the portmanteau,

brought out a flat parcel wrapped in a cloth and tied round with string. "This is all I have."

He took the package from her and unfastened it. Inside he found a sheaf of poetry written in a niggling hand. Beneath it, fastened with tape, was the flowing manuscript of Louise Parmeter's memoirs.

He held up Louise's document. "This isn't yours."

"It was my recompense for the money she lost me when she sold my work short." Agnes sat down on the bed, gestured wearily at her things. "I don't have the diamonds. Look for yourself."

He put the papers on the dressing table and upturned the portmanteau, scattering hairbrush, mirror, pins and jars. No jewels. He rummaged through the clothes in the case with the same result, turned his attention to the box of books.

"Louise had made money out of me," she said. "Why shouldn't I make money out of her? There are lots of people who will pay well to make sure the memoirs aren't published."

He paused in his search. "Is that why you went to see Lord Hawkhurst? To blackmail him?"

"Not blackmail. To offer him first refusal on the manuscript. But there were all those men. You were so kind, Mr Foster. I don't know what would have happened if you hadn't come along."

"Were you going to try him again? Or approach someone else?"

"There are certainly others who are more deserving of the opportunity. If they could read the things she said about them! She wasn't a kind woman, you know."

"She was generous to you."

"Oh, yes, she was generous enough. She loved being generous. It gave her such power. She liked playing patron to native genius, but she couldn't bear a rival. She couldn't bear that Cadell and Davies wanted to publish my poems, so she had to interfere with them, delete, rearrange, take out the best lines for herself. She couldn't bear it when I outshone her in company, so she made me dress like a maid of all work and paraded my wit and originality as things of her own creation. She couldn't bear it when Lord Hawkhurst paid attention to me, though she'd discarded him. She couldn't bear the thought that I might make a good marriage and be free of her. She cloaked it all behind her cant of women's rights: better independence in a garret than subservience to a husband. She was willing to please the men when she had her own fortune to win, but once she'd got all she wanted, she must preach to the rest of us about freedom and rights, and devil take other women with their own way in the world still to make."

"You could have refused her money."

"And do what? Rot my life away in an attic sticking feathers on to bonnets? Have you ever known what it is to be poor, to struggle, to face the future with nothing but uncertainty? The rich wallow and guzzle, and what choice do the rest of us have but to run at their heels, curtsying and bobbing and treating them like little gods for a small share of prosperity? There is a life that is more like death and I will never go back to it."

She sat with her head turned from him, her hands limp in her lap, her shoulders bent. Misery had leached the beauty from her face. Her fine, gaily printed dress hung off her as if it did not belong to her, as if she did not know how to wear it, exposing her for what she really was: a poor girl in another woman's clothes. That other woman had taken the wearing of good clothes as a thing of course, along with the food in her belly, the perfumes on her skin, the fireplace that warmed her, but these things still sat uneasily on Agnes.

Poverty and the fear of poverty were ugly. A picture flashed before his eyes: a child's thin hands clutching the bars of a cot, and beyond the bars a woman and man tumbling in rags on the floor. The smell of gin, chamber pot, sex, damp plaster, mice. The grunting and slapping, and out beyond the bare walls, shouts and curses echoing around a filthy courtyard. Dogs barking, running footsteps, bumps and scuffles, knuckles on soft flesh, the wails of women. The feel of his breath snuffling in and out in the cold air, the slime of snot on his face, the wet blankets at his feet, the terror of making a noise and reminding his mother of his existence.

Agnes did not have the diamonds, but she had lied, wasted time, stolen evidence. Now, like all thieves when they were caught out, she was pathetic, scared, pitiable. That didn't change the lie. He should arrest her, charge her with theft, cart her off to Newgate, start the fall which would lead sooner or later to her destitution and death.

All for a bundle of paper.

"Here are your poems," he said, thrusting them at her. "Finish your packing and go."

For a few seconds the manuscript lay on her lap. Slowly she moved her hands and took hold of it, and as she did so hope came back into her face. He did not stay to see it. He put the memoirs in his coat pocket and left.

Chapter Twenty-Eight

Dan opened the door on to the scent of coffee and the companionable murmur of voices. He passed the long, age-darkened table in the middle of the room with the cluster of smaller ones around it. Many of the seats were occupied by men absorbed in their newspapers, some drawing thoughtfully on their pipes. The rows of coffee pots and cups on the shelf behind the counter glinted invitingly. Trays of the Rainbow's renowned fresh breads and cakes sat temptingly in front of them.

A waiter leaned on the counter gossiping with his colleague, who was busy with the gleaming urn of hot water and jars of aromatic beans. Dan went straight to the table in the corner beneath the window. He hung his hat on a hook beneath the high shelf of blue and white Delftware which ran the length of the room, and placed the papers on the table.

He was vexed by the discovery that the memoirs had not been the motive for the murder after all. He did not look forward to telling Townsend he had been right about that. Still, at least he could counter Townsend's crowing by proving the man's own mistake. In the light of Agnes Taylor's revised story, Townsend would have to admit that his theory about the timing of the murder was wrong. When Agnes Taylor knocked on the study door, Louise Parmeter's killer had already been and gone, taking the diamonds with him.

It was still not absolutely certain that the diamonds were the only motive for the murder. Setting aside Townsend's jewel thief who had so far left no trace that Dan had been able to discover, Cruft and Hawkhurst were the most likely suspects.

But Louise had had other lovers, other men who knew their way into the house, who knew her routine. Where better to look for information than in her memoirs? In their pages Dan could hope to discover who she counted as friends and who as enemies. He knew he ought to hand the manuscript in to Sir William Addington, but if he did it would be whisked off to the Prince of Wales and he would never get a chance to look at it.

The waiter glided up to the table. "The usual, Mr Foster?"

Dan agreed, and minutes later the steaming pot was on his table.

Hidden away in his favourite spot in his favourite King Street coffee house was not a bad way to spend an afternoon, he reflected, as he sipped and read. He was chuckling over Louise's remarks about a young Mr Specie, a banker's son whom life had blessed with great wealth by way of making up for his want of brains and character, when a thin boy slipped into the room. His pinched, anxious face turned towards Dan, who did not notice him weaving noiselessly between the tables under the stares of the company that had suddenly discovered a concern for the contents of its pockets.

Dan heard a sniff and looked up. "Nick? What are you doing here?"

"Looking for you, Mr Foster. I tried the office and the Brown Bear and I was on my way to Berkeley Square when I thought of coming in here. You have to come home."

"Why, what's happened?"

"It's Alex. He's been took."

Not my boy, not my boy. Running across the Piazza, Dan pounded the words into the stones, drew them into his lungs, hammered them into his heartbeats. In Russell Street a group of constables, patrol and watchmen had gathered around his door. Many of them were off duty. When they saw him, they fell silent and lowered their eyes. No one knew what to say to him.

They parted to let him through. He ran into the kitchen, Nick at his heels. Half a dozen Bow Street officers stood around the table: Carpmeal, who combined running a tavern close by with his work as a law officer, Fugion, Taylor, Rivett, Miller, and Sayer. Sam Ellis knelt on the floor talking to Mrs Harper, who was rocking herself back and forth. Caroline sat opposite her mother, staring at the floor, dry-eyed, white-faced, her arms tightly folded across her hunched body. Eleanor sat beside her, her arm around her sister's rigid shoulders.

Dan had not seen Sam and Eleanor since their wedding. He had managed to be out whenever they called. Whatever he had dreaded about that first meeting was irrelevant now.

"Foster," said Carpmeal, "I've got more men on the way." As he was the most senior officer, the rest ceded control to him.

Dan nodded acknowledgement. "What happened?"

Sam patted Mrs Harper's hands, stood up and joined the others. They huddled around him, conferred in low voices.

"It's hard to get much sense out of her," Sam reported. "Seems she was alone in the house with Alex when a man knocked on the door. Said the landlord of the house next door had sent him to ask if he could look at your cesspit as it was leaking into his cellar. He shoved her into the yard and bolted the door on her. She's not sure how long she was locked out. She shouted and knocked, but it wasn't till Mrs Foster came home that she was let in."

Dan looked over at his mother-in-law. She caught his eye, screamed, flung her apron over her head and rocked faster.

"Any description?" he asked.

"Not much. Tall, gaunt, shaven head, wore a leather apron."

"Mr Foster!" Nick tugged at Dan's sleeve.

Dan's attention was taken up by Caroline, who had pushed her sister away, saying, "Go to Mother, Nell." She came to Dan's side, clutched his arm. "I was only gone half an hour. Sally said she'd do my hair for tonight. It was only half an hour. Oh, Dan, why would anyone do this to our little boy?"

Dan had not noticed that Caroline's hair had been put up. He had a moment's confusion while he tried to make sense of 'tonight' before he remembered Sheridan's gift of a box at the theatre. He pictured his wife and her friend gossiping over a glass of gin and hot water, comparing notes about shoes and hats, discussing Sally's latest romance amidst shrieks of laughter.

He put his arms around Caroline, let her sob into his coat, but his mind was not on her.

"How long has he been gone?"

"We reckon an hour or so at most," Carpmeal answered. "Allowing half an hour for Mrs Foster to make her visit, get back, release her mother, the servant to get to Bow Street, and us to get here." He cast an unfriendly glance at Nick, who stood at Dan's elbow, his fingers still grasping Dan's sleeve. "Seems the boy had gone to fetch some bread."

Nick returned the look with a sullen glare. There was no need to doubt him. The loaf was on the table, untouched. He had obviously taken his time over his errand, though. The market was only at the top of the street.

Mrs Harper stopped wailing and uttered low moans into her apron. With a look, Dan appealed to Eleanor for help with Caroline. His wife would have clung to him, but he gave her into her sister's care, had put her out of his thoughts before Eleanor got her back to her chair. Caroline dropped her head into her hands and sobbed, while Eleanor tried to comfort her.

"Has anyone sent for Dad and Paul?" Dan asked.

"I did," Sam answered. "Have you any idea who's done this? Is there anyone with a grudge? Any threats lately?"

"There's plenty with grudges, but no names I can think of. There is one man, though. I don't know who he is or why he might have it in for me, but from what Mother remembers of him, it could be the same. I tracked him to a tavern in Orange Street. The landlord told me he was a tall, shaven-headed, sickly-sounding man."

"What's he done?" Sam asked.

"Only played nasty pranks up till now. If it is the same man, kidnapping is something of a step up. Though there was an incident at the gym last Friday. Someone attacked Paul, maybe mistook him for Dad, though Dad thinks it's me he was after."

Nick shook his sleeve again. "Mr Foster! It's him as came for the pie. The dead spit."

Dan looked down at him. "Are you sure?"

"'Cepting the leather apron. Tall, shaved head, looked at death's door."

"Can you remember anything he said?"

"He said the pie was good, and you was lucky to have a wife who cooks such food, and I said Mother Harper made it, and he said was I your son, and I said no, he was indoors with his mammy and granmer, and he asked if he went to school and I said he was a hinfant, but I was learning my letters and he said, thanks for the pie, and went."

"Meaning," said Carpmeal, "that you told him everything he needed to know about Mr Foster's household."

The other officers murmured agreement, turned hostile eyes on the boy.

"Mr Foster, I didn't! He asked all pleasant and friendly, like you was old friends."

"It's all right, Nick." Dan looked at Carpmeal. "We should get the men organised into search parties. A man carrying a child is likely to draw attention. Someone might have seen something. I'll work round the Piazza; I know most of the people there. I'll take Dad with me when he comes. Sam, would you go with Paul, head down to the Strand?"

"Of course."

"I'll sort out the rest of the men," Carpmeal said. "And I'll get a description, such as it is, circulated out of the office."

There was a rap on the door.

"That'll be Dad and Paul." Dan hurried to let them in.

It was not Noah Foster and Paul who stood on the doorstep

but an impressively cloaked and booted John Townsend, gripping a hefty cudgel in place of his elegant cane.

"Foster," Townsend said gruffly, "I've come straight from the Prince."

He stalked in, glanced at the weeping women, greeted his fellow officers, and announced, "His Royal Highness has offered to call out the militia if you need them."

Dan considered this. "It's a generous offer, but no thanks. At least, not yet. It might scare the kidnapper into doing something stupid."

There was another knock. This time it was Noah and Paul, and with them half a dozen clients from the gym.

"I shut up shop," Noah said, "and they insisted on coming with us."

Dan, who recognised them all, had had friendly spars with most of them, nodded. "Thanks."

The pugilists waited outside with the other men while Noah and Paul went inside.

"Do you know who took him?" asked Noah.

"No. Could be the man who attacked Paul. Have you remembered anything else about him, Paul?"

The old soldier shook his head. "All I know is that if he harms a hair on that child's head, I'll pay him back a hundredfold."

They had not noticed that Caroline had stopped sobbing and was listening to their conversation.

"You never said he'd attacked someone," she cried. "And now he's got my baby!"

"Hush, Caroline," Eleanor said. "This isn't helping Dan. He needs you to stay strong."

Caroline drew in her breath, was on the verge of making a sharp retort: *How do you know what help my husband needs?* Instead she sank into silence. Her fear for Alex was exhausting enough and she hadn't the energy to rake up ancient resentments alongside it.

"What's this, Foster?" said Townsend. "You were attacked? Why didn't you report it?"

"It wasn't me who was attacked. And I didn't need to report it. I was handling it."

"While you are working for the Prince of Wales, you must keep me apprised—"

"Mr Townsend," Carpmeal murmured, "this is not the time."

Townsend bridled, but recollecting the circumstances, blustered, "Oh – ah – we should get started, Carpmeal. We need to get the villain's description circulated and set up search parties."

"Good idea," said Carpmeal. He picked up his hat from the table, bowed to the women and followed Townsend out of the house. The other officers muttered their goodbyes, turned and trailed out after them.

"What about me?" asked Nick.

Dan thought of telling the boy to stay at home and look after the women. On second thoughts, he knew Caroline would not welcome it, and it would be hard on Nick to be forced into inactivity when he was so eager to help.

"You can come with me and Dad."

He took Louise Parmeter's manuscript out of his pocket, dropped it on top of a sporting magazine on the sideboard. Carpmeal's voice drifted in from outside.

"You leave nothing unturned. Every outhouse, every alleyway, every market stall, every courtyard and area. Anywhere and everywhere."

"Remember, men, this is no ordinary case," Townsend added. "The Prince of Wales is taking an interest."

Dan turned his back on the women, said quietly, "Did you bring pistols?"

Noah, Paul and Sam said they had.

"If it comes to needing them, I want you to leave it to me, if it can be done without putting my boy in danger."

Sam looked away, avoided looking into the darkness in Dan's eyes. Paul straightened his back, accepting his orders, whatever they might require him to do. Noah nodded once. They all understood. If Alex was already dead, it would be his father who put a bullet in his killer's heart.

Chapter Twenty-Nine

Dan and Nick worked their way along the shops and stalls on the south side of the Piazza, Noah the north. Gossip about the unusual police activity in the area had already spread and everyone was eager to talk and be a part of the excitement. In Feterson's glove shop, the assistants and two ladies they were serving at the counter volubly shared with Dan the nothing that they knew.

"A dreadful thing, Mr Foster," said Feterson, a slight, dapper man who just came up to Dan's shoulder. "An attack on a child is the act of the most miserable coward." He broke off and waved his fist at the door. "Of all the impudence!"

Through the glass, Dan saw a young woman in a gaudy dress beckoning to him. He recognised her as one of the women he often saw looking for business in the Bedford Arms in Tavistock Row. He threw Feterson a thank you and hurried outside.

"I heard you're looking for a missing child," she said. "Thought you might like to know I saw a man hand a baby over to an old woman by the church steps. Ugly old biddy, she was, wall-eyed, looking every way at once. No wonder the babe squalled at sight of her."

"Did you see which way they went?"

"She went towards St Martin's Lane. I didn't see which way he went."

Dan sent Nick to fetch Noah. The boy sprinted off. A few moments later, the woman repeated her story to the two men. When she had finished, Dan brought out some coins.

She shook her head. "Hope you find him." She flashed him a gappy smile that almost cracked the paint on her cheeks, and tip-tapped on her high heels back to her pitch on the colonnade.

"Now we're getting somewhere," Dan said. "Where's Nick got to?"

"He was here a minute ago," Noah said.

"I'm not waiting. We'll go on without him."

"Where now?" asked Noah.

They stood at the end of Spur Street looking into Leicester Fields. The area was packed with people drawn to the many wonders and entertainments on offer in and around the square: miniature theatres showing moving images of Niagara Falls, shipwrecks, and water spouts; displays of living sea monsters; spinning models of the universe. For those seeking something more intimate, there were brothels and bagnios. Lights shone from tavern and coffee house windows. Street hawkers accosted the hurrying crowds, yelling: "Buy matches, baked apples, roast chestnuts". Women stood about waiting for clients. A fire-eater performed his tricks by the railings, the flames shooting up from his mouth, illuminating the upturned faces of his audience.

Dan watched a trio of boys creep through the crowd, helping themselves to the contents of pockets. It was a neat operation: one did the diving, passed his haul on to the next, who passed it on to the next. If the pickpocket was caught and searched, there would be nothing on him. But it was not likely he would be caught. He was quick and nimble, had been well trained. As Dan had been.

The last in the chain was a stunted and ugly youth, anonymous in his filth and rags. Put him next to a child from a good home and you would hardly recognise them as the same species. All most people would see if the scarred, wizened street urchin intruded on their line of sight would be the threat of crime, the danger of disease. If he was taken off the streets now, could he be turned into a clean, bright boy with a future? Or had his mind and imagination been too deeply infected by sin and want?

What if it went the other way and a child was taken from his home and made to fend for himself? Could Alex ever look like that? Of course he could.

Dan wrenched his gaze away from the children. The trail had gone cold; had never warmed once they left the Piazza. They had circled endlessly down streets and alleys, knocked on every door, spoken to everyone they met. No one remembered seeing an old woman carrying a child.

"We'll go home, see if there's any news," Dan said.

It was gone eleven when they got back to Russell Street. Eleanor and Caroline rose to greet them, their question unvoiced and as wordlessly answered. They had persuaded Mrs Harper to go to bed, and made a pot of soup. Eleanor ladled out a bowlful, handed it to Noah with a slice of bread. He ate it where he stood.

Dan refused the food. "Is there any coffee?"

Eleanor moved between the fireplace and the cupboards, busy with kettle and pot. Caroline, her elbow resting on the side of her chair, her head in her hand, watched listlessly. Dan did not sit down. They would be going out again in a few minutes.

Eleanor handed him his cup. A look passed between them; the first that had not been weighted with hurt, anger and disappointment for many a day. It was gone in an instant. His features resettled into haggard lines, and in his eyes was a hard, vengeful glint that only the death of his enemy would extinguish.

He sipped. "Isn't Nick here?"

"I thought he was with you," Caroline answered. "Fat lot of use he's turned out to be."

There was a light tap on the door. Dan put down his cup, went and found Nick on the step. Seeing Dan, relief flooded the boy's excited face. He followed Dan into the kitchen.

"I've found him, Mr Foster."

Dan looked at the boy in astonishment. Eleanor, on her way to the hearth with the coffee pot, stopped. Noah, bowl in hand, lowered his spoon. Caroline stood up.

Nick, ignoring the other three, turned his face up to Dan's.

"I went to see Sparrer. Him and his boys seed the law is out in force tonight so they're keeping out of the way, but I knew where to find them. I see him for a smoke sometimes…" His voice trailed off.

Dan understood. Nick still sometimes sought the company of his old acquaintances, slipped back into the world of the streets like an animal returning to its pack. It did not augur well for his future. If he did not break the habit soon, he never would. But the boy had calculated correctly that Dan would let it pass for now.

"There's been stories lately of children disappearing off the streets," Nick continued. "Talk of a Mother Poison. They say she's got eyes in the back of her head, can see you even if you're behind her. So when the girl on the Piazza says about her eyes, I guessed it was her. Sparrer says you fall into her clutches and it's all up with you. I asked if they knew anything and one of 'em says he'd been talking with someone who knew someone who said he'd seen Mother Poison on Cow Lane carrying a child. But it wasn't no street child, it was proper dressed. And they knew the nabbers were looking for a Runner's child, and even despite it being a Runner they says it's a shame for she's the very devil, and then I says it's Mr Foster's and he's been good to me, and Sparrer thinks a bit and says, 'It won't fadge.' So I says will you tell me how to find Mother Poison and he sends out the word and after a bit word come back from Bungey that she's got a ken at Smithfield. And Sparrer's outside waiting to show us the way."

"What's the creature talking about?" demanded Caroline. "How could he know where Alex is? Why doesn't he say?"

Nick's gaze flicked towards her, his face tight with dislike. "I am saying."

"And that's your idea of helping, is it?" Caroline said. "Running off to play with a bunch of street arabs, then coming back here to spin some stupid tale about a bogey woman you probably saw in the bottom of a gin bottle. Mother Poison!"

"She ain't no bogey. And she's got Alex."

"He's trying to help," Dan said. "But look, Nick, we used to tell stories like this when I was a boy, about baby-eating beadles and witches who turned children into slaves, and God knows some of those stories weren't far from the truth if you got taken up by the parish and put out as an apprentice. The woman you call Mother Poison is probably just some parish nurse minding babies from the workhouse. We both know there are plenty of her kind you wouldn't want to be left with, but that doesn't mean she's got Alex."

"But it all fits with what the doxy said," Nick said.

"For God's sake, Dan, get him out of my sight or I'll swing for him, I swear I will," Caroline said.

"The boy could be on to something," said Noah. "We should take a look. It's not as if we've any other leads to follow."

"Sparrer's outside," Nick prompted.

"For heaven's sake," Caroline said, "Alex is missing and you're going to follow this – this – idiot to the other side of town?"

"We are," Dan said. "Tell Carpmeal and the others to follow on to Cow Lane when they get back. We'll keep a lookout for them."

Chapter Thirty

If Mother Poison didn't kill you, Dan thought it likely that the filth of Smithfield would. The streets radiating out from the empty pens, warehouses and market halls were a morass of animal droppings, mud and offal. The reek of terrorised cattle and stale blood rose from the gutters and cobblestones. A miasma gathered in the alleys where the decaying houses added the stench of overcrowded rooms and overflowing privies.

They passed a beer house from where, despite the lateness of the hour, came the sound of voices shouting and cheering, intermingled with the desperate snarling of fighting dogs. A man lay on the ground outside, where he had fallen or been thrown. Noah almost stumbled over him, but Dan strode by without giving him a glance.

Sparrer and Nick led them by little-used byways: narrow, foul tracks linking dens of drinkers, opium eaters, murderers, beggars and thieves. None interfered with them; their pistols gave them indisputable right of way. Rat eyes and human eyes, indistinguishable in their cunning and viciousness, glinted at them out of the shadows.

Their only light was the occasional gleam of moonlight which managed to penetrate the smoke and fumes, with every now and again a grudging glow escaping through a grimy window or from beneath an ill-fitting door. They squeezed after the boys into a gap between the blank walls of small warehouses. The children disappeared, their footsteps plashing through the muck. Instinctively Dan and Noah lightened their tread.

Each put out a hand to feel the wall on their left, kept his right hand close to his pistol.

A small space opened out where a building had collapsed, its bricks long since carried away, leaving an overgrown, rodent-infested gap dotted with midden heaps. Ahead stood a ruinous house with a sagging roof and cracked walls. Smoke rose from its broken chimney. A foggy patch of light drifted from a front window. There were no lights in the upper rooms, and, since many of the windows were broken and there were wide cracks in the brickwork, it appeared they were not inhabited.

They gathered in the wide, deep doorway of a storage shed opposite. The door had not been painted in years, but the padlock on it was new. Under other circumstances, Dan might wonder what was inside that was worth hiding away in this desolate place. Nothing legal, he'd guess.

"Mother Poison's is over yonder," Sparrer rasped in his husky smoker's voice. "Bungey, give us the lay."

A sandy-haired, lantern-jawed boy emerged from the shadows. "The room wiv the oldest childer is at the front, next to the one wiv the glim. Mother Poison sits in the one wiv the glim, the babbies' cot at back of it."

Dan looked over at the house. The room with the light was on his left. "I wonder if there's a back door."

"Yers," Bungey said. "One winder at back 'as a rotten frame. Took a peep earlier," he added. He held out his palm. "That's me done."

Dan handed over some money. "I'm grateful to you, Bungey."

The boy glanced at the money, whistled softly. Sparrer took his coins with a nonchalant air.

"Shall I take the back?" asked Noah.

Dan took out his pistol. "I'm going to have a look first."

He crept up to the house, his boots sinking into deep puddles which released a stagnant, rotting smell. The front window was shutterless, cracked and dirty. It took a moment

197

for his eyes to adjust to the dim and dusty light, but gradually the room came into view.

It had bare floor and walls, was furnished with a rickety table covered in a muddle of dirty dishes alongside a pile of clothes, most likely stolen. It was too dark to see if Alex's blue frock was amongst them. There was a trestle table at the back of the room covered in jars, herbs and potions representing the trade in herbal remedies that gave Mother Poison her name. Dangerous cures for syphilis, crabs, the itch, unwanted pregnancy.

A pair of candles burned low on the mantelpiece over a sinking fire. Beside it sat a woman, legs straddled, warming her feet on the ash-covered hearth. She wore a ragged russet-coloured dress with a filthy apron, shabby slippers, a dirt-coloured shawl. Knots of grey hair hung down from a plain cotton cap. She was fast asleep, snores shaking her frame, her slumbers steeped in gin from the bottle on a low stool at her side.

A man sat opposite her, his back to the window. All Dan could see of him was the top of his head, flung against his chair, and a huge pair of hob-nailed boots stretched out in front of him. On the floor beside him was a frying pan from which he had eaten his supper. A mangy cat nibbled at the remains.

Mother Poison's son or husband? Or accomplice – perhaps even the man who had taken Alex? Whoever he was, Dan sensed he wasn't there just to keep the old woman company. He was her bully, might be armed with a cudgel, even a pistol.

Dan scanned the darkness beyond the fireplace. A line of her infant charges lay in a cot at the back of the room, still and quiet. He crept back to Noah, was surprised to see the boys were still there.

"She's in there, sleeping on a chair by the hearth," he said. "There's a man with her, also asleep. Both dead drunk."

"And Alex?" asked Noah.

"There's five or six babies in there. Can't tell if he's with them. But I can tell one thing. Those children aren't staying there."

Noah nodded. "What's the plan?"

"Simple. Break down the door, take them by surprise."

"That's it," said Sparrer. "Me and Bungey'll go round the back in case the old bitch tries to hop the twig that way."

"You don't have to do that," Dan said.

"We knows it," Sparrer said. "But this is 'istory, ain't it, Bungey?"

Dan would have felt the same in Sparrer's place. The downfall of Mother Poison would indeed be a major event in their world. The boys would live on the legend for many a day. It would not do Sparrer's position as a leading light in his community any harm either.

"Yers," Bungey said in answer to Sparrer's question. He did not look all that excited at the prospect of his part in an epoch-making battle, but knew he faced ruin if he backed down in front of Sparrer.

"Then I'm glad to have you with me," Dan said. "Carpmeal should have got the message at Russell Street to follow on with some men by now. Nick, you go and keep watch for them and guide them here."

"Should we wait for them?" asked Noah.

"I'm not leaving my boy in there a moment longer than I have to."

"If he's there."

Dan ignored this. "Nick."

Nick hesitated. He would have preferred to stay with Sparrer and Bungey, but Dan was in no mood to have his orders questioned. Besides, the other boys could not go. They might make an exception for Dan, but ordinarily nothing would get them within a mile of the Runners. Nick jumped up and disappeared into the darkness.

"Off you go then," Dan said to Sparrer and Bungey.

They sped off, gave the house a wide berth, circled back and disappeared behind the ramshackle structure. Dan did not fancy Mother Poison's chances if she ran into them. But that was up to her. She could take her arrest calmly, or she could try and bolt.

A few minutes later Dan and Noah positioned themselves on either side of the front door. Dan held up his hand. For ten seconds they stood there, guns at the ready. Then Dan lowered his hand, stepped in front of the door and kicked it open. He sprang into the room, Noah close behind.

"Bow Street Officer! You're under arrest."

Mother Poison's bleary eyes shot open. She screamed. Her companion jerked awake and leapt cursing to his feet. He threw himself at Noah. He was the bigger, heavier man, had swollen, fight-scarred fists, but Noah had the better of him and nimbly delivered a right to his jaw that sent the drunk tottering back. He stumbled on the hearth and fell, cracked his head on the mantelpiece as he went down. That was him out for the count. Noah hauled him away from the fire and shoved his inert body against the wall.

The woman went for Dan, feet and fists flying. He raised his arm to beat her off, but before he could make contact two screeching shapes rushed past him. Sparrer jumped on to her back, wrapped his arms around her neck, kicked her sides with his heels. Bungey laboured her about the face and body with his sharp little knuckles.

"Get 'em off me! Get 'em off!" Mother Poison squealed. Dan left it to Noah to sort out. He grabbed one of the candle stubs and hurried over to the cot.

There were five babies tightly tucked under a rough, flea-ridden blanket. Two were almost starved, had evidently been there some time. The next two had a bit more weight on them, though one was flushed and feverish, ill from all the flea bites he had suffered. One was still clean, plump and healthy, but his round face was stiff and pale and he lay like the others in a deep, unnatural sleep. Dan snatched him up. He was wrapped in a coarse length of cloth, but was otherwise naked. Dan clutched Alex to his breast, showered his solemn face with kisses.

"It's him, God be praised!" Noah cried. "Shut up, you." The last was addressed to Mother Poison, whom the boys had got back into her chair. They were cheerfully engaged in tying her to it with lengths of fabric and anything else useful they could find. Dan threw a pair of cuffs at Noah, who used them to manacle the bully as he groaned back to consciousness.

This done, Noah came over to the cot, looked down at the babies. "What's she done to them?"

"Laudanum," Dan said. "What about the other children?"

"Bungey, go and let 'em out," ordered Sparrer.

Bungey hurried out of the room. They heard the sounds of bolts being drawn back, Bungey's imperious voice.

"Go in there."

Partly because they were used to doing as they were told, partly because they did not know what else to do, the released children filed across the cold passageway into Mother Poison's kitchen and cowered together. There were seven of them, ragged, thin, the bruises on their skin barely distinguishable from the grime. Dan guessed the oldest, a girl, was about sixteen, the youngest ten, possibly older but stunted by hard labour and want.

Their dull eyes flicked from the sight of Dan with the baby in his arms, Mother Poison being turned into a maypole by Sparrer as he capered around her chair and wrapped her in makeshift bonds, Noah with his gun in his hand. Then they lit on the man sprawled on the floor and into their misery flickered a glimmer of delight. Their tormentor lay powerless, his hard hands shackled, his feet in their great boots twitching weakly.

"I think she's safely trussed," Dan said.

Sparrer stepped back to admire his handiwork. The old woman, her cap gone and the bald patches on her head exposed, cursed him soundly. He laughed, mimicked her cries.

"Take him," Dan said, handing Alex over to his father. Noah pulled his scarf from around his neck, wrapped Alex in it.

Dan stood in front of Mother Poison. She aimed a gob of spittle at him. It landed at his feet.

"Who brought you that child?"

"Go and fuck yourself."

"I asked, who brought you that child?"

She tried to outface him, failed, dropped her eyelids and muttered, "His mother asked me to take him in."

"I told you to have nothing to do with a rich man's child, you stupid bitch," the cuffed man cried. "You might have known someone'd come looking for him."

"You didn't argue when you were drinking the daffy," Mother Poison snarled back.

Dan grinned. "Now this is something I always enjoy: villains turning on one another. So which of you is going to tell me the truth and save themselves from the rope?"

"The rope?" Mother Poison wailed. "When I've taken these waifs in out of the goodness of my heart, clothed them, fed them, treated them like my own?"

"Your heart is open for all to see," Dan said. "You've snatched these children off the streets, sold them, made them work for you, starved and beaten them. But that one is no street child, is he? So I'll ask you again. Who brought you that child?"

"I had nothing to do with it," the man put in. "It's all her doing."

"I expect these children have a different story to tell," Dan answered. They gazed at Dan, too frightened to so much as nod their heads. It would be a long time before their stories could be coaxed out of them.

"All I know," the man said, "is that she went out to meet a man and came back with that child. I told her it wasn't no good. That one would be missed."

"He was missed. Not by a rich man. By me."

"God in heaven!" the man cried. "He's a Runner's child. You stupid cow, you've only gone and taken a Runner's child. We're fucking done for now."

The network of broken veins under the old woman's skin glowed red against her white face. She gabbled, "I never knew, I swear it. I thought he was some rich woman's mistake he was helping her get rid of. It's the God's truth, I didn't know he'd been stolen away."

"I doubt you and the truth have been friends for a very long time," Dan said. "What's the man's name?"

"Smith. That's what he told me."

"I'll bet he did. What did he look like?"

"I never got a good look at him. He sat in the shadows over there, away from the fire, kept his face covered. A big man, scrawny, like he'd lost flesh too quick. The skin around his eyes was sunburned, like a sailor's, but he didn't walk like a sailor."

"He came here? How did he know how to find you?"

"He never said. One of the girls told him maybe."

Mother Poison's services would be well known to the women who worked the streets.

"When did he come here?"

"Night before last. Told me to meet him this morning outside Lovejoy's bath house on the Piazza and take the child off him."

The door shot open and Nick appeared in the doorway. "Carpmeal and half a dozen men headed this way."

"That's us out of here," Sparrer said. "Come on, Bungey!"

The boys scrambled out at the back of the house as Carpmeal, Townsend and the other men came in at the front. Sam Ellis was with them. He and Dan clasped hands, the gesture standing for all that could be said at such a time.

"You haven't left much for us to do, Foster," laughed Carpmeal when Dan had given an account of the raid.

Dan pointed at the pile of clothes on the table. "Stolen clothes there. Haven't searched the rest of the place. These children were kept prisoner. They need feeding and clothing."

"You can leave it to us. You get home to your wife."

Dan took Alex off Noah, tucked him inside his coat. Followed by a chorus of cheers and congratulations, they left. On Holborn Hill they took a cab. Caroline and Eleanor already had the front door open by the time they climbed out. They tumbled into the house, Caroline clinging to Dan, who still had the baby in his arms. The couple came to a halt in the kitchen.

"He's safe!" said Eleanor, giving Noah a teary embrace. "Oh, Mr Foster, he's safe!"

"He is," said Noah. "And we got the villains who took him. Captain Ellis is still there, but it's just the clearing up now."

"We got 'em!" Nick said. "Didn't we, Mr Foster? We got 'em!"

In his excitement he skipped up to Dan and Caroline, put out a hand to touch the baby, make himself part of their circle. Angrily Caroline pushed his arm away. The boy looked up at Dan, expecting a kind word to smooth over the rebuff, an acknowledgement of his part in the rescue, his place in Dan's affection. Dan only had eyes for his son. Nick recoiled, his lips pressed together, his eyes narrowed. Dan did not see the expression in his eye as he looked at Alex.

Chapter Thirty-One

"How is she?" asked Dan when Caroline came back into the kitchen.

He shifted Alex's weight on his lap so that he could turn over a page of Louise Parmeter's memoirs. He had stacked the breakfast plates at the end of the table to make space for them. Nick sat opposite him, unconsciously mirroring his reading attitude while puzzling over an alphabet.

"She's asleep," Caroline answered. "I gave her some of the drops the doctor left."

She shut the door and carried the tray with the glass and spoon to the sink. Mrs Harper, who blamed herself for what had happened to Alex, had worried herself into a fever and taken to her bed.

"She needn't take on so," Dan said. "It wasn't her fault."

"She needs to hear it from you."

"I'll talk to her."

Alex whimpered and Dan gently bounced the boy up and down. "Here's another one who won't stop grizzling."

Alex's drugged sleep had done him no permanent harm, but had made him teary and fractious. The doctor had said the effects would wear off in a day or so.

"What's that you're reading?" asked Caroline.

"Something for work."

She sat down at the table next to him, slid the pages he had finished towards her. Nick frowned; she had disturbed the companionable silence between himself and Dan. Dan, rocking the baby, went back to his reading. He looked up when Caroline burst out laughing.

"This is really funny. What is it?"

"It's Louise Parmeter's unpublished memoirs. And it's meant to be secret." He reached for the sheets, but she snatched them away.

"Don't get in a fret. I won't tell anyone. I wish I'd met her. What's her house like? Did you see any of her clothes? I'd love to see them."

"I don't know what you find to admire in her. When it comes down to it, she was no different from the girls on the Piazza."

"Those dirty things? There's a world of difference. Louise Parmeter was beautiful, accomplished and clever. She played the men at their own game, and won."

"If you call ending up murdered winning."

"Are you saying she deserved it?"

"I said nothing of the kind. I just think there's no need to lionise her."

"But it's all right for you to lionise men who smash one another up in the boxing ring?"

"It's not smashing up," Nick said. "It's science, isn't it, Mr Foster?"

She gave the boy a cold look. "You men and your science. Seems to me science is whatever you like, while whatever we like is just silly nonsense."

Dan rolled his eyes. "How is it the same thing?"

But she had flounced away from him to concentrate on Louise Parmeter's book. Dan and Nick exchanged glances. Women!

Dan did not find the book as entertaining as Caroline did. The heroine bored him with her incessant self-justification and inability to give a thing its proper name. Sordid transactions were cloaked in the language of romance. Money was never paid for sex, her threats to publish her lovers' letters were never blackmail, and the lovers themselves were a succession of aliases. No doubt the Prince of Wales and his circle would recognise the originals of Mr Pinchbeck, Sir Matthew Mite, Admiral Flogemall, or Judge Scragging – scragging being a cant word for hanging – but Dan had no idea who they were.

It was not until he was near the end of the manuscript that he came upon two men he did know: Lord Hawkhurst as the rakish Lord Eagleton and the Honourable Charles Bredon as his lanky friend Lord Beanpole.

> *Beanpole, a man of good birth and outward gentlemanly appearance –* Dan read *– is a pander, a pimp, a procurer, a blaster of innocence, a ruiner of youth.*
>
> *This Lord Corruption attached himself to Lord Eagleton when both were young. Lord Eagleton was a fine youth, destined to shine in the world, but Lord Beanpole led him into a pit of vice and turned him away from that lustrous promise. There are still glimpses of the man Lord Eagleton once was, but as long as Lord Beanpole clings to him, that man can never reveal himself.*
>
> *This reptile, this Lord Beanpole, hates to be refused, and my refusal of his passionate advances stung him. He vowed vengeance and took it by coming between me and His Lordship, spreading lies and falsehoods until he had convinced Lord Eagleton, whose mind he had long prepared to believe any evil of his most disinterested friends, that my love was mercenary. That proud dignity and delicacy of woman's nature which will not stoop to ally itself with undeserved calumny and reproach dictated that I could no longer remain in Lord Eagleton's company and with my own lips I pronounced the fatal doom that rent my heart in twain.*

That was a new way of seeing Hawkhurst, Dan thought. Had he been such a promising youth? Was Bredon to blame for his dissipation? Or did Louise seek to justify her affair with a notorious libertine by presenting it as an attempt to redeem him? If that had been her aim, she had failed miserably. The funerary gifts he had sent her were proof enough of his lasting ill-nature.

Dan was not sure what to make of the suggestion that Bredon had been in love with her. If her book was to be believed, a man had only to look at her to fall at her feet. If it were true, it did not seem to have affected the two men's friendship, unless Hawkhurst did not know what part Bredon had played in the end of his affair. Her lady's maid, Sarah Dean, had been in Louise's confidence, and she had not mentioned that Bredon bore any malice towards her mistress. Malice enough to murder her? It might be worth speaking to Sarah again.

He finished the last few pages and pushed them over to Caroline. Absorbed in her reading, she reached for them without lifting her eyes from the page. She smiled as she read; sometimes laughed out loud. It suited her, brought back all the bright beauty she had possessed when they were younger, when he first started courting her. He realised that at some point he had stopped noticing how lovely she was.

Even as he enjoyed rediscovering her beauty, part of his mind was working on the case. The memoirs hadn't opened up much in the way of new leads, or added a great deal to what he already knew of Cruft and Hawkhurst. John Townsend was still wrapped up in Pickering, but the coachman would be safe enough now he knew he was being followed. He had the sense to stay away from the Martins and avoid any more attempted break-ins for a while. No one expected Dan back in the office yet, not after what had happened. That gave him a couple of days free to pursue his investigations without worrying about Townsend's interference.

As soon as he could get away, he would call at the Crufts' mansion. If Randolph Cruft was not there, Dan had made up his mind to travel to Hertfordshire tomorrow. He should be able to get there and back in a day if he was lucky with the coaches. All being well, he would be in London on Thursday to meet Jones when the wagon got back from Tewkesbury and ask him about the man who had been waiting outside the Feathers. If he was the man who had taken Alex, and Jones knew anything about it – but there was no use Dan thinking about what he might do now. He would ask Noah and Paul to keep watch at his house while he was gone. His family would not be left unprotected again.

He pulled his watch out of his pocket: nearly midday. Punctual to the arrangement made last night, a knock sounded on the front door. Eleanor had promised to return in the morning to help Caroline look after their mother and Alex. Sam had listened with pursed lips when the offer was made. He did not much like the idea of his wife coming back to run his sister-in-law's house for her. Like everyone else, though, he had to accept that Caroline would not cope on her own.

Dan passed Alex to Caroline and let in their visitors. He stayed behind in the passageway to put on his hat and coat, watching the bustle of kisses and greetings through the open kitchen door. Sam put a heavy basket on the table. The smell of stew and fresh bread rose from it. Eleanor started to clear away the dirty dishes. Caroline sat down by the fire, Alex on her lap. Dan went back into the room, gathered up the memoirs and put them in a drawer in the dresser.

"You're not going out?" Caroline exclaimed.

"There are a couple of calls I need to make," Dan answered.

"Today?"

"Sam and Eleanor are here. I'll be back soon."

"I thought you'd stay with us today at least."

"Sitting around here isn't going to lead me to the man who took Alex. Sam, if you have to go before I get back, send for Dad."

Sam hesitated. Eleanor gave her husband a warning look. He forced a smile.

"We'll be here."

"Thanks."

Dan stooped to kiss Caroline, pat Alex's head. She pulled away from him.

"Make sure you shut the door on your way out."

Chapter Thirty-Two

Randolph Cruft wafted the handkerchief he held between thumb and forefinger in front of his eyes. "I will never love another."

The young man was sprawled in a chair by the fire in his bedroom. He wore a silk dressing gown over fawn breeches, billowing shirt, embroidered waistcoat, white stockings and Turkish slippers. With a loud sigh, he sank his head on to his hand and curled his fingers against his right temple to show the polished nails to best advantage. After a few seconds he sighed again, flung back his head and pressed the handkerchief to his left cheek.

Dan, standing in front of him, looked out through the window at the lawn and shrubberies which ran down to meadows and woodland. He glimpsed the loop of a river in the distance. Thinking longingly of cold water and chill air, he edged as far away from the fire as he could.

"When did you last see Miss Parmeter, Mr—" It was on the tip of Dan's tongue to call him Mr Namby Pamby, one of the names Louise Parmeter had given him in her memoirs. "—Cruft?"

Cruft struck himself on the forehead. Not too hard, Dan noticed. "Oh, Louise, Louise! Parted from me by a cruel, remorseless parent, slain by a ruthless assassin's hand! Ah, Mr Foster, it is a poniard to the heart!" Cruft placed his hand over that organ and fetched another sigh.

Dan glanced around the opulent bedchamber. He didn't think Mr Cruft senior such a cruel parent; his son had been provided with every luxury. And if he didn't buck up the young man, he'd be here all day watching him strike poses in it.

"Now look here, Mr Minimy—" Hastily Dan corrected himself. Not Mr Minimy Piminy. "Mr Cruft, this is a murder investigation and I need you to concentrate. When you last saw Miss Parmeter, did you part on good terms?"

"We were one and indivisible."

"Did you know she was one and indivisible with other men? That she had other lovers?"

Cruft waved his hand like a sultan pardoning a slave. "The purity of our love expunged whatever she had been."

"I don't think it did. And from what I've gathered, she wasn't in love with you at all. Thought you something of a nuisance in fact." Mr Mincey Wincey. "As I recall, the kindest thing she had to say about you was that you were a kind of neuter, a creature somewhere between male and female."

"You must be mistaken. I offered to lay my fortune at her feet. She would have been my Cleopatra, my Helen, my—"

"She turned you down, though, didn't she?"

Cruft pressed his hand to his head. "Really, Mr Foster, I must ask you to desist. I feel quite faint."

"Made a bit of a fool of you, all in all." Dan didn't think Cruft needed much help with that. "And then she got you sent into the country like a naughty schoolboy."

"To wander in solitary, melancholy groves in a rapture of devotion."

"While she was treating your attempt to throw your life away for love of her as a subject for gossip and humour. *At the sight of half a dozen tiny drops of blood, he squealed like a stuck pig, a creature which he very much resembled.*"

"What?"

"That's what she wrote about you."

"The damned jade!"

"You might very well think that. Might very well decide to do something about it. While everyone thinks you're wandering in solitary groves, you sneak back to London, go to Louise's house, confront her, lose your temper, and strike her. Dead."

"Yes, yes!" cried Cruft, clasping his hands. "Driven by a cruel, imperious mistress to a crime of passion, to spend the rest of his days in bitter solitude, far from the empty, shallow world, his noble soul consumed by a love so pure that even the worthlessness of its object cannot destroy it."

"Or hanging from a rope at Newgate."

"What?"

"Mr Cruft, you do realise I'm asking if you murdered Louise Parmeter?"

Cruft sat bolt upright. "Murder her? Me? But – but – I couldn't. I wouldn't. I didn't."

"So you were here at Childwick Hall all the time?"

The colour rushed back into Cruft's white face. "Oh, yes, that's it. I was, wasn't I?" He tittered. "I'd forgotten."

Dan had known men bluster and lie through their alibis, or repeat them by rote, or produce scores of dubious witnesses, but he had never come across a man who forgot his. It hardly mattered. Cruft was not the killer. Dan left him to enjoy weaving epic tragedies with himself as hero.

The steward was waiting for Dan outside the room. He led him down to the kitchen, where Dan was given bread, meat and cheese. The meal was welcome. He had caught the 5 a.m. coach from the Bell and Crown in Holborn that morning and had eaten nothing since breakfast. His appetite had been further sharpened by walking the couple of miles from Watford.

While he ate, he asked the steward about his master's movements during his stay. There had not been many of them. Cruft spent very little time wandering in solitary groves, passed most of the day in his room, often only emerging at dinner time. Sometimes he had guests, pallid young ladies and gentlemen, to share languid evenings of music and conversation.

There could not have been much to alarm Cruft senior

when he received the steward's reports of his son's activities. Nor did Dan have any reason to doubt the man's account. It was clear that the young master was no favourite of his. He spoke in incredulous tones of Cruft's preference for poetry and a roaring fire when there was such a fine sporting estate to enjoy. With a disbelieving shake of the head, he mentioned that Master Cruft had always preferred the library to the gun room.

When Dan had finished his meal, he took his leave and walked back to Watford. Several coaches to London passed through the town daily; with luck, he would soon be on his way home. From questions put to other servants and grooms on his way out, Dan left Childwick convinced that Cruft had not made a mad dash to London to commit murder in a fit of passion.

It was nearly eight when he got back to London. There was still time to call on Sarah Dean and ask her what she knew about Bredon's relationship with Louise Parmeter. He preferred not to wait; the house would soon be closed, the servants gone, all signs that a murder had been committed swept and scrubbed away. But when he reached Berkeley Square, he was already too late. The house was shuttered and silent, a dark gap amidst the brilliantly lit buildings.

Chapter Thirty-Three

Dan turned away from the front door of the Berkeley Square house and went round to the lane. He scanned the track, listened to the watery bustle from the laundry, the lowing of cattle in the dairy, muffled hammering from one of the workshops. It could have been a street in some obscure village or country town were it not for the sense of the city pressing in on every side. The traffic on the main streets kept up a continual low roar, and the sky above the myriad rooftops was smudged with light and plumed with chimney smoke.

He spotted the shadowy bulk of a man leaning under the branches by the garden gate. The man straightened up and turned to face him.

"You drew the short straw again," Dan said.

"Mr Foster!" cried Patrolman Grimes, who had been keeping watch on Pickering last time Dan was here. "How do things go with you? Is the little fellow well?" Grimes had done his share during the search for Alex.

"He is safe and well, thank you," Dan answered.

"If anyone did such a thing to one of my little ones, I'd rip his liver out."

"And so I will, when I find the villain." Dan jerked his head towards the large stable gate, which had been fastened for the night. "Anything doing?"

"Not much. Pickering seems to be lying low mostly. I did follow him to a drinking den near Monmouth Street last night. Mr Townsend thinks that's where he's going to fence the diamonds, if he hasn't already. He thinks it might be worth raiding the place."

He would, Dan thought. "I need to ask Pickering some questions."

"Right you are, Mr Foster."

Dan tried the wicket gate, found it was still open and went inside. Jacko, the stable boy, was filling a bucket at the pump in the yard. He beckoned Dan to follow him into the stables where Pickering was giving one of the horses his last grooming by the light of a lamp hung on the wall, before settling him down for the night. The boy unlatched the stall next door and went inside with the pail, clucking softly at its occupant.

Pickering looked up from his work and nodded a greeting. The stall door was open, and though the animal was tethered, Dan kept a cautious distance from his restless hooves.

"Fine beast, isn't he?" Pickering said.

"If you say so."

Pickering laughed, gave the glossy coat its last few brush strokes. "Hold these," he said, handing Dan the brushes while he checked the horse's hooves. Finally, he patted the animal and left the stall. He looked over the partition at the boy, who was raking the straw bedding.

"Pile it higher against the wall," Pickering said. He drew his keys out of his pocket and handed them to the boy. "Bring out the lamp and lock up when you've finished. Bring me the keys." To Dan, he said, "Come on up."

They went outside. Dan gave him the brushes. "I didn't know if you'd still be here. The other servants have gone. I was hoping to speak to Miss Dean."

"I've been asked to stay on to look after the horses until we've found a buyer for them." Pickering broke off. "Jacko! Move that shovel! I've told you to keep the yard tidy."

The boy appeared at a run from the stables, hastily grabbed the offending tool and scuttled off with it. Pickering winked at him, softening the rebuke. He ducked into the tack room to put the brushes away, resumed his conversation with Dan when he came out.

"Shouldn't take long. They're prime stock."

In his rooms, Pickering lit a lamp with a spill from the stove, set a kettle to boil, reached for a bowl, sugar and lemon from a shelf. Dan took off his hat and sat down while Pickering peeled the lemon into the bowl, poured in hot water, added a good measure of gin. He went to the door, called "Jacko!", came back into the room and put three glasses on the table.

"None for me," Dan said.

The boy raced up the stairs and burst into the room. Pickering handed him a steaming glass. "Take this to Mr Grimes." He met Dan's look of surprise with a grin. "We always have a tot of something around this time. It's cold work for a man standing out all night. If you won't drink gin, how about some coffee?"

"That would be welcome. What will you do when the horses have gone?"

"Thanks to Miss Parmeter, I'm going to set up on my own account." Pickering took a swig of his drink. "Her will, Mr Foster. I'll have enough to start my own livery stables."

"Miss Parmeter left you money?" As if Townsend hadn't got reason enough to arrest Pickering, here was a nice fat legacy to make another one. "Did anyone else get anything?"

"The bulk of the estate goes to her brother, but there was something for each of us. Mr Parkes has already found himself a grocery shop on Piccadilly and asked the first housemaid, Miss Evans, to marry him, which didn't sit well with the housekeeper, I can tell you. Miss Dean is going off to her next job with a trunk full of Miss Parmeter's shoes, hats and gowns, as well as a tidy little nest egg. Cook, footmen, housemaids… she left out no one. As I told you, she was a generous woman. There aren't many like her."

"What about Miss Taylor? Was she mentioned?"

"Only to say she's to be paid the money Miss Parmeter had in safekeeping for her from the sale of her books."

"Nothing more?"

"No."

"I wonder if she was expecting any more?"

"None of us were expecting anything and we'd been with Miss Parmeter for years. I don't see why she would. Besides, Miss Parmeter had already done a great deal for her. You don't seem very pleased with our good fortune."

"I am, of course."

"You think one of us murdered her for the money."

"You can't deny it does offer another possible motive to someone who's looking for one."

Pickering slammed his glass on the table. "But it's as I told you. No one had any idea she'd left us anything. You can ask her lawyer if you don't believe me. And if you got on and found her killer instead of hanging around here, you wouldn't be trying to put the blame on us. You're all the same. You get one idea in your heads and you'll make the facts fit and devil take the truth."

Dan pushed back his chair, placed his hands on the table and pushed himself to his feet. "Damn you, Pickering. You can come outside and say that."

For a moment the two men glared at one another, anger snapping between them. Then Pickering ducked his head and ran his fingers through his hair. He looked up at Dan and said, "I'm sorry. I spoke out of turn. It's this damned murder hanging over us."

Dan settled back in his seat. "Apology accepted."

Pickering grinned, poured himself another drink. "It would have been a good bout between us though, don't you think? I hear you've something of a reputation at fisticuffs."

"What makes you say that?"

"Grimes told me."

"Did he, now? Well, if it's a fight you want, why don't you come to my dad's gym in Cecil Street some time?"

"You're on."

"After the case is over."

"I hope that will be soon," Pickering said. "Sarah is still in town," he added.

"Yes, Parkes gave me her address. I'll have to look her up tomorrow. I'd better be getting home. I've been away since early morning."

Jacko's arrival with the keys delayed Dan's leave-taking.

"I'll wish you good evening, Mr Pickering," Dan said, when the boy had gone to his pallet bed in the harness room.

"I'll come down with you. I'm off out to meet someone."

"I hope it's a social engagement. No more housebreaking."

The coachman laughed. "Oh, she's sociable enough."

He put on his hat and locked the door after them. In the lane, he called out, "Ready, Mr Grimes? Let the game commence!" To Dan, he said, "He's really very good, you know. I haven't yet succeeded in shaking him off."

From the shadows, Grimes spluttered into his glass. Dan grinned at the patrolman's embarrassment. Serve him right for gossiping.

Mrs Watson sat on a chair outside the laundry. A girl stood in front of her, holding up her skirt and testing the strength of her left ankle by pressing her weight on it.

Pickering doffed his cap. "Good to see Miss Julia is up and about again."

Mrs Watson nodded at her daughter's plump limb. "Good as new. And a good thing too."

Pickering, with the quick glance of a man used to judging the severity of equine strains and sprains, said, "I wouldn't let her do too much to start with, Mrs Watson. It was a nasty accident."

"It was no accident!" Mrs Watson retorted. "He ought to be made to pay for my loss and inconvenience. The laundry basket knocked out of her hand, everything rolled in the mud and all to do over again, and what with one of the girls leaving and this one being laid up, we've had to work every night this last fortnight to keep on top of the orders. Then there's the apothecary's bill, and Lord knows doing business with them is a robbery in itself." She shifted her grievance on to Dan. "You're a law officer. Don't you think there should be a law against it? There should be compensation, that's what I say."

"Unless we catch the thief, I'm afraid there's nothing we can do," Dan said.

"It wasn't a robbery," Julia said. "He knocked me over and left me lying in the street."

"I'm sorry, but if you didn't report the attack when it happened, there's not much likelihood of catching the man now."

"Well, I like that," Mrs Watson said. "A young girl can be knocked flying by a man just because he's a gentleman and all the law's got to say is, 'On you go, sir, why don't you come back and trample her while you're at it?'"

"The law hardly says that," Dan said. "But if you want to report an assault, you've left it a bit late. Unless you know who did it."

"I'd recognise him if I saw him again," Julia said. "If he'd stood sideways you wouldn't have known him from one of the area railings. I'd just turned into the square when he came rushing up behind me on his skinny shanks as if all the devils was after him."

"He ran out of the lane? When did this happen?" asked Dan.

"The Friday morning before poor Miss Parmeter was killed, wasn't it, Julia?" said Mrs Watson.

"No, Ma, it was Saturday. It was trotters for supper."

"That's right," Mrs Watson said. "The Saturday."

Dan wondered how this had been missed when the constables made their enquiries. A moment's reflection suggested an explanation. Julia Watson had been laid up in bed with a sprained ankle when the constables called. Besides, the men had been asking about the day Louise Parmeter died, the Monday.

"Can you remember what he was wearing?"

"A brown coat," Julia said confidently, adding, "It could have been blue." She tittered. "He looked like a mop someone had dressed in fine silks."

"Which direction did he take?"

She flicked her lank hair. "I was too busy being knocked over."

She had already told him enough. An excessively thin gentleman had been seen rushing into the square from the direction of Louise Parmeter's garden. Dan could think of one man who matched the description. Lord Beanpole: Bredon, Lord Hawkhurst's friend and, according to the memoirs, one of Louise's ex-lovers. Julia's story might mean nothing, but if the man who knocked her over had been Bredon, it put him at the scene of the murder only two days before it happened. What had he been doing there and why had he left in such an agitated state?

"Got to go," Dan said. He broke into a run, leaving the three staring after him.

"La!" Mrs Watson cried. "Aren't they wunnerful? Off to catch the villain just like that!"

Chapter Thirty-Four

Dan stood by the railings outside Lord Hawkhurst's house in Cavendish Square, avoiding the light cast on to the pavement by the lamps outside the front entrance. It was cold, winter still clutching at spring. He could see his breath on the air.

He looked down into the area, where a door opened on to damp flagstones. There was a small barred window next to it. The sound of laughter and voices drifted up from the domestic regions. The servants were having a party. In a well-run household he would assume that meant the family had gone out. In Hawkhurst's establishment that was not such an obvious conclusion. Still, if there was carousing below stairs, it was likely there was just as much above. Whoever was inside, master or servant, would be befuddled by drink. Even so, it was too risky to attempt breaking in through the basement door.

There was no way of getting into the house from the street either. Because of the railings and the drop into the area, the sash windows at the front were inaccessible. Even if he had been able to swing over and get in at a window, he would be visible to any passer-by.

He was about to set off for the rear of the building when he spotted a faint light bobbing in the window below. It grew brighter, steadied, and seconds later the basement door opened.

"You should have known better, Dan Foster," he muttered. In his days as a sneak looking for easy ways into a house, the first rule he had learned was that it was always worth trying a door before you assumed it was locked.

Harry, the footman, appeared on the threshold. He was in

his shirtsleeves, his waistcoat unbuttoned. A tomcat shot past him into the night. He aimed a kick after it, clutched at the lintel as he missed and overbalanced.

"And stay out."

A woman's voice slurred behind him. "What are you doing, Harry?"

"Bloody thing shat in the pantry."

"I'll get the girl to clean it up." She staggered up behind him, slid her hands around his waist. "Come on. We've just opened another bottle."

Harry turned, pulled her towards him, pushed the door shut as he covered her face with a slobbering kiss. Dan waited, but no key turned in the lock, no bolts slammed shut. He crept down the stairs, peered in through the window. The couple had finished pawing one another and were stumbling along the corridor arm in arm, Harry lighting their way with a lantern. They turned a corner and the light disappeared. Dan opened the door and slipped inside.

Ahead of him a door opened on to the revelry. It snicked shut and the din faded. Dan passed the open door of the pantry where the tom had disgraced itself and turned the corner into a brighter section of the passageway. Candles guttered in sconces, and light also came from a line of uncurtained plain glass windows overlooking the corridor. He crept up to the last of these and peered into the servants' hall. Slovenly men and dishevelled women sat around a long table making free with their master's food, drink, and one another. Dan ducked beneath the windows and hurried by.

Stone stairs brought him up into the hall, which was as muddy and untidy as last time he had seen it. The door to the room where he had fought Hawkhurst stood open. It was empty, the furniture disarranged, dirty glasses and empty bottles uncleared. No sound came from any of the other rooms. Dan opened the doors and looked inside: a drawing room where a fire burned; a cold but tidy library.

Hawkhurst and his crew must have gone out on their nightly round of pestering actresses, night watchmen, waiters, whoever was unlucky enough to cross their path. Dan went up the broad staircase to the bedrooms. He looked into Hawkhurst's room first. It was scattered with rumpled clothes and discarded shoes. A fire gasped its last in the grate. Next to it were an armchair and reading table. There was just enough light from the coals for Dan to make out that the open book on the table was in Latin. There were more classical books on the bedside table, along with a brandy bottle and glass.

The neighbouring rooms were empty, smelt stale and damp, but the chamber two doors down was in use. Here there was evidence of the work of a conscientious valet: clothes put away, combs, razors and stoppered bottles neatly arranged on the dressing table, curtains closed, fire tended. Dan stepped inside, shut the door and lit a candle. He opened the dressing table drawers, sifted through pill boxes, jars, shaving brushes, buttons, buckles, handkerchiefs. He went through the wardrobe, hat and boot boxes, and a pistol case.

A drawer in the desk yielded a stash of letters addressed to The Honourable Charles Bredon. With these were bundles of IOUs, some from him, others to him, some for wagers, some for wins and losses at cards. Dan read the half-written letter on top of the desk:

I am sorry that I have been obliged to disappoint you respecting payment of the five hundred guineas. I extremely regret that I am not immediately able to command the money. However, I cannot help adverting to the circumstance which misled me into the expectation that you would allow me any reasonable time I might want for the payment. The circumstance is the total inebriety of myself when I made this preposterous bet.

Dan wondered what he would do with five hundred guineas. Not waste it on a bet, that was for sure. Look for a bigger house, perhaps. He put the letter back, pulled out the drawer on the other side. To his surprise, it shot out and he had to move quickly to catch it before it crashed to the floor. A glance showed him that it was shallower than the aperture. He laid it down, knelt, and groped inside the cavity until he touched something wrapped in a cloth bag at the back. He pulled it out, untied it, tipped the contents on to the palm of his hand. A diamond necklace and one diamond earring, the match to the one he had seen in Louise Parmeter's left ear.

He sat back on his heels. "Got you."

Bredon was obviously a man who insisted on his comforts and it was likely that, drunk as he was, his valet would come in at some point to make up the fire. It was also possible that someone would attend to the fires in Hawkhurst's bedroom and drawing room before his return. Dan decided it would be safer to wait in one of the empty bedrooms. He slipped the jewels into his pocket and went into the disused chamber next door. He carried a chair over to the door, opened it a few inches and sat down.

The valet and one of the housemaids had been upstairs, noisily pleasured one another, and put Hawkhurst's and Bredon's rooms straight by the time the revellers banged on the front door. A nearby church clock struck two. Dan tiptoed on to the landing and looked over the banister. Harry ran into the hall carrying a branched candlestick in one hand, struggling to tuck in his shirt with the other.

"About time, too, ye lazy dog!" Hawkhurst shoved him aside. "Bring some claret, if you haven't drunk it all." He took off his hat and threw it across the hall. It landed on the head of the bullet-pocked ancestral bust, the sureness of his aim exciting cries of admiration from his company.

The footman veered back to the servants' hall. Hawkhurst led his friends into the drawing room. Bredon stepped neatly behind him. Fotheringham, the erstwhile poet, zigzagged, his hands hanging at his sides. Ormond, the Irishman who had seconded Dan for his sparring match with Hawkhurst, picked his way with exaggerated care.

Dan waited until Harry had served their wine and been dismissed with a kick and a stream of abuse from his master before he left his hiding place. Downstairs, he listened at the door for a moment, trying to get a sense of where the men were in the room.

"And I swear yours was a man, Fotheringham!" Bredon's voice, high and mocking.

"No – upon my honour – I insist—" Fotheringham tried to make himself heard above the shrieks of laughter.

"But what I want to know," Bredon continued, "is why you stayed with him. Something you should tell us about? Better be careful not to turn your backs on him, you fellows!"

"She was a girl and we went at it like – like rabbits!" Fotheringham protested. "I fucked her three times if I fucked her once."

"Aye, in her—"

Dan had heard enough. He opened the door and stepped inside.

For a moment, they stared at him. Then Fotheringham jumped up from the sofa and jerked his fists about.

"A burglar! Where are the rest of the brutes? Let me at 'em!"

"Sit down," growled Hawkhurst, who was sprawling in a chair by the fire, a wine glass in his hand. He booted the poet in the backside and Fotheringham's tenuous balance gave way. He landed on Ormond's lap, jogging the Irishman's arm and sending the contents of his glass cascading down his front. Ormond swore, pushed him away, and dabbed at the spilled wine with his sleeve.

Fotheringham hauled himself to his knees and sparred with the air. "Where are they? I'll give 'em this! And this!"

"Oh, shut up, Fotheringham," said Hawkhurst. "What do you mean by breaking into my house, Foster?"

"I'm here to arrest a murderer."

Fotheringham blinked at Dan, his wine-dimmed brain working at top speed yet coming up with nothing to account for Dan's presence. He rubbed his aching brow, crawled back on to his seat and seized a glass of wine.

Dan drew the diamonds from his pocket and held them out to Bredon. "I found these in your room."

Bredon did not move, but Hawkhurst sat up and reached for the jewels. Dan passed them to him.

"They are Louise's," Hawkhurst said. "How did you come by them, Bredon?"

"Isn't it obvious? That myrmidon of the law placed them there."

"You think it was me who hid them in the back of your wardrobe?" Dan asked.

"They weren't—" Bredon broke off before he fell into Dan's trap. Not a very good trap, but enough for the others to see that Bredon was rattled, if only for a few seconds.

"You were going to say they weren't in the wardrobe," Dan said. "For you well know I found them in the desk."

"No wonder in a man finding what he put there."

"But why would he put them in your room?" asked Hawkhurst.

"Perhaps he mistook it for yours. Certain it is that the fellow has come here in an attempt to force a conclusion to his inept investigation."

"If I was going to do that, I wouldn't be so obvious about it," Dan answered. "It was you, wasn't it, Bredon? You were furious when Miss Parmeter rejected your advances, so you killed her."

"You think I had any interest in a faded demirep?" Bredon turned to Hawkhurst. "The fellow should be kicked downstairs."

"You had such an interest in her that you couldn't bear it when she and Lord Hawkhurst became lovers," Dan said. "You poisoned your friend's mind against her, told him she was only after his money."

"Which was no more than the truth," Bredon retorted. "As for her turning me down, the woman could hardly refuse to grant what she'd already given... I'm sorry, Hawkhurst. Louise and I were lovers when she met you. She didn't tell you that, did she? When I saw how besotted you were, I said nothing either. I didn't want to cause you any pain. Besides, I thought the thing would soon burn itself out and no harm done. When it became apparent that she had her hooks in you, I had to warn you what kind of woman she really was. She dropped me as soon as a better prospect came along. She'd have done the same to you sooner or later."

"But you wanted her back," Dan said. "And when she refused, you killed her."

"I take her back? Hell would have to freeze over first."

Fotheringham gave a loud sigh, shut his eyes and slid slowly on to his side. His glass fell from his fingers, the wine spreading its crimson stain across the cushions. No one took any notice of him.

Dan pressed on. "You were seen leaving Louise Parmeter's house in a rage two days before the murder. I think you went there to demand that she resumed your former relations. Maybe that wasn't the first time you'd had that conversation, wasn't the first time she'd refused you, but refuse you she did. Only you wouldn't take no for an answer, so you went back on Monday morning to make another attempt. When she still spurned you, you killed her and took the jewels to make it look like a robbery."

"Bredon?" said Hawkhurst.

Bredon gave a rueful shrug. "So I was there on Saturday. You said it yourself: the woman was a whore. I had at least as much right as any man to make a purchase; more than most. Do you know the arrogant strumpet actually believed me when I wrote hinting that you wanted me to sound her out, in a private conversation, with a view to a reunion? She was so desperate to get her claws back into you she couldn't agree to a meeting quickly enough."

Hawkhurst raised his eyebrows. "I ask her for a reunion?"

"I know. Was there ever such a presumptuous drab? And then she had the nerve to threaten to call the servants if I didn't leave. Is it not enough to drive any man into a rage? But Foster has no proof I was there on Monday morning."

"Only this." Hawkhurst trailed the necklace over his fingers, said wonderingly, "It was you." He smiled at Bredon over the glittering stones. "But why, for God's sake? There are plenty of other women."

Bredon returned the smile, relaxed into his seat. "I lost my temper. Bloody females giving themselves airs and graces. Going on about their right to independence, parading their ingratitude, refusing to recognise that man is their master. The world is well rid of such monsters."

"So it was Miss Parmeter who let you in on Monday," said Dan.

Bredon, still looking at Hawkhurst, said, "No, only Saturday. But she'd forgotten I still had a key to the gate. I'd come in that way often enough in the past. To hear her outrage, you'd think I'd violated a virgin's bower."

"That's all I need to hear," Dan said. "You're guilty of murder and you're coming to Bow Street with me."

"Of course I'm not coming to Bow Street," Bredon said. "Put the jewels back, there's a good fellow, and we'll say no more about it."

Dan did not move.

"Come now. If it's money you want, state your price."

Still Dan stood his ground.

Bredon clicked his tongue. "I see you are determined to make a nuisance of yourself. All the worse for you." To Hawkhurst, "The man has broken into your house and tried to plant evidence. That must be good for a criminal charge or two. Send for Townsend, let him sort this out."

Hawkhurst rubbed his chin. "Burglary. Perjury. Blackmail. Extortion. There's enough to hang a man several times over."

Bredon laughed. "You're so right, Hawkhurst. What do you think of arresting me now, Thief Taker?"

"Hold on now," Ormond cried. "You have just confessed to killing Louise, and you're plotting to send this man to the gallows to save your own neck? I will not stand by and let you do it."

"But you will," Bredon said. "Unless you wish your father to hear of your marriage."

"Damn you, Bredon!" Ormond started to his feet, fists clenched. "It was you who tricked me into the marriage in the first place, you who made sure I didn't find out till too late that my wife is nothing but a common strumpet. And for what? Because it amused you."

"A fool is always amusing," Bredon said. "None more so than this Bow Street clown."

"I thank you, Mr Ormond, but there's no need to worry," Dan said. "Send for Mr Townsend. You'd be saving me the trouble."

Bredon smiled up at Dan. "John Townsend won't be able to save you, even if he wanted to. It's the word of four gentlemen against one thief taker. You retrieved the diamonds from one of your flash-house fences and you decided to turn them to profit for yourself. A sad story of greed and corruption. You've finished yourself with this little jaunt, Foster. And when they're tying the rope around your neck, you can comfort yourself that it was all for the sake of a worthless drab. Ormond, ring the bell."

Ormond turned his face away from Dan and shuffled towards the bell pull.

"I'll give you one last chance, Foster," Bredon said. "Leave now and we'll pretend this regrettable little incident never happened."

"For God's sake, man," Ormond said. "Go."

"No. Bredon, I am arresting you for the murder of Louise Parmeter."

Bredon and Hawkhurst exchanged glances and burst into laughter.

"You have to give him the belt for tenacity!" Bredon said.

"You do indeed," Hawkhurst agreed. "He's going to make an impressive show in the ring next week, I think."

Bredon guffawed. "If only he wasn't going to be in Newgate this time next week."

"No, Bredon. It's you who will be in Newgate. Arrest him with my blessing, Foster."

"Ha, ha! Very droll, My Lord! An excellent joke."

"No joke," Hawkhurst said. "At long last I can be rid of you."

"Be rid of me?" Bredon's eyes narrowed. "You'll never be rid of me, Hawkhurst. You forget all you owe me."

"I forget nothing. You're a vampire. You've done nothing but suck the life out of me ever since we met."

"I've always got you what you wanted."

"And helped yourself to plenty into the bargain. No, Bredon, I'm done with you. If Foster can get you to Bow Street, he's welcome to you." Hawkhurst leaned back in his chair, the diamonds wrapped around the knuckles of one hand. He swirled the wine in the glass in his other hand, stared into its winking lights.

"Foster will get him to Bow Street," Ormond said, "with my help."

The Irishman was as good as his word. When Bredon uncoiled his lanky figure from his seat and made a bolt for it, it was Ormond who brought him down with a heartfelt left hook to his jaw.

Chapter Thirty-Five

"Her companion had this?" Sir William tapped his forefinger on the memoirs which Dan had placed on his desk.

"That's right, sir. Agnes Taylor," Dan answered.

"And Foster discovered them on Monday," said John Townsend. "He should have informed me straight away."

"I know," Dan said. He made a shameless play for sympathy. "But what with Alex…"

"Quite, quite," said Sir William. "Perfectly understandable. Other things on your mind. All well at home now? The little fellow unharmed? Good, good. Foster has done well, eh, Townsend?"

Townsend grunted. "It's a pity he followed the leads I gave him in such a roundabout way. I said all along the lady's book had nothing to do with it. And, as I pointed out in my report, it was obvious that Miss Parmeter must have known her killer. However, I have now interrogated Mr Bredon and obtained his full confession."

Last night Dan had sent word to Townsend as soon as he got Bredon to Bow Street, and tactfully refrained from interviewing him until his colleague arrived. It was no surprise that Townsend had immediately taken charge of the proceedings. Even less of a surprise that Dan's gesture had done nothing to lessen his resentment.

Townsend shifted in his seat to avoid looking at Dan. "I've always said, sir, that a man distracted by family doesn't make an effective officer. Of course, I don't blame Officer Foster for what happened, and I'll be as happy as the next man when the villain who took the child is hanging from the gallows. An attack on one officer is an attack on us all. But if he'd had his mind on the case, this arrest could have been made days ago."

"Perhaps if you weren't so busy policing dinner parties at Carlton House, you might have paid more attention to the investigation yourself," Dan retorted. "Instead we wasted time arresting Pickering and trying to pin it on him."

"With good cause," Townsend responded. "Pickering's a shifty cove, definitely hiding something. I think it's only a matter of time before we find out what."

"The man's taking part in illegal fights, with plenty of lively betting. Why don't you arrest him for that? And while you're at it, you might as well arrest the Prince of Wales too."

"There's a difference between a private sparring match before His Royal Highness and a mill in a drinking den."

"Only difference is the quality of the audience."

"That will do, Foster," Sir William said. "I don't think we need to bring the fight into it. You should have kept Officer Townsend informed, but in the circumstances, I am sure he can overlook the lapse. What's important is that we have arrested the killer." He eyed the manuscript eagerly. "You can leave this with me. I will pass it on to the Home Secretary."

After Sir William had had a chance to read it first, thought Dan. Though he could have told him that Louise Parmeter's memoirs weren't as racy as he might think.

"His Royal Highness has first claim on it," Townsend said. "I don't think he'd like to hear it went to the Duke of Portland instead of himself."

"Dear God!" Sir William muttered. Give the book to the Home Secretary, and annoy the Prince. Give the book to the Prince, and have the Home Secretary asking the reason why.

"It can be delivered to His Highness with all due discretion," Townsend added. "The Prince is always mindful of those who oblige him." He coughed. "And administrations don't last for ever."

Sir William did not need reminding that obliging a prince made more sense than obliging a politician who might one day be out of office at that prince's pleasure. He had said the same thing to Dan about relations between the Duke of Portland and the Prince. He pushed the bundle across to Townsend.

"Do what you like with it. But I never saw it."

"I'll take it to Carlton House right away, sir. No need for you to come, Foster."

Leaving the way clear for Townsend to claim all the credit for himself. Let him, Dan thought. As far as he was concerned, he was well out of it. Mixing with those in high places brought nothing but trouble. And he had something else on his mind: talking to Jones the carrier.

Having to report to Sir William first thing this morning meant he had missed the arrival of the wagon at the Feathers. But after he had tracked down Jones at his sister's house in Cripplegate, he was no closer to finding the man who had kidnapped Alex. The carrier knew nothing about him.

When Dan got home, there was a message from Sir William telling him he had been summoned to Carlton House on the following afternoon. It seemed there was no avoiding the great ones after all.

"Your men have done a splendid job, splendid," said the Prince of Wales.

"Thank you, Your Royal Highness," Sir William Addington replied. "It has been an honour to serve in the matter."

From the bow window, Dan watched Sir William and John Townsend engage in a chest-puffing contest. Unable to decide the winner, he turned his attention back to the view of the gardens. His head was still spinning after their long walk from the Pall Mall entrance of Carlton House to this room where, after waiting for an hour in an anteroom, they had been shown into the Prince's presence.

The green, browns and greys of damp trees, shrubs and sky were restful to eyes dazzled by acres of pink, red and black marble; green walls, yellow walls, red and blue walls; spears of light hurled from gilded surfaces; aching expanses of brightness in huge windows hung with shining swathes of silk and velvet. On every side crouched strange creatures transformed into table legs, handles, stands for urns: dragons, gryphons, unicorns, lions, men with the legs of goats, dog-like creatures with women's heads. Dan wondered why a grown man would surround himself with such fairy tales.

Everywhere he looked there were servants in livery, gliding here and there with trays, standing in groups, moving about the rooms. One of the chambers they passed was draped in dust sheets and a group of workmen were removing a marble chimney piece in order to replace it with another marble chimney piece. Another was circular and furnished with a large dining table. Inside an army of women wearing white gloves and over-sleeves dusted and polished under the anxious direction of a male supervisor whose heavy responsibility was the survival of a warehouse-worth of knick-knacks.

Snatches of hammering, cheery voices and whistling drifted up from the grounds. Gangs of workmen swarmed over the lawn. They were building a wooden awning. It faced a staked-out square and was flanked by two small pavilions. A setting for one of the Prince's famous entertainments, no doubt.

Dan, remembering his manners, turned back to the company. The eyes of the Prince's companion, who sat beside his royal master, were fixed on him with an appraising stare. Richard Sheridan acknowledged him with a friendly nod.

The Prince, a tub in blue on a pink sofa, crossed his fat legs and drank from his goblet.

"I want to know everything, Towney. How you found the memoirs, and how you discovered it was Bredon who murdered Louise."

Townsend beamed and bowed. "Intuition and intelligence, sir, intuition and intelligence."

"And Foster here was a great help in the matter, was he not?"

"A promising officer in many ways, sir," Townsend answered.

Dan caught Sheridan's mischievous eye, quickly looked away.

"I heard it was Mr Foster who apprehended Mr Bredon," Sheridan said.

"What, you actually made the arrest, did you, Foster?" asked George.

"I did, sir," Dan answered.

"Then tell all."

"Well, sir, I—"

"Perhaps," Sir William said hastily, "the less said about Foster's methods, the better."

George laughed. "A little rough and ready, is he? Well, well, I won't pry into your police secrets. Answer me this at least. Is it true that Hawkhurst turned on his old friend and refused to protect him?"

"It is," Dan said. "And it was Mr Ormond who helped me convey him to Bow Street."

"Ormond... Ormond. Irish, I take it. D'you know him, Sherry?"

"No, Your Royal Highness, I have not had that pleasure."

"Strange fellow, Hawkhurst. You'd have thought nothing could separate him from Bredon. Do you know why I think it was, Sherry?"

"I am sure that with your usual perspicacity, you will fathom his character," Sheridan answered.

The Prince gave a self-deprecatory titter before sharing his insight. "I think he loved Louise Parmeter more than he was willing to admit."

"He had a funny way of showing it," Dan said.

"Foster!" Townsend reproved. His promising officer was putting himself too far forward.

"No, no, Towney, I like to hear him speak," said George. "Why do you say that?"

"Because of the cruel gifts he sent her. Mourning gloves, a black hatband, a silver coffin plate engraved '*Here lies*—'" Dan broke off, ended in confusion, "Your Royal Highness."

"A whore?" the Prince finished for him. "Something to the same effect. I thought Hawkhurst was more subtle than that. I wonder if it was Bredon's idea? It's no matter." He stood up, signalling that the audience was over. "It's enough for me that the memoirs are in my possession and that the murderer will hang. You will see my treasurer on your way out."

Townsend bowed. "Thank you, Your Royal Highness."

Dan also bowed and thanked the Prince. He gave a last look out of the window. Noticing his interest, the Prince came to stand beside him.

"What do you think, Foster? Will it do?"

Sir William took advantage of the Prince's distraction to corner Sheridan. "You will notice, I think, that Act Three is a highly original way of introducing the themes of love and honour. Lord Aramand's passion for the charming captive who he is determined to cherish in spite of his father's vengeful fiat is quite a new situation."

"It was old when Dryden used it," Sheridan muttered. "But, as I say, Sir William, I have not had time to read the play. Perhaps we could defer our discussion until I have?"

Sir William edged closer to Sheridan. "The character of Jacarantha is handled with great delicacy."

Dan, recollecting that the Prince was waiting for an answer, took his attention away from the eager playwright.

"I am no judge of such things, sir."

"But you think everyone will have a clear view of the ring?"

"The ring?" Dan looked at the stand again. He had been told that the bout was to take place before a few select friends.

"For your fight next week." George frowned. "You had not forgotten?"

"No, I had not forgotten."

"Good… Sherry."

Sheridan escaped from Sir William to join the Prince. Dan and Townsend followed the chief magistrate out of the room, Townsend stepping on Dan's heels. He plucked at Dan's sleeve. His voice grated in Dan's ear.

"I hope you don't get too mashed up next week, Foster."

Dan pulled away and strode off, leaving Townsend smirking after him.

Chapter Thirty-Six

Dan climbed the stairs to Pickering's apartments. He heard voices and hesitated, wondering if Pickering had forgotten his invitation. Dan had received his note at Bow Street earlier in the day. Pickering had asked him to join him for a celebratory drink, and Dan had replied that he would call in on his way home.

While he was in two minds about whether or not to knock, the door shot open and Pickering appeared in the doorway.

"Thought I heard footsteps. Come on in, Foster."

"You have company. I don't want to intrude."

"Of course I have company. They're here for you."

Dan took off his hat, looked round at the welcoming faces. Louise Parmeter's former butler, Parkes, was resplendent in an embroidered waistcoat, black breeches and black silk stockings. His appearance was bound to impress any gentleman seeking a purveyor of high-quality groceries. He sat next to Miss Evans, his attentiveness to her suggesting that she meant more to him than the capable helpmeet he had described to Dan at the start of the investigation.

Mrs Watson's face was as red as ever, thanks more to the hot water in her gin than the heat of the laundry. Miss Julia's dress seemed to have been chosen to advertise their skills, so beribboned, crimped and ruffled was it. Even Sarah Dean greeted Dan with a warm smile, abandoning her haughty manner. The stable boy, Jacko, sat on the floor, gobbling a plate of food, and paused only long enough to wave a friendly chop.

"What will you have?" asked Pickering. "Not wine, or gin, I know. I have soda water, or ginger beer I got in for the boy."

"Ginger beer, thanks."

Parkes pulled up a chair for him and he sat down. Pickering refilled glasses all round and they drank a toast to "Principal Officer Foster" which ended in cheers. They followed this with a solemn toast to the memory of Miss Parmeter, another to the success of Parkes and the future Mrs Parkes, one to Miss Dean's appointment as lady's maid to the Duchess of Gornall, one from Pickering to the end of slavery. Then Pickering threw in an appreciation of Mrs Watson's laundry, with long life and happiness to the simpering Miss Julia. There was another toast for "Principal Officer Foster" and then, overflowing with goodwill, they begged Dan to tell them how he had discovered Bredon was the murderer.

"I never liked the man," Parkes said when Dan had done. "Very mean with his tips."

"And to think," Mrs Watson said, "that my poor girl here was trampled underfoot by the murderous villain still reeking with Miss Parmeter's blood!"

This brought gasps of astonishment and they all turned to her, eager for an explanation. Dan let her get on with it, embellishments and all. Miss Julia would always be known as the girl who stopped a murderer in full flight, whether or not he pointed out the incident had happened two days before the crime.

Pickering, having seen to his guests' glasses, flopped down in the seat next to Dan. He winked.

"Two burglaries in two weeks. Sounds to me like you missed your true calling."

Dan grinned. "How else was I to get into Hawkhurst's house? And if I was you, I'd show a bit more gratitude."

Pickering laughed. "I am grateful, Foster, as you well know. And glad that you kept going. If you hadn't, it might be me at the end of the rope. Mind you, I almost miss Patrolman Grimes."

Dan smiled. "How are your plans for buying your own stable coming along?"

"Good, good. I've found the place I want, off Tottenham Court Road. Just arguing the price with the owner. Truth to tell, it's worth what he's asking, but I'm not telling him that." He cast a sly glance at Dan. "You must come and see me whenever you fancy a gallop around the Park."

"Not for me, thanks," Dan said. "Not a great one for horses."

"I could tell. But really, Foster, how do you get along without being able to ride?"

"I get other people to do it for me."

Pickering laughed again. "Well, if you ever change your mind and want to learn, come to me. I'll have you racing at Epsom before you know it."

Dan put down his glass. "I doubt that. And now I must be getting along."

He shook hands all round, wished everyone well, and went out into the night in a chorus of goodnights and God blesses. The Parmeter case was over, and well over. But he still did not know who his enemy was, or what had become of him.

He descended carefully into the lane and hurried towards the lights of Berkeley Square. He was near the middle of the square when a shadowy figure stepped out from behind one of the plane trees.

Chapter Thirty-Seven

Dan's hand flew to his pistol, fell to his side when he saw it was a young woman. She clutched a shawl around her shoulders, making up for the lack of cover from her low-cut dress. Her cheeks were spotted with rouge and her lips painted red, a garish contrast with her grey complexion.

"Hallo, darlin'."

"Not for me," Dan said.

She smiled. "I weren't offering, but now you mention it."

"Move along, else you'll find yourself in the nearest watch house."

She recognised the hollowness of the threat, laughed up at him. "We ain't got time anyway. Dark Peg's waitin' fer yer at the Beak."

"Dark Peg? What does she want?"

"She don't tell me 'er doin's. All she says was, it's about the business you spoke on."

Dan walked into the heat, smell and racket of the Old Blind Beak's Head. The sound of a fiddler playing a maniacal jig cut above the babble of voices. In the middle of the room half a dozen couples stamped drunkenly to the music. A few people scowled at him and one or two bold souls muttered threats, but no one dared to challenge him as he made for Dark Peg's table.

She drained her glass of gin, stood up and beckoned with a pudgy finger. He followed her to a door at the back of the room and up a flight of stairs to the foul chambers where the working girls made her profits. He could still hear the sounds from the bar, catch eddies of movement through the gaps in the floorboards.

She led him into one of the rooms. It contained a bed covered with a set of dirty sheets, a table with a candle on it, and a ragged mat beside it. A wash stand stood in the corner supplied with a jug of water and a grubby towel. A couple of lewd prints had been nailed to the wall.

A thin girl aged about eighteen sat on the bed. She was not painted like the woman who had spoken to him in Berkeley Square and her dress was more modest, though the neckerchief across her bosom was not so demure that her profession was not obvious enough. One side of her face was blue-black, and there was a red gash on the corner of her mouth. She rose when Peg came in, dropped something like a curtsey.

"This is Hetty," Peg said. She nodded at the girl. "Go on."

Hetty pulled off her neckerchief, began to unlace her bodice.

"I've not come here for that," Dan said, but Peg put her finger to her lips.

"Wait."

The girl took off her bodice, unlaced the ties at the neck of her shift and lowered the fabric, exposing her breasts. Wincing, she lifted her arm, displayed the bruises along the side of her prominent ribs. It was nasty, but girls rarely reported such injuries. Peg would have her own bullies to deal with rough customers.

Dan glanced at the older woman. Stone-faced, she signalled that he should keep his attention on the girl. Hetty shuffled in a circle, revealed her back covered in bruises. Peg took the candle from the table, held it close to the battered, broken skin.

"Look."

Dan leaned forward, followed Peg's finger as it sketched a blurred shape between the shoulder blades. A boot mark, and at the toe a red V-shaped weal. He recognised the wound. He took out his pocket book and extracted the sketch he had made of the marks on the dead woman at the Feathers in Holborn.

"That's the one?" Peg asked.

"It is," he said. To Hetty, "Cover yourself up. Who did this to you?"

She hitched up her shift and glanced at Peg, who said, "Tell him."

"I met him last night on Holborn Hill. We went back to his room at the Thatched House on Field Lane."

Field Lane was off Holborn Hill, north of Fleet Market. Fleet Ditch ran – or more usually stagnated – behind it. It was part of the network of rookeries around Chick Lane. It was a convenient lair for a rapist and murderer.

"Did he give a name?"

"No."

"What does he look like?"

The girl's eyes gleamed. "He's got a bleeding great cut on his head."

"You gave him that?"

"With a bottle."

"What else, apart from the cut?"

"He looks like someone sat on the side of his head and squashed it all together. His teeth're all crooked, crammed into his gob, and his top lip slobbers out over them. A tall gangrel cove, all hands and feet. Thick wrists. Dressed smart, had a watch in his fob. I don't think he'd come by it honest, either."

"What makes you say that?"

"The Thatched House is a flash house, and he seemed well known there."

"Did you try to take the watch? Is that why he hit you?"

"I never. He slapped me a couple of times when we was doing the business and after I said he should pay more because of it. He knocked me down, ripped the dress off me back, started kicking me. I crawled to the table, grabbed the bottle, lammed him and ran. I knew there had to be a back way out. You know."

Of course; a rookery landlord would make sure there was an escape route for his customers.

"Which room was he in?"

"Upstairs."

"Which room upstairs?"

"Don't know."

Peg shifted her feet, folded her arms. The girl said hastily, "At the back. Don't remember which one. The bottom panel of the door was all splintered and rotten along the edge."

"Anything else?"

"Can't think of nothing else."

"Sounds useful, yes?" said Peg.

"Very," Dan agreed. The girl's eyes widened as he handed Peg a bank note. He doubted she would see any of it, took some coins from his pocket and handed them to her.

He eyed Peg sternly. "Earned in her own right, Peg. No sharing."

Peg, grinning happily at the note, nodded. "Understood, Mr Foster."

"Make sure it is. Ladies." He put on his hat and left them.

Chapter Thirty-Eight

It had started to rain. Icy water gurgled along gutters, poured from eaves. People splashed through the mucky pools that had collected in the cobbled street. Dan welcomed the filthy weather; it was good cover for someone who did not want to be seen or heard. He stood in the doorway of a narrow, dark house, the cracked canopy over the step providing some shelter from the downpour.

People passed in and out of the doors of the crowded lodging houses, many of them working girls with blind-drunk clients, a few working boys. Most of the shops were little more than stalls set up outside the houses and hardly ever ceased trading. Tripe shops, pawnbrokers, beer houses; an old iron shop whose owner was known as a receiver of stolen lead and ironmongery, but who had so far avoided prosecution; a house where a mother and her daughter were suspected of making and selling false money.

Dan had no time for any of that tonight. The Thatched House opposite him was an old two-storey building with a steep gabled roof that may or may not have been thatched at one time. Through the thick latticed windows, he watched a blur of brightly dressed figures moving around inside. People came and went: footpads, highwaymen, and their doxies, swaggering about in their misgotten finery. There was a light over the door which gave a good view of their faces. After half an hour, it illumined thin, wedge-shaped features atop a skinny, slouching figure which could only belong to the man who had beaten Peg's girl, Hetty.

Dan followed Hetty's hint and went round to the back of the tavern through George Alley. There was a cramped path where the rain lay dark and deep between the dank walls of the houses in Union Court which backed on to Field Street. He walked along until he found a nondescript door half-hidden behind piles of wooden crates. It had no handle on the outside, but it took only a few minutes' work with a knife to release the latch and let himself inside.

He was in a long, dark passage, lined on one side with empty barrels. At the end, a door half-glazed with coloured smoke-stained glass led into the bar. To the side of this a flight of uncarpeted stairs ran to the upper rooms. He slipped past the bar, put his hand on the creaky banister and tiptoed upstairs.

He came out on a landing facing a row of doors, all closed, the rooms within dark. All except for one at the end where a light shone through a large, jagged gap along the edge of the bottom panel. Shadows flickered back and forth.

Dan crept up to the door, put his ear to the board and listened to someone dragging something heavy along the floor. There was the click of a key, the squeak of hinges. Dan crouched and peered in through the gap, saw the profile of a man kneeling by the bed in front of a box such as servants use to store their belongings. He was wrapping up some small object, placing it inside the chest. A candle burned on the table near the bed, the flame glinting on the barrel of a pistol beside it.

Dan straightened up, rammed the door open with his shoulder. The man's startled face turned towards him. There was an ugly red slash across his forehead. His hand flew towards the pistol, but Dan was across the room before his groping fingers found a hold on the weapon. He hauled him up by his lapels.

"Bow Street Officer. You're under arrest."

"Fuck you!"

The loose, long-limbed body was tough and wiry, the large hands Hetty had described accustomed to fisticuffs. In their struggle, they knocked the table over, sent gun and candle flying. In the sudden darkness, Dan felt his adversary squirm out of his grip, sensed rather than saw him lunge for something that lay on the bed. A hard object swung into the side of Dan's head. He staggered back, blinded by the explosions behind his eyes. He made a wild grab after his adversary as he sprang past him, but a shove sent him spinning to his knees. The man flung open the door and disappeared down the stairs.

Dan clutched the side of the bed and dragged himself to his feet. He raised his hand to his head, felt the blood sticky on his fingers. He had been hit with some sort of bludgeon, which had probably just been used in the theft of the plunder the man had been adding to his stash.

He listened for a moment. The carousing downstairs continued unabated. The thief had preferred escape and abandoning his chest of stolen goods to seeking the company's help – and letting them know he had led a Runner to their bolthole. Dan groped for his hat and ran out after him.

Dan was just in time to see him dodge out of the top of the alley into another half-hidden track. He twisted, turned, doubled back, but every time he looked over his shoulder, Dan was still there, and gaining on him. He did not know he was dealing with someone who was used to finding his way around London's rookeries.

After a while they were running between buildings so ruinous and decayed that only the rats found a home in them. The ground was littered with spars of rotting wood, glass, rags, metal, ash, clinker, oily pools of poisonous by-products from who-knew-what manufacturing processes. Rivulets of sewage trickled down to join the ditch which crossed the bottom of the sloping track. Two planks had been laid across it to form a slimy bridge.

Dan thought the man would make for the bridge, but he swerved off to the right and ducked through a gaping doorway into the ruins. Dan skidded after him into what had once been a room, but which now lacked walls and roof. Unpromising as it was as a shelter, people had been here. A charred circle in the middle was evidence that a large fire had been lit not many days ago. Empty bottles flung around the foundations suggested the gathering of a canting crew.

The rain had stopped and the clouds had divided to let down faint beams of moonlight. The fugitive was on the other side of the room, clambering over the low brickwork.

Dan pulled out his gun. "Stop or I'll shoot!"

The man froze and slowly straightened, his hands in the air.

"Lie down. On your front. Hands flat on the ground above your head."

The man twisted his face over his shoulder. "Come on, mate. All this trouble for a few watches? I can share. Let me go and I'll pay you."

Dan gestured at the ground with the gun. The man scowled and dropped down. Dan knelt on the beaten earth beside him, held him captive with one knee pressed into his back while he patted his pockets with his free hand, keeping the pistol in the other. He found no weapon.

"What's your name?"

"Fuck off."

That earned him a smack across the head. "Your name."

"Blake. Tom Blake."

"And the girl's name?"

"What girl?"

"The girl you raped and beat to death at the Feathers in Holborn."

"I never touched no girl."

"Girl in a blue dress."

"I never touched her."

Dan increased the weight on his knee, grabbed Blake's jacket collar and twisted it tight. He pressed his lips to his ear.

"What was her name?"

Blake coughed and spluttered into the mud, his fingers scrabbling. "I don't know any girl! Get off me!"

Dan pressed the muzzle of his pistol against Blake's head. "I'm going to ask one more time. And this time if you don't answer me, I'm going to blow your brains out and leave your body in that river of shit down there. What was her name?"

Blake whimpered. "I don't know. I swear to God. I don't know. She was just some whore."

Dan ground his face into the dirt. "She was a whore, was she? Was she?"

"I offered her money. Bitch had only to take it."

Dan pushed himself up from his knee, dragged Blake up after him and slammed him back to the ground. Having half stunned his prisoner, he pocketed his gun and felt for his cuffs.

"You're under arrest for murder."

He dragged Blake's right arm behind his back and manoeuvred the shackle towards it. Blake, recovering his breath, began to put up a struggle. Then Dan felt him relax in his grasp, saw his eye swivel round, realised too late that there was someone behind them. He heard a pistol cock.

"Move away," said a voice. "Hands where I can see them."

Dan started to get up, but the man snapped, "On your hands and knees. You, get his gun."

Blake was happy to oblige. He rolled on to his side, came to a sitting position, leaned over to Dan, who knelt on all fours, and took the gun from his pocket. He got to his feet and gave Dan a kick in the ribs which sent him sprawling. The cuffs flew from Dan's grip. Blake pointed the gun at him.

"Ain't so cocky now, are you, lawman?"

"Let him up," the other man ordered. "Slowly. Keep your hands high. Turn round."

Dan did as he was told. Blake stepped back, kept his distance in spite of his gun. Dan ignored him. He looked the stranger in the face.

"It's you who's been following me," he said.

"It is. You know who I am?"

"Yes. I know who you are."

Chapter Thirty-Nine

"Bob Singleton of Barcombe. Last time I saw you was in the assizes court at Taunton. Seven years' transportation," Dan said. "Why didn't you go?"

"I did. I was on the *Lady Jane* which left Portsmouth just after the mutiny in the fleet started. It must have got into our blood; come August, we had our own mutiny a few days out from Rio de Janeiro. The soldiers took over the ship. Most of them were only in the army to avoid being hanged. Such is the wisdom of the law they'd put the worse criminals in charge of the convicts. They'd kept us in chains and stole our rations, but it was go along with them or die. They hacked the first mate to death, put the captain and his crew in a boat and turned them off. I got away from them in Montevideo and worked my passage back by weary, roundabout ways. I said I'd be back to kill you no matter how long it took. Just happens to have come about quicker than I'd hoped."

Blake guffawed.

"You're a fool, Singleton," Dan said. "You could have given evidence against the mutineers, might have had a chance of avoiding the rope that way. There's no hope of it now. It's a hanging offence to come back before the end of your term."

"There's no chances in the law for men like me."

"No chance now, no. And after what you did to my son, I'll make sure of it."

"I wasn't going to hurt the boy. I was going to bring him back in a day or two, but when I went to get him, Mother Poison had gone and the child with her. I'm not like you, Foster. I don't take innocent lives."

"You weren't innocent. You were convicted of poaching."

"We took what was rightfully ours. The land is ours, the right to hunt on it is ours. You lived amongst us long enough, spied on us long enough, to know that. You could have turned a blind eye, but no, it's a rich man's law and you're the rich man's lackey. You like the power it brings, don't you? You give yourself the right to choose who goes to prison, who doesn't; who hangs, who doesn't. So tell me, Foster, who deserves to hang? That thing for the rape and murder of a defenceless woman? Or the man who seeks justice?"

"Oi!" Blake said. "Who are you calling a thing?"

"I'll tell you what justice means here, Singleton," Dan said. "You put my family in danger and I'll see you hang before you do it again."

"You held my life or death in your hands once, and you chose death. And now it's me who can choose whether you live or die." Singleton raised his gun, cocked the pistol, pointed it at Dan's head.

Blake sniggered. "Go on, do him! Kill the pig! Eek – eek – eek! Squeal, piggy, squeal."

Singleton stood, arm outstretched, the pistol steady in his hand.

"Go on!" Blake said. "Lost your nerve? If you won't do it, I will." He raised Dan's gun.

Dan might stand a chance of avoiding Singleton's bullet if he went for him, dived beneath the shot, crashed into the other man's midriff. Now there were two guns trained on him and his chances of survival plummeted. But it was that or nothing. His only hope was that he could move quicker than Blake's sluggish mind worked. He tensed himself to spring at Singleton. The flare from Singleton's gun fizzed into the shadows.

Blake screamed and fell to the floor. The gun flew from his hand and landed against a tumble of bricks. He clutched at his leg, brought his hand away covered in blood.

"What the fuck d'you do that for?"

Singleton lowered his weapon, useless now the shot had been fired, stood with it hanging loose in his fingers. In the darkness between them, Blake rolled on the ground, sobbing.

"You stupid whoreson, you shot me. Fuck you, fuck you, fuck you."

The clouds scudded over Singleton's head. His haggard face was spectral in the moonlight, his eyes dull and sunken, his silence deep as the dead. Dan had a fleeting image of him as he had been, the powerful blacksmith working at his forge, his hammer ringing on red-hot metal, the jug of village ale ready at his elbow, the soft autumn breezes of the Somerset countryside playing around him. He had not carried an ounce of spare flesh then, had been all muscle. He carried hardly any flesh now, was nothing but jutting bone. From village smithy to the hell of a convict ship on a glaring ocean, to bloodshed, suffering and sickness.

You chose death, he had said.

Then Dan knew. Only his will to seek revenge had kept Singleton alive. He would not long survive whatever disease he had picked up on his journey.

Dan's gun had not been fired, lay where Blake had dropped it. He had only to pick it up and turn it on Singleton. He left it lying. For a moment the two men looked at one another. Then Singleton turned and walked slowly out of the ruin.

"Aren't you going after him?" Blake yelped. "He shot me."

Dan retrieved his gun and the cuffs. He pulled his scarf from his neck, tied it around Blake's thigh to stop the bleeding, shackled his hands behind his back and dragged him to his feet.

"But he shot me," Blake whined. "You're letting him get away and he shot me."

"Shut your trap, or I'll shoot you myself."

Dan half carried, half dragged his prisoner across the threshold. Rather than head back into the rookery, where there would be plenty willing to come to a brother villain's aid against a lone Bow Street officer, he got him over the plank bridge and started across the open wasteland.

Singleton had already vanished.

Chapter Forty

Dan stood in the middle of the ring, breathing heavily, his head still buzzing from the punches he had taken. The grounds of Carlton House were a blur of snapping banners and streaming pennants. Rows of faces gazed at him from the spectators' stand, all bearing the same stamp of their unshakeable belief that it was the duty of the world to lay its good things before them. Even those who had made losses on their bets – who would draw first blood, who would win a round, who would win the fight – were satisfied. The pugs had served them with a good measure of skill and pluck.

The Prince's poker-faced flunkies, immobilised by servility, winked at Dan over their trays. The patrolmen who lurked under the trees on the edge of the lawn forgot to look out for crazed radicals or French assassins, and clapped and cheered. A smiling Sir William Addington, his jowls shaking with approval, stood next to the Prince of Wales. Today Dan was the hero of the service.

George had risen to lead the applause, his podgy hands meeting beneath his doughy, paint-smeared cheeks. Sheridan raised his wine glass to the victor. John Townsend stood at the Prince's elbow, almost exploding with rage, his little eyes dark and bitter, his lips white. The failure of his plan to see Dan humiliated was hardly likely to improve relations between the two men. Not that Dan cared much about that.

Other faces pressed close enough for Dan to feel the gusts of their breath, catch snatches of their talk. Lord Hawkhurst, who had sponsored the fight, was in the ring consulting with the referees and umpires. His complexion was clear, his eyes bright, his stance upright. Losing Bredon had done wonders for his health and temper. He had also shaken off his young hangers-on. Only Ormond was still admitted to his company. The Irishman, a fastidious judge of the science, nodded appreciatively at Dan.

It was for all these gawping faces that Dan stood half-naked, his torso sheened with sweat, blood running down his face from the cut over his half-closed right eye. It was for them that his opponent sat on his second's knee, his head lolling as his trainer wafted smelling salts beneath his bleeding nose. A blue stain with a gash of red in the centre spread across his left cheek, the flesh having finally given way thirteen rounds in with the final knock-down blow. His eyes were still glazed, his mind disorientated, his swollen lips trembling.

The betting on the man's identity had been going on up until the moment he had stepped into the arena. The names Paddington Jones and Bill Ward of Bristol had been bandied about. Others, influenced by Ormond's inclusion in Hawkhurst's entourage, opted for the Irish fighter Andrew Gamble. Some hoped for the return of Daniel Mendoza, who had retired to a public house in Whitechapel. Many were certain that only Gentleman John Jackson, who had wrested the championship from Mendoza, could make the bout worthwhile. The subject had long since been exhausted, the conversation grown desultory, before Dan's opponent had finally emerged from his pavilion.

He had been dressed in black breeches, a contrast to Dan's own, which were white. He had approached the ring surrounded by his entourage, his dark, cropped head bent, droning over his clasped hands. As he drew close, Dan had made out the words of his prayer.

"Oh, Lord, smite thou my enemies! Crush my foe before me! Beat down my enemy! Break the teeth of the ungodly!"

Paul had looked up at Dan and Noah from outside the ring, where he had been arranging bucket, sponge and bandages.

"Bill Willis, the Fighting Quaker. He's heavier than Dan, and a real hard hitter."

Noah, who had been massaging the tension out of Dan's shoulders, had summoned spittle to his mouth, lobbed it over the ropes. "A humbug. If his last fight wasn't a cross, I'd like to know what was."

No one really believed the man who called himself the Fighting Quaker ever prayed, or that he had any connection with the Religious Society of Friends. It was just part of the show. In spite of his reputation, there had been no humbugging in his battle with Dan. He had fought fairly and bravely. Paul stepped in front of the defeated man, cutting him off from Dan's view. The old soldier's craggy face loomed close to Dan's, his grin exposing his battle-shattered teeth.

"It's deliverance he's praying for now."

Dan closed his eyes. Paul moved behind him and he felt the rasp of a towel rubbing down his back. Shadows flicked in front of his eyes, once, twice, three times. His eyelids fluttered open.

"Son! Son! Can you hear me?"

Dan focussed on Noah's clicking fingers, the bright face behind them.

"I'm proud of you, boy. As I knew I would be. Come now, the Prince is waiting to present you with your prize."

Noah led Dan towards the ropes, but Dan stopped, turned back and crossed over to Willis. The Fighting Quaker was on his feet, benefitting from the temporary revival a good slug of brandy afforded. Dan held out his hand and the two men shook.

"Till next time," Willis said.

"There'll be no next time," Dan answered.

"'T'ain't doin' unto others not to give a man a chance to even the score."

"Then you'll just have to turn the other cheek."

Willis gazed at him for a moment, then laughed. He winked with his good eye. "You better go and collect the wages of sin."

"Loser's purse shouldn't be too shabby."

"No. The Lord's provided all right on this one. Lord Hawkhurst, that is."

"Good luck."

"Good luck, Dan Foster."

Willis gave a duck of the head and stepped back. Dan turned to see Lord Hawkhurst behind him.

"You don't mean that, Foster," Hawkhurst said. "You've got a great future ahead of you."

"Not in the ring, My Lord," Dan said.

"Nonsense. I thought you had it in you and today you've proved me right. You rid me of Bredon, and in return, I'm going to make you a champion."

"I arrested a murderer."

Hawkhurst smiled, though there was a flicker of displeasure in his eyes. "If it's a question of keeping your father and his old friend on your team, I can accommodate them. I intend, however, to send you to Captain Barclay to get you in training for your next match."

"No, thank you, My Lord. I do not have my mind set on a career as a pugilist."

"Come, man, don't be so shy. A few more fights like this and you'll be a rich man. You'll never make so much at Bow Street. You have a family, don't you? You must think of them and their future."

Dan thought of how hard his money was usually earned, of the dark nights spent in filthy, shadowed streets where the hatred, want and despair were palpable. The days away from home, away from Alex, on the trail of some vicious criminal. The murderous hostility of the criminal fraternity, and the scarce-hidden contempt of respectable society. The ring had its perils, but they were nothing compared to the risks faced night and day by a Bow Street officer.

He thought of his family's future, had been thinking of it for years. Added to what he had already saved, the £200 reward from the Prince for catching Louise Parmeter's murderer had substantially increased his worth. But Lord Hawkhurst was right. He could earn more in the ring. For this hour's work he was five hundred guineas richer. Perhaps he should have felt more grateful than he did, but he knew from the notes he had found in Bredon's desk that such a sum meant little to people who could throw as much away in a single bet.

He thought of Noah and Paul, who were listening to the conversation while pretending to be busy packing away the fight paraphernalia. Though they would never say so, Dan knew they hoped his victory had changed his mind. They had always believed he had the skill to aim for the championship.

He thought of the nameless girl in the blue dress, her suffering marked on her body, whose poverty had led to her death. There had been no reward for arresting her murderer.

He squared his shoulders, looked the lord in the eye.

"I never wanted this fight," he said. "And I never want another."

Hawkhurst almost flinched, so taken aback was he by the bold rejection. He drew himself up haughtily.

"Well, Foster, since you feel like that about it. I had no idea."

Dan thought he had made it clear enough, but let it go. With a dismissive gesture of his hand, Hawkhurst moved away and clambered out of the ring. Noah and Paul moved to Dan's side, a silent declaration that they stood by him whatever he decided. With the match officials tagging behind, the three followed Lord Hawkhurst between the ropes and across the grass to the waiting Prince. Dan hoped the presentation would not take long. The sooner it was over, the sooner he could get back to Bow Street.

THE END

Notes

Bagnio

A bathing house, which might also be a brothel.

Broughton's Rules

In 1743 champion pugilist Jack Broughton (c.1703–1789), who ran a boxing academy for the gentry in London (the amphitheatre on Oxford Road), formulated the first set of rules for the sport. They included the requirement for the chalking of a square in the centre of the ring where the fighters were placed on the lines opposite one another at the start of a round or after a fall. Defeat was signalled by a fighter failing to come up to the line within the allotted time (thirty seconds), or if his second declared him beaten. The rules banned hitting a man when he was down, and a man on his knees was counted as down. Originally intended only for use in his academy, Broughton's Rules were widely adopted and were not replaced until the introduction of the "New Rules" in 1838.

Bum fodder

Toilet paper.

Canter

A rogue, thief or beggar (who uses the language or 'cant' of thieves).

Cross

A fixed fight.

Daffy

Gin.

Demirep

A woman of doubtful reputation.

Diver	A pickpocket.
Doxy	A female prostitute.
Glim	A candle, shuttered lantern or fire.
It won't fadge	It won't do.
Ken	A house.
Lumper	A labourer who loads or unloads ships' cargoes.
Mill	A fist fight.
Mungo	A racist epithet: a black person or slave; also used as a proper name.
Nabbers	Police officers.
On the cheating lay	A lay is an occupation, enterprise, adventure or line (as in job).
Pug	Pugilist.
Regrate	To buy up commodities (especially food) in one market and sell them in the same or another market at a profit.
Rhino	Money.
Rookery	A crowded slum, usually the haunt of criminals; 'a rook' is a cheat and 'to rook' is to cheat.
Snowball	A racist epithet.

Square Toes	An old man; a precise, formal, old-fashioned person.
Tagtail	Parasite, hanger-on.
The Fancy	Followers of boxing. (Also used of other sports, e.g. pigeon fanciers.)
To hop the twig	To run off.
Trull	Female prostitute.
Up to scratch	A scratch (or mark) is the line drawn in a boxing ring to which boxers are brought at the start of a fight.
Wiper	Handkerchief.

Acknowledgements

I would like to thank all the people who have helped me in the writing of this book. I am grateful to Richard Tearle and Debbie Young for their thoughtful comments; to Alison Jack for her editorial services; and to Helen Hart and the team at SilverWood Books for being so lovely to work with. And, as ever, I couldn't manage without my husband, Gerard, to keep me well supplied with cups of tea, encouragement and grammar lessons.

Bow Street Runners and bare-knuckle fighters, radicals and pickpockets, resurrection men and bluestockings…

Find out more about Dan Foster's world at www.lucienneboyce.com